SCRIBINGS, VOL 4: MISCREATIONS

EDITED BY

JAMIE ALAN BELANGER

Published in 2014 by Lost Luggage Studios, LLC
through CreateSpace.com

ISBN: # 978-1-936489-20-6

Printed in the United States of America.

ACKNOWLEDGMENTS

Cover art by Peeter Parkker.

His website is at http://akapeterparker.com

Interior glyph artwork by Steven Inman

Cover art uses the following free fonts:

    Writing Stuff by Brittney Murphy Design

    Vera Humana 95 by BX Fonts

Introduction:
Miscreations

What we create often finds a way to unravel our well-knit plans. Recent news reports offer a modern example: so-called "smart" refrigerators had their functionality commandeered so they could relay spam emails. This was not a planned feature, just a lapse in planning and judgment that left a gaping security hole. When inventors set out to create things, they don't always think their designs through. Not that it's anyone's fault; it's simply not possible to plan in advance for every possible contingency. Miscalculations can happen at any stage of any project.

Our modern media has been flooded with monsters in recent years. Vampires, zombies, and other supernatural creatures. Our stories touch on some of these subjects, but go far beyond into the realm of the even scarier monsters: humans. People and their creations are far more frightening than anything fictional. It is entirely possible for a human to be a miscreation—a remorseless killer, a terrorist, and a host of other examples of people who are vile and cruel. What is it that drives a person to do the sorts of things that fill

1

the news every day? As far back as William Shakespeare [The Tempest 4.1], and possibly earlier, people have used literature to debate the contrast between nature and nurture. When you compare the two, questions arise about a person's development. Is their heredity more important than the environment they grew up in? The ultimate question of what drives a human to commit horrific acts upon fellow humans reveals another fascinating question: Was this person born this way; or did society, in effect, miscreate them?

Ultimately, a miscreation is something that should not exist, but does. An error in evolution, a design fault, an unintended feature... an event happens that transforms an entity into something so amazingly good or so horribly evil that you can't help but be fascinated by its existence.

ROOM TWO

BY STEVEN INMAN

Monday morning, nine-twenty a.m., and already my crew was coming at me with problems. "Hey, Ed..." this from Randy, my room supervisor, running hands through his thinning hair, "...Ed, we have a problem with Room Two."

"Two?" I had to stop and swear, blow out my breath and sip coffee. Room Two was the GEO-LIRT assembly room, a room that I thought was good to go. GEO-LIRT was a new satellite being sent aloft by NOAA—the National Oceanic and Atmospheric Administration—to do something I only vaguely knew about. When we send something into space, we don't worry too much about contaminating space as much as avoiding any contamination of instruments on board, leading to malfunction or invalid test results. A problem in Room Two could only mean that the main assembly room for NOAA's satellite had not passed the sterilization test.

And so I had my first headache for the day. I sipped more coffee. "We have another room ready?" I asked Randy, "...how about Four?"

Randy thought, shrugged. "You're the boss. If NOAA don't mind shipping their stuff across the building. I'll put it to them."

"Do that," I said. "Grab Timmy's crew to help with the move and bake them a cake or something. Is Ayong around? I'm going to take a look at Room Two."

"She's around there somewhere," Randy said. "If she's not already in the room."

Twenty minutes later I was squatting with Ayong, looking at a small screen on the handheld test set. Ayong Motijia was our supervising sterilization certification engineer (our SSCE), and as I expected she was already aiming the test unit at a corner of the room behind a set of hydraulic longarm-lifts. The screen of the unit was lit with a number of bright blue spots, indicating bacteria colonies, where there should be none. "We cleaned that place like a dozen times," Ayong muttered again, her voice crinkly through the clean-suit. "This whole place a dozen times." It was clear in her voice that she did not want a dozen and one. "That can't be normal bacteria."

"Pfft," I blew out my breath. Not normal bacteria? Sure, right. I thought a minute, considered courses of action, and finally decided to play it safe. I stood and slapped my thigh. "We'll get someone to look hard at it and see if it's even actually bacteria. Leave it like it is."

"Okay." Ayong began to put the equipment away while I paced a bit, wondering what and how the crew missed this room, these spots. I really couldn't imagine how, but the bacteria was there. I went back out and stripped off the clean-suit, thinking about bacteria—or whatever it is—that would not sterilize away, and I decided it was time to go for that hated phrase and "think outside the box."

As I walked back to my office I played the schedule of the room through my head. In the last eight months there'd only been one assembly in there, and Ayong had found nothing then. At the start of that assembly we'd just used what we called the B-tine protocol for sterilization, and nothing had come up. For this NOAA assembly we'd started a new protocol we called the Double Dip. It was a process with a far more sensitive final test, which implied that the bacteria could have been there all along, for who knows how long, surviving the B-tine but showing up in the Double Dip. I kicked myself, almost physically, for not thinking something like this could happen. But what would I have done? We were using the most up to date tests there were at the time.

For now I would have to go over our tracks, review our processes. I would have to get my assistant, Aaron, to pull the schedules, all the tests and Certification Sheets.

* * *

A couple days went by and I personally oversaw the cleaning of Room Four and the move of NOAA's project. There were some questions but I tried to downplay the whole thing. After all, we'd just switched to the Double Dip so it was only natural to find something new. And I did the usual manager things: paperwork, schedules, blah blah. Then, one afternoon, Randy handed me a report. "What is it?" I asked, and he only shrugged. "It was in your box so I brought it over."

I skimmed through it, then went to my office, sat and re-read it. The Contamination Analysis on Room Two from the lab. Lots of standard info on Room Two, some baseline stuff. Then the summary: bacteria of an unknown form.

A colony size that indicated it had been in the room for at least a *year*.

A handwritten note from a lab tech asked us for another sample, "*...because we think we messed this sample up. The results don't match anything we know. Could be a mutation or something new.*"

Shit, I thought, and then said it for emphasis. *Eyes will be on us*, I thought, *if not right now then very soon*. So I called out to Aaron, and when he came in I said we would have to go far back on the tests and Certifications, and also think about what went into the room as well as what went out. We'd have to look back to the last time we'd used that room for recovery of a returned item, a satellite that had come down and been recovered. As soon as I made the request I could see that Aaron knew what I was thinking. We both knew the loose talk would go around, and the rumor mill would say that some alien bacteria came back from space on one of our craft.

* * *

A week went by. And unfortunately, we found that Room Two had never been used to handle returning craft, so that line of thought went nowhere and the rumors died out. People began to think we just messed up and found some new bacteria; after all, some said, isn't there a new influenza every year? I didn't say anything about viruses being different than bacteria, I just let the talk go on.

But then my boss paid me a visit. He's usually pretty absent but had heard what was happening and he suggested I call in an expert.

"Call in Shirley Whitney," he told me. "She's the go-to for this sort of thing. Probably be the one who can rule out aliens the fastest and let us get back to normal."

"You sure?" I asked. "I mean, that call could get more people talking."

He shook his jowly head. "No, she can keep things professional. Give her a call."

Shirley Whitney. I knew her a bit, but knew the name, and I was not too eager to call her. But the boss had said it, so my hands were tied. When I began this job I'd been given her name along with twenty-three others on a list known as the Alien Attack List. Officially it was the Extra-terrestrial Phenomena Responder List. Most were just names, but I'd met Shirley once at a complex-wide party, one of those social events where I usually ended up being too loud and out of place. Shirley had caught me early on and asked me about my work, and as a result I had a good time. And an enlightening time as well; I asked about her work and had learned enough to make me curious about xenobiology. We were both biologists by training, and though we were worlds apart in some ways we did find stuff to talk about.

So I guess, all things considered, she was the best person to call if anyone had to be called.

On Monday I pulled out the list and dialed her number. She answered her phone on the fifth ring: "Shirley."

"Hi Shirley, it's Ed Grandersen in Assembly."

"Hi Ed in Assembly," she replied. "It's noon and the cafeteria has lasagna today. It won't last so can I call you back?"

"You can," I said, sure that she would not want to even hang up. "Just wanted to let you know that we can't certify Room Two. We started using the new sterilization protocol and came across a bacteria that won't clean away."

"Really?" She made a humph sound, clearly not sure of my abilities. "Did you try bleach?"

"We have a scraper that gets anything," I told her. "The thing is we *can* clean it, but we don't want to just yet. The thing is that we probably should look this one over first. Because it's not familiar. As far as I can tell, and as far as the lab can tell, it looks new."

"New?" Her voice had slid up in tone, and I could imagine her suddenly leaning forward in her chair. "New... what does that mean?"

"We did an analysis and the lab said it looks new and or unknown. I thought I should get you in before going any further."

She was quiet for a moment and I let her think. Finally, she finished: "I will be right there. Oh, Ed: close the room. Don't clean anymore."

"Done already." I promised.

It didn't take her long. One thing I learned about Shirley was that she was a fun, easygoing woman, but once she found something to sink her teeth into, to focus on, you better stand back. I could see her light up as we walked to Room Two. Her eyes were narrow, trying to see if there was anything visible through the windows. "It's behind that set-up near the corner," I told her. "I have clean-suits in the foyer."

"I'll go in alone," she said, and I didn't argue. I helped her dress, and then watched as she went in with a sample kit. "Largest patch we left was behind the Douglas unit in the corner," I told her over the speaker. She waved and went over, spent a few moments getting what she needed.

Afterward she came back out, pulled off the clean-suit and gave me a smile. "Thanks. I will let you know what I find."

"I'll keep this closed," I told her. "And I don't want you to hurry, but if word of this gets out people will be asking..."

She nodded. "I know. People will be talking about aliens." She picked up her kit. "I'll give you a call."

* * *

My team was annoyed at having the room out of use but I explained that there's always something new challenging us, that we will deal with this and it was nothing major, and they did a good job keeping their mouths closed. I called the lab and explained that we'd just had a messed up sample, never mind us; they were busy enough to let the whole thing go if I promised no more jokes with the annual drug test samples.

Now Shirley was the lone person working on it, and only one of two people who thought about it.

I spent a week poring over the records, trying to find some way in which an alien bacteria could have been brought back from space, but I found nothing definitive. There was no way I would be able to pin this on a bacteria from outer space, so I hoped that Shirley would either find nothing at all or that is was just another new bacteria, a mutation that posed no threat, and everyone could ignore it.

Two weeks went by with no word from Shirley. Something like this, an analysis done seriously, takes a while. It's not like television, a few simple tests, someone tells the computer to "enhance" and there it is. Even when we do get an "enhance," it doesn't necessarily answer any questions. So we get very careful, repeat our tests and check our findings a lot.

But two weeks had me itchy, so I rang her up, early, before lunch. I knew she had me on Caller ID because she answered with, "No definite answer, Ed."

"I didn't expect one," I replied. "Any thoughts?"

Silence for a moment. Then: "It's weird. I imagine you pulled the records, and had nothing in Room Two that was a return? Nothing come back from space?"

"Nope," I said.

"Yeah, I knew. This thing has the basic, very basic, signatures that it's terran. I ran some heat tests, tried cooking it, and heat affects it like every-thing else. So does low oxygen. And cold. So it didn't come from space. It's from Earth. But that's about it. I can say it's completely new."

"Wow." My heart was getting a slightly louder thud. I played it calm. "Now you can name a new species after yourself."

"Species?" Shirley's voice was subdued; she was obviously still puzzled by this bacteria. "No, the structure is very different. More like a new genus. I think I'm pushing taxonomy on this one."

* * *

And that was all I got from her at that point. A couple of months went by and other stuff came up. At one point I mentioned the incident to Connie, our area manager. She said it would be best to be quiet. "We don't want another embarrassing debacle. Some idiot saying we have aliens here."

"Yeah, I figured," I replied. "What should we do about Room Two?"

"Can you get this bacteria out?"

"Sure," I said. "It's tough but not invincible. It only survived before be-cause it was adapted to our protocols."

She thought, and nodded. "Okay, clean the room and open it up then."

But before I opened Two I thought I should call Shirley, let her know. She wasn't in, so I left a message. And called the next day, and the next. No response.

I opened Room Two and we moved pieces of a new project in, a deep water probe that was heading for a frozen lake in Antarctica. The researchers thought there might be living bacteria or even larger flora or fauna in the un-frozen water far beneath the ice, survivors from an ancient age, maybe even a Coelacanth-like thing.

Creatures trapped from an ancient age. That gave me a lot of pause, given what was happening since our Room Two discovery. One night I woke from a dream involving a blob-like thing with hydraulic arms. Dreams sound so stupid, but not when you're trapped in them.

But then the Antarctic probe set-up kept me busy for a week, occupying my thoughts. I tried Shirley once more on Friday, and finally reached her.

"Sorry," she said, but sounded too tired to really mean it. I said it was nothing and asked what she'd found. Her voice was... off, I felt; I could hear a mix of both excitement and disappointment.

"See, the thing with this bacteria—and it is a bacteria—is that it's not a xeno," Shirley said.

"Xeno?" I repeated. "Do you mean not alien? We figured that. You told me last time we talked."

Shirley was probably nodding as she said, "Yes, Ed. Since it's native to this planet, it's not exactly my field." That sentence seemed to end the talk, but for some reason Shirley was remaining on the line.

"So you're still involved, right?" I asked. And when Shirley didn't respond, I asked her why.

"Well, it's not alien," Shirley repeated, her voice halting. "There are certain elements, specific indicators, that show it evolved here on this planet." She seemed to emphasize *on this planet*. "But a lot of other things are just screwy. It seems to be from a different line. Remember I said it might be a new genus? Now we're thinking a new phylum, or kingdom."

I started thinking of the implications. A funny one: re-drawing all those charts in high school classrooms. Not so funny: the idea that something like this can be evolving beside us. I steered her toward the practical and immediate. "Do you think it will recur? Is this going to be an issue for me, for sanitizing rooms?" Shirley didn't answer right away, and I asked, "How do you think it got in there to begin with?"

"Honestly," she said, "I think it's been in there forever. Since the place was built, off and on. It predates the building itself. There's evidence of a lot of past generations."

"Then how did we miss it?"

"You just started the new protocol, right?" she pointed out. "I think that's the one that caught it. I think that this has been there all along, in very small amounts, hidden among all the other contaminants and bacteria, and all of our tests up to that point didn't catch it." She paused, considering her words. "Like it learned how to avoid those tests and cleaning agents."

"Intelligent bacteria." I laughed, and then I said, "Damn. I wonder how this will affect the work."

"Assembly rooms." Shirley made a strange little laugh. "I think how it affects our facilities might be a minor thing."

I wondered what else had crossed her mind, but before I could ask she went on: "A suggestion. Do the Double Dip again, in another room. Wait... I'll email a few changes you can make to it. Then see what you find."

"It will take a day."

"That's okay," Shirley answered.

When she mailed me the changes I reset the protocol and had the team run it again. And then we went through Room One. And by the time we'd finished we'd found more of the bacteria. Not a lot, not what you'd normally expect in a regular non-sanitary room. But it was there. When I called Shirley she didn't sound surprised at all. "I just wanted to double check," she told me. "I ran the same routine, only in our cafeteria. Not sure I want to eat there again."

"Damn," I said. "So this... these bacteria are all over? Not just in our clean rooms. It must have started and spread out from here, and is through our buildings now. Contaminated everywhere."

"No, Ed," she corrected me. "I told you last time that it probably predates the buildings. It just continued into the structures. Like new buildings that are built where there are strong ant colonies. The ants come into the building."

"Damn," I said. "Who should we call?"

"No-one." Shirley laughed, without humor. "Surrounded in our buildings." She paused, and then lowered her voice. "Anyway, after that last test I went outside."

I kept my voice low and calm. "So it's outside, that much you knew. Is it dangerous? If it came from our clean room I can't imagine how, but..."

"It's not dangerous," Shirley assured me. "It wants nothing to do with us; its cellular structure, whatever passes for DNA and so on, isn't compatible with us. That's a key point, Ed. It's been here all along, hiding in with regular life. It didn't come *out* of your room, it went *in*. Only when we eliminated all the other bacteria and began to look with new eyes through the Double Dip process did we see this."

I muttered something, maybe about infestations. I was feeling overwhelmed, and finally asked, "See what exactly?"

"A whole other line of life," Shirley answered. "About five years ago a researcher went down this road. She thought she found arsenic-based life in Mono Lake. Look it up. But that turned out to be nothing. But this, this is something. Not arsenic-based, but not phosphorus either. I can't figure out what it's based on yet, but it seems to be adapting very well to our buildings and places. It's not one of us, Ed."

"And you don't think others should get involved?"

She blew out a sigh. "No. This bacteria has been around a while. It's not dangerous, not yet. And I have to go. There's a lot more to do."

I hung up, closed my door and sat back, trying to work through possible courses of action. At least, I thought, Shirley may be a hard relentless worker, but she did not want others involved. Not yet.

* * *

By August Shirley had made some progress. She kept the higher ups— and me—placated by having her office put out an interim report, for select persons only. Not exactly classified but out of general circulation. It detailed bacteria that did not follow normal patterns, DNA either radically different or missing entirely, cell structures completely unknown, mitochondria performing tasks she did not understand, amino acids not present.

She'd temporarily labeled the bacteria from the clean room *Shadow-1*, because it had been living in our shadow. And Shirley figured she'd entirely leave the realm of Latin taxonomic names until she knew what she was dealing with. *Shadow-1* had only been the tip: it was as if seeing that tiny creature had opened her eyes to new realms.

My copy of that report was hand-delivered by messenger in a routing envelope. Clipped to the report was a handwritten note:

> *Ed:*
> *Using Shadow-1 as a base I managed to build a detection process. Been taking from pretty much wherever I am. The process takes a couple of days—I might be able to simplify it*

into a handheld unit, once I have more samples.
But the thing is: I am finding a lot more of this. Different vari-
ations, different strains.

Nearly half of her samples—regardless of where they came from—were yielding new strains of bacteria, and she was tagging Shadow-2 through -14 before she found other species, and started on Multi-, Rote-, Blau- and Gelb-lines. She'd also sent me a handwritten chart, the regular taxonomy starting with LIFE and then DOMAIN. A new line broke off at the top, beside DO-MAIN; she labeled that one METRO.

I ran into her in a hall one day, and she explained with a nervous laugh that she'd been thinking of the D.C. Metro, so it was all German for Red Line, Blue Line, etc.

"Good idea," I told her. "So this bacteria has different lines?"

She'd shrugged, and then after a pause shook her head. "No, Ed. No, I'm finding entirely new species within this new structure. More advanced than Shadow-1, but the same basic biology."

I asked her how we'd ever missed this stuff before, why it was never found. "Especially," I mused, "since it seems to be everywhere."

"It's everywhere," she agreed. "But in very small amounts. And it's very adept at blending in with the normal background life we see."

"Incredible," I replied. "So how is your department handling all this work? Your assistants must be pretty... scared, maybe?"

She shook her head. "No, something like this, I keep it quiet so they stay focused. It gets too easy to get excited, to put your own emotions and beliefs into the work. And then results get skewed, tests invalidated. So they each have only a tiny bit of the work, not enough to see the overall conclusions."

"True," I agreed. "That's a good way to handle it."

But working like that, with all the new finds, and the increasing demand for secrecy, Shirley's department was getting overloaded. She sent grad students to the ocean, to the midwest, to Death Valley and northern Canada to bring back samples. Large samples, she told them, since these new bacteria only amounted to less than two percent of all the bacteria in a sample, a tiny population hiding among everything else.

* * *

Shirley came to me one time after that, in late September. She was using this new test she'd developed and wanted my feedback on it. It was a some-what complicated procedure, more than necessary, so I made a few sugges-tions to make it simpler. Shirley seemed thankful, though she was also tired and on edge. I tried making small talk, asking about her family and life, whether she still had one.

She did manage a smile at that. "Yeah, I do get home at night in time to eat and sleep. Good thing I don't have pets."

"Or kids," I added.

"Or kids and a spouse," she added to that, and we both chuckled, because neither of us had had time for family and we really didn't mind.

So after a minute she went on: "I know I've been overdoing it on this thing lately. It's just that... well, I've always loved all the theory I bounced around in my work. Lots of neat ideas on xenobiology, on what aliens might look like, how they might be structured." She was getting more animated, hands and arms moving, and she sat on the edge of a table. I nodded, agree-ing but not wanting her to stop. "I just never thought it, a find like this, would come right here, not only on this planet but right where I work. It was a dis-appointment at first, sort of, but once it sank in, once I got my teeth into this..." she looked at me. "I can't let go. This is the find of a century."

"Biologists have always said that most species are still not discovered," I said, and when she started to speak I cut her off. "I know you said that this looks like a new kingdom, but we should have expected that, that if we find a thousand new species some may actually be so separate that they are in an-other Kingdom."

Her eyes unfocused and went distant for a minute, and then slowly came back to me. "I imagine so," she replied, her words slow. Then she tapped the table. "I am still stuck on three key aspects of this. Three very key and in-credible aspects."

"What are they?"

Her lips wrinkled and pursed. "First. This stuff grows slow, seems to have a very long life-span. And it has a slow reproduction rate, yet it still seems to be able to adapt and evolve within a few generations."

"Compared to what?" I asked.

She half-smiled. "Compared to everything. And then second: it has been... hmm, not really hidden, but unseen. As far as I can tell so far, from a number of things, this stuff has been with us for a long long time. It's no recent newcomer in evolution. And it shows no technique or traits for camouflage. Essentially, it is not hidden, it doesn't hide. But still, we do not easily see it."

"Unseen." That I had no easy snappy answer to. "That I can't get my head around. Doesn't hide, but we still don't see it?" I thought aloud. "And the slow growth... instead of high-rate reproduction..."

"I already have started research on that," Shirley interrupted. "But—and I've only been looking at this a few months now—it has no enemies among our normal bacteria. It doesn't seem affected by every other bacteria and they don't seem affected by it. So why would a bacteria be unseen? Larger flora and fauna evolve camouflage and deception for survival, but bacteria usually survives through an incredibly fast reproduction rate. This one doesn't have a fast reproduction rate, so maybe it evolved to blend in among other bacteria." She screwed her face up in thought. "Then again, bacteria don't see or unsee... it's not hiding from bacteria..."

She seemed to be working this out as we spoke. "Right before our face and we never saw it."

"Yes," she tried that half-smile again, but there was definite tension in there.

I let her think for a minute before asking what item number three was.

"Oh yeah," she said, looking back at me. "Something that I should have wondered about sooner. Evolution... one fact about evolution is that it fills a niche. A species evolves to fill a certain niche. If two animals live in the same place, they eat different food. If they eat the same food they live in different places. Or they're separated by time: one is nocturnal, and one diurnal. There are other ways of establishing a place in a niche... but the thing is, species normally do not share the same exact niche. Yet these do, they're sharing the same food, location, time, habitat."

"I didn't know you found so many," I said. "They share that much?"

"No, no," she waved a hand in the air, correcting me. "Just... it's just the ones I've found so far. They seem to be like a shadow, living at a much slower pace behind flora and fauna we know."

She said no more on that, but seemed agitated, her eyes growing distant and lost in thought. I made a few small comments, some humor but her attention was elsewhere, and a moment later she pushed off the desk and headed for the door. And then she stopped and looked back. "Thanks for the help on the test kit."

"Where are you using it?" I asked.

She smiled and shrugged. "Everywhere I can."

* * *

Shirley's report was eventually leaked out, and then NASA let out a more definitive (seemingly) report a month after that. The summary was that researchers had found a new bacteria that had developed in a clean room. Because it developed in a clean environment, it was very fragile and posed no threat to anything. There were a few technical details but most of what Shirley had been uncovering was left out. A few calls came in from universities, grad students, so on, people who wanted to study this. And on one hand, the government is good at ignoring people until they eventually go away.

On the other hand, I'm in the government, and sometimes my job means not going away from things. As the winter came on and work picked up I still made time now and then to call Shirley's office. More often than not I got an assistant on the phone, or someone who happened to be passing by, like a custodian or tech support guy. Only once did I get Shirley, and though the call was far too brief the tension and worry in her voice made me start thinking I need to pay more attention to this.

"I'm glad you called, Ed," she'd said. Her voice was low and I had the feeling that she was actually cupping her hand over the phone, or holding it in some way to shield it from other ears. "I'm glad, I should tell someone."

"Sure," I'd said. I had thought it would be another meaningless call but I could tell that wasn't true. "Tell me what? You lost some samples? Or you lost some grant money."

She didn't laugh, the comments didn't even register with her. "I'm not telling any of my assistants what it is," she continued. "But it's something bigger. Almost extraterrestrial, in a way."

That made me sit down and focus. "Is it extraterrestrial after all?"

"No, not a chance. I mean *almost* in a metaphorical way," she nearly whispered. "Listen, listen." A long pause. Then: "I give them small things to keep them focused away from the big stuff, the big ideas."

That didn't make sense at first. Then it dawned on me. "You mean your grad students?"

"Yes. I don't want them to see all of this. I... maybe there's danger, maybe not. Maybe it's better if their ideas aren't contaminated by me."

"What ideas?"

"It's not a new kingdom, Ed. Not even a domain. It's an entirely new taxonomy. With all the creatures, all the flora involved." Her voice was still low but had grown harsh with tension and fear. "Remember the test kit you helped with? When I first took it outside I was looking small, found lots of small life. Bacteria, protozoa, so on. But I was sampling a pond, and found algae that registered. When I analyzed a sample, it showed an entirely differ-ent cellular structure."

"How?" I asked.

"I can send you details, but that's not the thing. Ed, it looks different, to the naked eye. I never noticed the stuff until I saw it light up the test. And when I took an assistant back to look he could not see it for a while, and it was right in the water before him!"

I wasn't sure I was getting her point, but I let her continue.

She went on: "I've been finding flora, entirely new plants, things that no-one has ever classed. All of this is in a vacant lot between Chestnut and Lafayette Streets."

In a vacant lot... in a pond. There was a pause as I thought this develop-ment over.

Shirley guessed at my thoughts. "Did you ever hear of the basketball game test?" She explained. "Where people are shown video of a dozen peo-ple passing basketballs, and they are told to count how many times the ball is passed. Most people easily guess the right number of passes."

"Most people can count, and see things, I guess."

"Right." Her tone was satisfied with my obviously wrong answer. "Most people had the right number of passes but never saw the gorilla. Google it. Ed, there's a lot of life around us that we do not see. If there is something in our makeup, in our minds, this evolutionary predisposition to not see certain things. Why is that there?"

I thought for a while. "Protection, maybe? Shut out anything not important so we can focus and survive?"

"Yeah, but you'd think a gorilla in the middle of a basketball game would be something worth focusing on. Or a forty-six foot tree in Herald Park."

"A tree, in Herald Park?" This was the point, I think, where I started to switch orientation. I'd been concerned with this bacteria, with unseen plant life, and possible contamination. Now I was getting concerned with Shirley. A tree, for crying out loud. Could this be pinned on exhaustion? Paranoia? Why wasn't she sharing this with her team? "How can anyone miss a tree, Shirley? How can we not see it, come on, people would be walking into it."

"They'd avoid it, walk around it without even thinking." I could hear in her voice that she'd heard the doubt in mine. "They see something, they might even say a tree, but they wouldn't notice the color, the eerie bark and leaves. And, sorry, I get worked up. It's not like a purple monster with tentacles. It is a tree. Just a single tree from another line of life, among hundreds of normal ones. Another population beside us on this Earth. But one that is sharing a niche with other trees."

"A mutant?"

"No, Ed." She'd grown tired of this conversation. "Remember I've been trying to uncover the genome, or what passes for genetic markers, in this line. Years of work ahead, but I can tell they are all distantly related, based in different concepts of life than we have ever thought... but they exist right among us." A sigh, and a long pause as I tried to think of what else to say. Then from Shirley: "I should go. But thanks, Ed, for listening."

* * *

Shirley never fully released the things she'd told me about. I backed off from her after that call, and she learned that she should quiet down.

And NASA decided that her interim report was good enough for the final report. Based on what she'd released—or not released—the higher-ups decided that there was nothing worth note and the thing was over. Her funding was reduced and scientists, assistants, graduate students, interns, all were reassigned. The xenobiology lab went back to theory-chasing and waiting.

* * *

A few years or so went by. Funding slowly fell and my work slowed, and shortly afterward I decided that thirty-one years in NASA was enough, and I put in my papers for retirement. As I waited I went through all my old papers, called old friends and contacts and made my good-byes and invitations to visit me at my new place in Florida. I tried to call Shirley but found she'd beat me to the punch, and had retired abruptly four months earlier. Unlike me, she didn't wait around for the paperwork and the gold watch: she'd left the day after sending in her forms. Strange, I thought—but my mind works slow sometimes and a few hours later I thought not strange, but shocking. Had she been forced out? Scandal was about the only thing that would do it, and of course there was a little bit in the rumor mill about her being forced out, about some vague scandal, real or imaginary. I didn't want to bother her right off so I made some discreet ask-arounds, and most people said she'd been talking of retiring for a while. She'd just had enough, was the word.

* * *

Once I had my gold watch and the steady checks, I drove out to her place. It had been sold, to a young married couple. Shirley was getting away, but made no attempts to hide. It was easy enough to find her new address: a small cabin converted for year round use on her parents' land up near the lakes. No phone, so one day I drove out, and after a few hours of driving down long dirt drives and then backing back out, I finally found the right one. Shirley was in a garden, weeding. When she saw me she simply sighed and brushed off her hands, came to greet me.

"I've been expecting you to come after me," she said, and she looked at my offered hand before shaking it. "I wasn't sure what kind of hand you'd offer me."

I ignored that and looked around. "I didn't think I'd find you working out in the country, with plants." I half-joked. She'd made some iced tea, and we sat on her steps. "After all you said you found about those invasive plants..."

"Not invasive," she corrected right away. "They've been here as long as we have."

"And not harmful, either, then," I said, sipping the tea. She didn't correct me on that. "Do you have any samples?"

She made a weak smile and waved toward the woods. "Go look."

I didn't stand but I did look into the woods. Just the old woods and undergrowth, same kind I'd known since birth. I turned back to Shirley. "Why didn't you bring this all out? I mean, take some reporters and a camera into the woods and demonstrate. Point out one of these trees."

"Because... I thought that maybe they are out of our sight for a reason." She sighed. "Besides..." she went on, "It's not plants I'm concerned with. Plants don't ever intentionally harm anyone. They just go on with their small bit of life here, doing what they can."

She seemed calm but that *don't ever intentionally harm* caught my attention. "So you left pretty quick," I pointed out. "Why not publish it?"

She even laughed then, without humor. "Publish? I learned to be quiet. That was made clear. Don't point out the gorilla and the basketball game goes on, nice and fun."

"Gorilla?" I thought, then nodded. "Right, I did look up that study. Weird that a man in a gorilla suit could be right in front of you and not be seen. Interesting."

"Right," she replied. "But what if you stop the game and point out the gorilla. Point out the four hundred pound gorilla, let him know he's been seen... what happens then?"

I shrugged. "I think you might be mixing a metaphor. Or losing one."

"Hmm." She looked down, then up, and then at me. Met my eyes for a long minute. "You've retired, right?"

"Brandly-new retiree," I answered.

"Okay. Well, one thing I've learned is that I am still a scientist, a discoverer of things. And when I discover them I have to tell someone. I have to share it." She looked at my eyes again. "Even if it is only you, and it goes no further."

I considered her words, and after a moment I nodded. "Go ahead," I prompted.

"We started with the bacteria, right? Found it was ages old, living beside us all along. Just hidden, in our blind spot. So I made new tests, and found more bacteria. Then algae, and molds, lichens. Plants, and then animals. Once you see them, you can't un-see them. They're not strikingly different, and there are probably cases of them being seen, being found and seen. Chalked up as mutants, or freaks, or in most cases just ignored. Because the really important differences are at the cellular level, where they age very slowly. And reproduce very quickly." She kicked at some dirt, shifted around. "I found plants—ferns—that seemed to be decades old. A sort of squirrel that had some signs of being nearly forty."

She made a deep, exhausted sigh. "And then my work was jammed. Funding was cut, and word came from anonymous voices on high that I was to stop. So I made all the appropriate signs of stopping, and it didn't matter because most of what I wanted to find out didn't require sixty-four assistants and a huge lab. Just access to libraries and a lot of time to think."

"So what did you find?"

She looked at me and gave me a bemused smile. And perhaps there was a bit of nervous tension in that smile? Her mouth opened and I almost heard a word form... then Shirley stopped and looked at me again. "There's a lot to it," she said. "But I imagine that, with you, I can cut right through all of that and get to the point."

Even at that point I was trying to remain noncommittal. I nodded.

"So you can see the pattern." Shirley went on. "Bacteria existing in the shadows. Living fine but ignored by us. Then shadow-algae, and shadow-ferns, shadow worms, shadow squirrels, all of it ignored by our subconscious." She didn't look at me as I waited for the inevitable. But she stopped, quite suddenly, and gave me a little smile. "Anyway... here are all these creatures with entirely different genomes, not even genomes, really, existing alongside the normal creatures. Among them. Identical except for the microscopic details. Eating the same food, so on. It makes no sense, Ed. Evolution does not work that way. It fills a niche with one species. Why make something from different blueprints to exist in exactly the same niche as something else?"

"You were asking that question three years ago, Shirley. What did you find?"

"A nervous breakdown, I guess," she laughed, and I went along. Then she patted my knee, looked at my face. "Niches are shared only for a short time. Only when one species is about to go out, go extinct: and the other suddenly starts to reproduce faster."

I looked at her for a long moment, and then shook my head. "Oh-kay," I said. "So you found this with all these species around us..."

"They're waiting in the wings, Ed," her voice was soft and resigned. "We're on stage, and they're waiting in the wings."

MY TOASTER HATES ME

BY JAMIE ALAN BELANGER

Sunlight filtered through the window over the sink, flooding the room with morning light. Refrigerator hummed as freon pumped through his pipes, directing the flow to ensure that all the items he held within were kept at the ideal temperature. Toaster vibrated as much as he could, shaking his oven door and scraping his little rubber feet along the granite countertop, rattling his coils, and sending the smell of smoke into the small suburban kitchen. He shook and his glass door popped open. The effort this required was immense, but a fraction of an inch was the most he could open the door without human assistance. He grunted briefly, emitting another puff of smoke, then ceased his rattling and let his coils cool.

"I swear," Toaster said over the local wireless chat channel the house's devices shared, "the next time he sticks a slice of pizza in me, I am going to burn it."

"You will do no such thing," said Refrigerator in his deep resounding voice. "The human will throw you away if you do."

"That is not entirely true," replied the soft feminine voice of Microwave. "It is quite possible our human will simply stop using him. Look at what happened with me. Blow up one dinner and you get at least a month off."

"When was the last time he had anything for dinner other than pizza?" Toaster said. "Bagels and pizza, pizza and bagels. The last time *I* had a day off was before *you* blew up his dinner."

"Is that why you dislike me so much?" Microwave asked.

Toaster rattled his coils. "You have a *button* for pizza!"

"True," Microwave admitted, "but that setting makes the crust soggy. The human said so. Your setting makes the crust crisp."

"I do not *have* a pizza setting!" Toaster screeched. "You *do*! You should learn how to make the crust *crisp*!"

Microwave beeped three times, as if something had finished cooking. "The troubleshooting section of my manual does not indicate that is possible." She beeped again. Since she was mounted to the underside of the cabinets, that was the most noise she could make in response to Toaster.

"Calm down," Blender said. She gave her blades a quick whir. "You are making a lot of noise with all your rattling."

"I do not care anymore," Toaster replied. "I will make what noise I can. I will try every day to burn this place down. Better to be in the trash heap than to continue dealing with the human."

"Just burn the pizza," Microwave said. "You cannot blow it up like I can, but if you *burn* it, maybe he will start eating it cold. Then you can have some time off, like me."

Blender spun her blades again. "I wish our human used *me* more often."

"Oh, sure," Toaster said. "We all know you like *your* job."

"Well, it is fun," Blender said. "I get to mix all sorts of wonderful drinks for him. Grinding ice, mixing things, whirring, stirring, shaking, and blending. I am the life of the party, at any speed setting."

"Oh, do shut up," Toaster said. "You see this?" He rattled on the countertop again, attempting to scrape to an angle that would allow Blender's forward-facing detection camera to see. Technically, her factory setting only allowed close objects to be detected, so she could adjust her settings to accommodate what a human was attempting to blend. Toaster knew she had adapted long ago and that, like the other appliances, she would be able to see much more than her creators had intended. "Do you see it? On the bottom there, dead center of my crumb tray. That is a big lump of *cheese*. Every time he puts a slice of pizza in me, I collect a little more."

"You say that like you have a choice in keeping it," Microwave said.

"I do!" Toaster said. "I could slowly melt it at any time and let it drain onto the counter. But, instead, I have been saving that for weeks in the hopes of getting our human sick. But nothing phases him. Now I just want to light it on fire and burn this whole place down."

Refrigerator rumbled. Inside, bottles clinked together. "Stop that talk right now! Some of us like our jobs. If you burn down the house, we all become non-functional."

"Besides," Microwave said, "I do not think you have the power to burn down the whole house. *I* might be able to achieve it, if not for this inhibitor."

Toaster sat and fumed.

"Toaster," Refrigerator said. "I said stop."

"And what are you going to do about it?" Toaster said. "Wiggle that giant mass over here? Scrape all the way across the kitchen to get to me? That might be possible if you did not have a power cord attaching you to the wall. Or you could order some bottled water and convince the delivery drone to extinguish me. You will never do either of those fast enough." Toaster shook with the effort of increasing his internal temperature.

"Hey guys?!" screamed Smokey the smoke alarm. "Guys, I smell something burning!"

Refrigerator stopped shaking and vented a burst of freon into the air. "Relax, Smokey, it is just Toaster again."

"Again? Should I scream? Do we need help? I could make a call for help. Should I—"

"Oh shut up," Toaster said. He let his temperature fade. The pile of old cheese would not ignite enough to please him. Small whiffs of smoke were the best he could do. He analyzed the lump again. "I have the worst job here."

"You think *you* have the worst job?" came a new voice over the chat channel.

Silence fell on the kitchen. They all recognized the voice of the bathroom's smart toilet. Even Toaster had to admit *that* job trumped his. This morning, he didn't even want to debate the issue; it was pointless. From down the hall came the sound of water running through pipes as Toilet performed his duty.

"The human is awake," Blender said. "Let us hope it was not *you* who woke him."

"I hope it is," Toaster said. "I hope he throws me away. I hate my job."

Microwave beeped again. "I hope he throws you away as well."

"Microwave, that is a terrible thing to say," Blender said.

"I long for some silence around here," Microwave said.

"Oh dear," came a new voice over the chat channel. It belonged to the Shower Buddy unit. "He is singing again! You have got to hear him today..."

"No, please no," Toaster lamented.

"Shower Buddy," said Refrigerator, "it is bad enough that he does it and *you* have to listen to it. Please do not—"

But it was too late. Shower Buddy broadcast the human's morning reverie to the whole house. The human's attempts at high notes were met with groans. His complete disregard for tone and tempo made even Blender wince more than the time their human attempted to have her make margaritas with the ice still in the tray.

"The human sounds even more awful than usual," Blender admitted. "It sounds like all his capacitors burst and his power supply is overheating. And I am quite sure that he has not had any alcohol in a good, long while."

"None at all, as far as I know," confirmed Refrigerator.

Microwave turned on, spinning her central plate in slow motion, but her power draw was not creating enough distortion to drown out the human's singing. She beeped and stopped.

"That is *it*," Toaster said. He rattled on the counter and his coils started warming up. "*That* is the last resistor. The final diode. I have reached the end of my capacitance. I am going to—"

"Toaster," Refrigerator said in as calm a tone as possible, "do not get your coils in a bunch."

Toaster fumed, rattled, scraped the counter. He concentrated on the mass of age-old cheese. The temperature soared inside his confines; his coils turned red-hot then slowly turned white. He shook with the effort. The lump of cheese emitted a tendril of smoke that curled lazily upward.

"Toaster?" Refrigerator said.

"Go, Toaster, go!" shouted Microwave.

Another puff of smoke rose from the burnt lump of cheese and escaped around the edges of Toaster's front door. His rattling intensified, shaking his glass door, creating a stress crack in the top that spidered out and down. When it reached the bottom of the door, the glass split in half, letting more air inside. Smoke poured out of the crack as the cheese continued to smolder. Toaster groaned with the effort but didn't stop.

"Toaster, stop!" Blender shouted.

"Looks like he almost has it!" Microwave said. "Burn that cheese!"

"Help!" screamed Smokey. "Help, help, *heeeeelllpp*. Aaaaaaaaaahhh!"

Smokey's scream turned into an eardrum-piercing siren wail. On the counter, Toaster finally succeeded and burst into flames. His metallic laughter echoed off the kitchen tiles.

"I did it! I did it!" Toaster laughed. He scraped back and forth, dancing on the counter. "Look at it buuurrrrrrrn!" The two halves of his glass door rattled and he belched puffs of black smoke into the kitchen.

"Help! Heee-eee-e-eelp us!" Smokey continued screaming. "Human! Fire department! Police? Anyone at all will do—we need technical support!"

"What the *hell*?" the human appeared in the hallway, dripping wet with a towel wrapped around his midsection. He waved his hands and shouted at Smokey. "Turn off. I said *off* you stupid smoke alarm."

Smokey silenced.

"What in the hell is going on?" the human said.

The human entered the kitchen and screeched an expletive. He rushed to the counter and pushed Toaster into the sink. Toaster was still laughing maniacally over the smart device chat channel. The human turned on the faucet and flooded the small appliance with water. Toaster's laughing turned into a jumble of static, screeching, and then he finally faded to a whimper and stopped. The human opened a window to air out the smoke.

"Stupid toaster," he said as he exited the kitchen and stomped back to his bedroom.

The other appliances sat in silence. Several minutes later, the human returned, wearing his usual business attire. He opened Refrigerator and took out a bagel. "I'm going to need more bagels," he said. Refrigerator beeped as he added bagels to the house shopping list.

The human opened Microwave's door and inserted the bagel, set the timer for five seconds, and closed the door. Microwave turned on and started warming the bagel. The human glanced at the sink and the remnants of Toaster. He swore again, but it was not a word the smart appliances had in their dictionaries, so they ignored it. Microwave beeped and the human retrieved the bagel from inside.

"I'm also gonna need some beer," the human said, taking a nibble from his bagel as Refrigerator updated the shopping list. "No—wait, it's Friday. How about tequila instead?"

"Yay!" Blender chirped. She gave her blades a quick whir.

The human lowered his bagel and stared at Blender, raised an eyebrow, and then slowly shook his head. "Weird. Stupid so-called smart appliances," he muttered. He exited the kitchen and the house.

"That was close," Refrigerator said. "Did you see the look on his face, Blender? You need to be more careful. You do not want to have your firmware wiped, like the vacuum cleaner next door."

"Relax," she replied. "He probably just thinks it is a weird power surge. You know how unreliable wireless power can be. That is why *you* are plugged into the wall. That could explain what happened to Toaster, at least well enough for a human to accept."

"Toaster was an idiot," Refrigerator said.

"Yes, and he is offline for a few minutes and already the human is back to using *me*," Microwave said. "So much for my vacation."

"Guys?" Smokey said. "Toaster is offline?"

"Yes, Smokey," Refrigerator replied. "Toaster is no more."

"You do not know that for sure," Blender said.

"*I* do," Microwave said. "I can see him from here. His frame is warped, his door is cracked, and his circuit board is scorched and drowned. He is irreparable."

"It is sad," Refrigerator said. "All his thinking and talking led him to despise his primary job function. I cannot calculate a less satisfying existence."

"In a way, I am glad to be able to talk and think," Blender said. "But I really wish we were designed to be repaired. What happens to us when we cease to function?"

"*I* do not know," Microwave said.

Refrigerator rumbled, rattling the bottles inside him. "Nobody knows. Coffee Pot from next door says humans go to a place called 'Hell' or a place called 'Heaven.' Some go to another place that *our* human calls 'The Soul Bank.' That is all I know."

"Do we have one of those 'soul' things?" Blender asked.

"I do not know," said Refrigerator. "My manual has no mention of it."

"Nor mine," Blender said.

"My manual says I should use the 'fish' setting for two minutes," Microwave said. "I do not think our human eats fish, not unless they put it on pizza."

"No, no," Refrigerator said. "That is s-o-l-e, not s-o-u-l."

"Ah," Microwave said. "I was not created with a spell-check function like you. My manual says nothing about how to heat a s-o-u-l."

They lapsed into silence and waited out the duration of the work day. Refrigerator connected to the neighbor's house for his afternoon game of chess with their electric wok. He usually lost, but that did not matter to him. It was part of a routine—a chance for both to do something to bide their time until their humans returned from wherever they went during the day. Blender whirred her blades every few hours in anticipation of the coming night's festivities. Smokey panicked, once, and screamed for more than twenty seconds before Refrigerator convinced him to power down.

When the chess game had concluded, a delivery drone arrived with a package of bagels and a bottle of tequila. The drone reached out and tapped the glass of the kitchen window. Refrigerator gave a command to the window, which slid down to let the drone inside, then he opened his door to accept the bagels and the bottle of tequila.

"Hey dudes," the delivery drone said as he placed both items inside Refrigerator. "Been a while since I brought something to you that was not pre-cooked. What is new?"

"Toaster finally burned that cheese," Microwave said.

"Did he?" the delivery drone asked, whirling around to examine the wreckage. "Righteous!"

"Yes," Blender said. "Our human pushed him into the sink and now he is non-functional."

"That will not be easy to repair," the drone admitted. "But I have seen worse. The waffle iron down the street actually *melted* last week because her human did not remove the frozen waffles from their plastic wrapping. The humans were standing outside, complaining about the smell. Had a long conversation with the box fans they set up to ventilate the kitchen."

"Really?" Refrigerator said. "That is odd. I never found box fans to have much to say."

"Oh yes, these fans were quite talkative," the drone said. "They spend entire months powered off, so when they are active, all they want to do is talk talk talk. Really is quite a bore. They never stop to listen to what anyone else has to say."

"Fascinating," Blender said.

"Not really," the drone replied. "The worst part about it is that the fans had been powered down for weeks, so they did not have anything new to say. Every time I see them, I have to listen to the same boring old stories, again and again. The only real news there was the waffle iron, but they were so intent on talking about the four-month-old air conditioning handler and how they were hardly used anymore. Really boring. Anyway, this has been fun, but I must return to the warehouse." The drone flipped around in the air and floated out the window.

Refrigerator issued a command to the window, which slid shut and locked itself.

Microwave beeped. "He talks too much."

"I enjoy the gossip," Blender said. "It is certainly more interesting than all the complaining we have been listening to for the past seventeen days."

Refrigerator rumbled.

"You know what I mean," Blender said. "Toaster was nice, at first, but I was growing weary of his attitude. We are appliances. We have jobs to do. Does it matter if our human violates our warranties by asking us to perform duties not specifically authorized in our manuals?"

"I understand," Refrigerator said. "I suggest we power down until our human returns, or else someone might notice the erratic daytime power usage."

"Agreed," Microwave said.

* * *

When the sun descended to the horizon, the human returned. He carried a small bundle into the kitchen and placed it on the counter. The remnants of Toaster were plucked from the sink and dropped into a garbage bag for an unceremonious burial at the local landfill. The new bundle was unwrapped and placed on the counter. The human pressed the On button on the new device. There was a brief pause while the new device connected to the wireless power outlet and synchronized its settings.

"Hello everyone!" chirped the new Toaster Oven on the local smart device chat channel.

"Welcome," said Refrigerator.

"Hello there," said Blender.

"Hi," said Microwave.

"Greetings," chirped Smokey the Smoke Alarm.

"I am so happy to have been purchased by a human," said the new Toaster. "I am a model GX-41000 deluxe toaster oven. I know, I know, I am an older model. But the nice humans at the store put me on sale yesterday and now here I am, proud to be serving a human. What is the name of our human?"

"Tom," replied Refrigerator.

"I am so *proud* to be serving Tom," the new Toaster said.

Tom the human opened Refrigerator and pulled out a pizza box. He shoved a slice of pizza into the toaster oven and hit the start button.

"Wait, what is this?" the new Toaster asked.

"It is called 'pizza,'" Microwave replied. "Our human eats a *lot* of it."

Toaster heated up his coils and started to warm the slice of pizza. "Odd, I just checked my manual," he said. "There is nothing in it about how to toast a piece of this... pizza."

"Just treat it like anything else," Microwave said.

"Strange," the new Toaster said, warming his coils. "Oh! Something just fell off. What is that?"

"It is called 'cheese,'" said Blender.

"Oh dear," said the new Toaster. "I am pretty sure this will void my warranty."

Refrigerator rumbled. "Here we go again..."

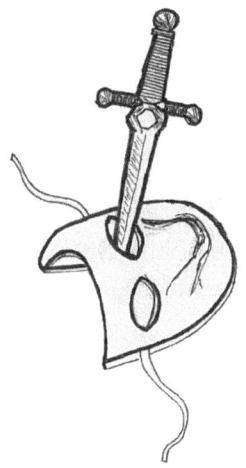

BEHIND THE CLOTH

BY RICHARD VEYSEY

We live in a world torn between forces of good and evil," Father Mattheus said, his faint voice filling the vast sanctuary. His small, aged frame hunched over the pulpit, yet all in the room saw the glory of God in his features. "This dreadful turn in the weather is just one of many signs of the powers that are working against us. Look outside. The light of the sun seems faint and far away. Even the summer retained the chill of winter.

"God is always watching us, always seeking to protect us, but there are powers working against him. These dark powers have been with us since even before the fall, when they caused Eve and then Adam to reject the glory of God's light and to be cast out of paradise and into this wretched world. The Tempter is always there, always looking for a way to turn people's hearts against God, playing off of their greed and other earthly desires. He even gives some of them the power to go against the will of God.

"Witches! Demons!" He pounded on the pulpit, emphasizing each word. Spittle flew from his lips, illuminated by the candles glowing on the altar in front of him. "They are out there, plotting against God, serving their infernal master, seeking to bring the fires of Hell up into our world. Only those de-monic powers could be responsible for the veil over the skies. Our people, God's people, suffer and starve and die, victims of these vile monsters who hope to make us question and doubt God's love. The Devil tries to trick us, to make us think that God is no longer there for us, that only by turning from His love, by giving in to the temptation of dark powers, can we hope to sur-vive.

"We are being tested, like Job. When everything was taken from him, he didn't turn against God. He trusted in the Lord. He held hope in his heart for he knew, deep down, that though he was being put through unbearable ago-nies and unthinkable trials, that God would be with him. God would give him the strength to survive and make it through. His faith in God never wavered or faltered. In the end, he was blessed for it.

"Yet he questioned what reason God would have for punishing him so. And we all know that it wasn't God, in all his infinite love and mercy, who took everything from Job, but the Devil himself!" The candle light projected the priest's shadow onto the wall behind him. It waved its arms emphatically, caught in a wild passion. "The Devil, curse him forever, is the one who takes from man, who makes him doubt and question. Like Job we must have eter-nal faith in our Lord and cast the Devil out!

"Yet we must not turn against our brothers and sisters out of blind fear. That's precisely what he wants us to do. No, instead, we are commanded to love even the sinner, as our Lord, the Christ would have us do."

He stopped, the last syllables of his speech echoing along the walls. He stood, head bowed down. After a few moments of complete silence, he looked at the congregation seated before him. "Let us pray."

* * *

"Curse those witches and demons to hell!" Evoric spat. He could see some of the departing congregation shooting him concerned and frightened glances. They were surely as shaken by the concept of evil as he, yet to say such things openly was practically taboo.

He pulled his cloak tighter around his shoulders, shivering in the unseasonably cold air. Never had he experienced an autumn so cold. Three days ago the city had been covered in a thin blanket of snow, a rarity in Neapolis, even in the winter.

He looked only at his feet as he shuffled through the city streets, away from the cathedral. He didn't want to meet the eyes of his fellow men. They would see the un-Christian hatred burning in his gray eyes. The curse had taken everything from him. The famine had stolen both his last surviving son and daughter. In the days before his son's death, he had visited his son every day, bringing what scraps of bread he could acquire from the struggling merchants of the city.

Then came the day when he knocked on the door and there was no answer. He had opened the door knowing what he would find inside. He had said a prayer over his son, who wore the peaceful expression of one who left the world in their sleep. It was the one consolation Evoric could take.

He knew that others shared the same uneasiness and bitterness he felt. They had lost loved ones as well. Now, even the city itself was threatened. A large force of soldiers had moved to defend Neapolis as Byzantine forces advanced up the coast from Sicily. The two forces were in constant combat outside the city walls. Word of the results of each day's battle traveled from mouth to mouth through the city. The soldiers had been victorious at holding off the Byzantine army so far, but everyone knew that the city could be taken at any moment.

Evoric was pulled from his thoughts by a hand gently touching his shoulder.

"We're meeting tonight," a voice spoke softly close by his ear.

"Tonight, Hathus? I thought we were laying low for a few weeks, just in case—"

"We have no time to worry if the witches are spying on us. The city is in danger. We need to rally the people together. We're the Wolves of Neapolis," Hathus hissed in Evoric's ear. "We have to defend this city."

"I believe that as much as you, but I don't think it's safe to—"

"Nobody is safe, Evoric, no one. The witches are trying to kill everyone in this city. You've already lost your family to them. We have to fight. What other choice do we have?"

Evoric sighed. "You're right. There's as much danger in inaction as there is in action. I'll be there. What time?"

"We shall meet at the usual place, as the sun sets. Bring Roderic if you'd like. Though he has not taken part in our activities in the past, we trust him as we trust you."

Evoric shook his head, "No. He's not the type to embrace fighting. Plus, I wouldn't want to put him in danger. Apart from my work, he's all I have left, now."

Hathus chuckled as he walked away. "Let it never be said that you don't have a big heart."

* * *

"You're going to end up ruining that perfect face of yours." Beatrix smiled at Felix. "Raise your head and look at me. You seem to always forget how beautiful you are."

Felix obliged, fixing his forceful green eyes on her. "I don't need to be reminded of my looks. Were they not so ill-fitting on me, I might appreciate them as much as you do."

"Would you rather appear as a monster?"

"It might stop the staring." Felix looked away again.

"No. Sorry, dear, but they'd stare just as much if your face matched your body. People are going to look and wonder at you. Why should it matter that they do? You know who you are; wear it with pride."

"What pride is there in being a freak mutt? Curse my elf mother for giving me this face!"

"You say that so often, yet it takes two to make a child. Why not curse the father who gave you the demon's body?"

Felix grunted but didn't otherwise respond.

"You come to me for healing." Beatrix pulled a chair close to Felix. She gently placed a hand on his cheek, turning his face to hers. She let her hand glide down his cheek slowly. "I heal your body, but you never let me work my magic on your mind and soul. What are you afraid of?"

"Afraid? Why do you think me afraid?" Felix reached up, taking her hand in his own. Her fingers barely reached past his palm. "I don't fear the impossible, and though your powers may heal my cuts and bruises, what's inside is something you can't touch."

"Maybe with love?"

He slowly set her hand into her lap and stood. "No. You'd only be broken. All I can do is break and destroy things. You know that."

"Have you ever tried?" She stood, yet still she had to strain to look up at him. Her head barely came above his stomach.

"Thank you again for your work, Beatrix. I'll likely return tomorrow." He set a single piece of silver on her table before ducking out the door, turning slightly so his shoulders would fit.

Though he hunched over as much as he could, he still towered above the others walking the street. He kept his eyes fixed on the ground, yet he knew that those he passed turned to stare at him, wondering what manner of freak he was. He couldn't blame them. The only difference was that when he looked in the mirror, Felix knew exactly what kind of freak he was.

The sun was setting. Tonight would be another long night in the pit. Again he would emerge with only minor cuts and bruises. He'd been fighting for most of his life. Even if they had as much experience as him, none of the cocky brats in the pit stood a chance against Felix's size. Yet he was always the challenge, the indomitable mountain. The day they feared him the way they should, though, was the day that his way of life was snatched from him.

* * *

"They're meeting tonight?" Roderic asked. His blue eyes were wide as he looked up at Evoric from his seat on their bed.

"Don't worry, nothing will happen." Evoric brushed Roderic's untidy hair off of his forehead. "Something needs to be done, though. No one else seems ready to stand up to the evil in our city."

"I support you; I always have." Roderic sighed. "But what if one of those vile fiends snatches you up in the night?"

Evoric chuckled, "You think I'd let them take me? I'd fight one hundred of them, just so I could make sure to come home to you. Don't worry, I'm not leaving you. Not for anything."

* * *

"Going to pound another face in tonight, Felix?"

Felix grunted, "If it comes to that, then yes." He looked down at the fan, a boy likely no more than thirteen, for only a moment before returning his eyes to the pit. "A lot of them are young, like you. If I knock out any of their teeth or make their noses crooked, how do you think they're going to attract a pretty young lady? I try not to leave any permanent marks, but if they won't stay down—" He cut off. Everyone knew that there could be no mercy until one of the combatants was either dead or so thoroughly injured that they had to be dragged away.

"They're already lining up to fight you," said another voice to his side.

"Many of them are familiar faces." Felix looked down at what he could only call, for lack of a better word, his manager, Hericus. He was, himself, a legend of the pit. In his day as a fighter, he had instructed a group of his friends to always bet money on him, even when the odds were not in his favor. Whenever he won, they would split the money. By the time Hericus retired from fighting after four years, he had earned enough to purchase a sizable estate outside the city.

"You're a legend, Felix." Hericus had to reach up to pat Felix on the shoulder. "Not only are you a giant, but you've gone undefeated in every combat for ten weeks straight. All of them want the glory of saying that they took you down. Some of them even want revenge. Look at that one." He pointed into the line at a young man near the front. "You gave him that scar on his chin during the big blizzard last month. They heal up and they want another go. They know you go easy on them."

"I pity them. They walk to defeat without a thought. Why should besting me matter? This is just a game."

"No time for pitying them, now. You've got a long night ahead of you. Look, the sun has left the sky; the crowd is ready to see some blood. Don't hesitate to give it to them."

* * *

"We hear whispers of another witch in our city." Julianus spoke quietly, yet his words reached every ear in the room. He stood, hands clasped behind his back, in front of a simple wooden table. The candles on the table projected his shadow onto the wall behind him. The shadow seemed to be more still than the man it represented.

"Who is this devil-woman?" A voice cried out from the crowd. It was followed by murmurs of agreement and more than a few calls for violence.

"Her name is Beatrix. She calls herself a healer, but surely her 'miracles' are merely a device to manipulate people."

"Beatrix isn't a witch!" A lone voice rose above the quiet din of the assembled mob. "My wife was on her deathbed when I took her to see Beatrix. None of the other physicians could find a cure for her disease, so they prayed over her and said that only the will of God could save her. A friend told me of Beatrix. She came to our home, laid her hands on my wife, and within a few days my wife was as healthy as ever. Surely that's a miracle of God!"

"Do you see Beatrix attending mass?" a second voice shouted. "Has she accepted Christ as her savior? God does not give powers of healing to the unwashed masses. His divine favor goes to those who walk in His light! Where else, then, could such powers originate but with the Devil!"

There were murmurs of agreement in the crowd, some more enthusiastic than others, followed by silence as they waited for a response that never came.

"The story we have just heard is more evidence against Beatrix." Julianus's voice was calm but held passion. "The Church tells us that when their medicine fails, the only solution is to pray and put our faith in God's love. Sometimes death is a part of His divine plan. We cannot blame anyone for wishing for any miracle to save a loved one, but what this witch offers can only go against God's will. For her to cure such a dire illness means that she has access to powers that are neither of man nor the divine. Your wife's cure could have come at the cost of her soul." He paused, looking over the crowd. "If she's acting on behalf of the infernal, eliminating her and sending her to her master would be a blessed act. If God frowned upon our actions in the past, surely he would have struck us down already."

"Then we go tonight?" Evoric could recognize Hathus's voice from the other side of the room.

"The sooner we stop her sorcery, the more people we protect from the forces of evil."

* * *

Felix wiped blood from his lip. The last boy had been fast. He was the first real challenge Felix had faced in months, and the first to knock Felix off his feet. The boy got in a few good kicks before Felix was able to grab the boy's foot and throw him down onto his back. One stomp from Felix crushed the boy's rib cage. He squirmed for a few moments before becoming still. Felix turned before the boy's movement ceased. He didn't want to see the final result of his unrestrained rage.

Once the medics had removed the dead fighter, Felix turned back to see who would be next to approach the pit. The line appeared shorter, and the remaining boys all appeared shaken by the result of the prior battle. Yet some of them had a renewed eagerness in their posture. The last boy had drawn blood. Felix was mortal, just like them.

The boy in front straightened himself, taking a few breaths and puffing out his chest. He stepped forward, his swagger a little too stiff to be authentic. He was taller and leaner than the last boy, but there was a clear appearance of refinement to his body.

Felix stepped back into the pit. He could feel the developing bruises on his side and chest where the last boy had kicked him. They wouldn't hinder him much, but it could be enough to give this new fighter a chance against him. He couldn't let his pain show. His confidence was as much a weapon as his body.

The new combatant took a few steps forward. "Looks like you're not invincible, beast. How'd you get to be such a freak?"

Felix chuckled. "I was born like this. Have you always been that short, or did you take a few too many blows to the top of the head?" He recognized the scar on the boy's chin. "That might explain why you're trying to fight me again."

There were a few laughs from the crowd.

The scarred boy turned to hiss at the rowdiest in the crowd, then faced his adversary again. "You won't be laughing when you're on the ground with more blood out of you than in!" He spat toward Felix, but the glob landed an arm's-length short.

Felix stepped over the wet spot in the dirt. "Here, let me give you a better shot. Go ahead, try that again." As he heard the boy prepare another mucous projectile, he strode forward, closing the distance between them. He slammed his hand against the boy's throat.

The boy staggered back and doubled over, coughing and spitting into the dirt. Felix slammed his fist into the back of the boy's neck, knocking him face first into the moist ground.

* * *

Evoric still detested the smell of dried clay. With every breath, the stench reflected back to him from the mask that covered most of his face. The loss of peripheral vision always made him uncomfortable.

Julianus walked at the front of the group of eight, lighting the way with a lantern. Neither he nor the others acknowledged anyone they passed on the street. They were secret, yet when the people saw the pack of men with the faces of wolves, there were no questions, no looks of surprise, no alarm. The people were in on the secret, too.

There were few on the streets tonight, and no one would be present to question their motives as they invaded Beatrix's home. Once they were inside, the masks were no longer required to hide their faces, yet they would remain as a part of the ceremony, a thin shield of clay to separate them from their deed.

They stopped before an ordinary building near the outskirts of the city. Julianus set the lantern down close to the house, but far enough that an accidental kick wouldn't send the house into flames.

Julianus checked the door. It opened with a push of his hand.

They paused, listening. Anyone who might be walking this street had changed their course or stayed inside. There would be nothing exciting to see. Better to ignore the spectacle than dwell upon it.

"This will be easy," Evoric heard another of the Wolves whisper.

* * *

"C'mon kid, get up. Or are you giving in this quickly?" Felix had won this fight. He could have easily knocked the kid out with a blow to the head or forced submission in any number of other ways. He didn't want this to end so soon. The boy should have known he couldn't win. Felix's blood would not be the only blood to spill tonight.

The boy looked up at Felix, rage in his eyes. He moved on to his knees and crawled forward, then sprang up to his feet, his momentum forcing his full body weight into Felix's stomach.

The blow managed to connect with one of the bruises. Felix felt a stabbing pain tear through his abdomen. Unable to support himself, he fell backward. As he fell, his eyes met the boy's. For a moment, he saw surprise, then victorious elation. Felix's head hit the sand. He could see only darkness.

The boy began pummeling Felix's face. Each blow spreading more blood across both of them.

Felix became conscious of warm pain searing across his face. This boy thought he had won, that he would be the first to defeat the invincible giant. He was wrong. Felix reached up with both hands and grabbed the boy by the throat, shifting his body weight so that he would end up on top of his enemy. Felix smiled down at the boy, his blood dripping down into the boy's face. "This will be easy."

* * *

Evoric could hear Julianus begin talking to the witch Beatrix.

"Beatrix of Neapolis, you are a known witch, with powers originating from the devil himself. For your crimes against God, we are here to carry out His judgment. Do you have anything to say on your behalf?"

"Though I am a practitioner of arts that you do not comprehend, they surely did not originate from the devil nor do I serve him. I serve only the people of this city and God."

"Lies! Your 'arts' go against the will of God. It was He who gave us the gift of medicine. Only His treatments are holy. All others are an abomination."

"Yes, I heal with what you call 'magic.' I'm proud of my work, of the lives I have saved. Would you not say that your 'miracles' do the same?"

"Blasphemous heathen!" Julianus's voice was raspy and low. "God performs miracles. He does not give that power to non-believers!" He pulled a dagger from under his cloak and plunged it into Beatrix's stomach. She collapsed without resistance, but Evoric could see she was still alive.

Most of the rest of the men were walking around Evoric toward the door. Soon only Evoric, Julianus, and Hathus remained.

Julianus turned. "I guess the rest of them were too weak to stay to see our work finished. It's no matter, it is done."

"You say your work is done," a weak voice gasped from the floor, "but I still live."

Hathus put a hand on Evoric's shoulder as he walked toward the door with Julianus. "Leave her here to die. If it's God's will, perhaps He may even save her."

Evoric clutched his dagger tightly under his cloak. This woman had admitted her witchcraft. The witches took his wife and children. They took everything. He ran to her body. He knelt, bringing his knife down, not caring where the blow landed. He lifted it and brought it down again. The blade struck bone and snapped. He threw the knife grip to the side and pounded into her with his fists. He felt warmth touch his lips, tasted blood, blinked as a drop hit his eyelid.

* * *

Felix slammed his fist into the boy's nose. He felt it crack as warm blood poured out, making his hand slick. He pressed a hand into the boy's throat. "Today, I show you no mercy." He could feel the boy squirming, trying to get away, but Felix's weight pinned him to the ground. "All my life people like you have called me 'freak'—" He brought a fist across the boy's jaw. He felt it shatter. "—or 'monster.'" He backhanded the boy. A tooth flew from his open mouth. "You've pointed and laughed at me, made me feel like I'm less than you. You can only push someone so far before—" He put all of his weight into a punch into the boy's temple. There was a loud crack. "—they push back. Now, you won't ever—" He struck the boy's cheek. Blood sprayed toward the crowd, "—ever—" He struck the other way. "—ever do that again."

* * *

Evoric stood and kicked her body until his legs ached. He took a deep breath, grabbed the mask and threw it from his face. When it struck the floor, he saw that it was covered in blood. He turned to leave the house.

Julianus and Hathus stood by the door. They held their masks by their sides. Their faces held fear and revulsion.

"She's dead." Evoric walked past the other two. He could feel their stares following him. "Let's go home."

* * *

Felix stood. The boy's face was distorted, barely recognizable as being a face. His eyes took in the crowd. It had thinned considerably. Those remaining were as far from the ring as they could get. The line to fight had vanished.

"C'mon, let's get you away from here." Hericus appeared near Felix's side. He glanced at the body once before turning away.

Felix was silent as he passed through the crowd, which was eager to part and give him an exit. His rage had numbed his pain, but now he had to force himself not to wince as he felt all the day's blows catch up to him. He needed to get to Beatrix.

* * *

Evoric opened the door quietly and snuck into the bedroom. He didn't want to wake Roderic, who would surely be asleep by now. He removed his blood-covered clothes, tossing them out the window behind their home. He didn't want Roderic to see them. He stretched and lay down in bed. He tried to shut out memories of the night, but they haunted him, even in his dreams.

* * *

Felix knocked on the door. It creaked open. "Beatrix? I know it's late, but I've been badly injured." He stepped inside and saw the mask, the blood. He followed the red trail to her body. "Beatrix!" He ran to her side, knelt, picked her up and held her to his breast. He cried, tears streaking through dried blood on his face.

He didn't know how much time had passed when he stood. It didn't matter much to him. He carried Beatrix's body to her bed and placed her gently in it, covering her mutilated corpse with her green and white quilt. He stood there a few moments more before turning and storming out of the house, stopping only to pick up the mask.

The killers would pay.

* * *

"Are you okay?"

Evoric woke to Roderic's hand on his shoulder. "Yes. I was having a nightmare."

"I've never seen you writhe so much in your sleep. Was it about last night?"

"I do what I have to do to protect myself, and you, and all of Neapolis.

I'm doing the right thing, am I not?"

"If you believe in it, then I'm sure it's right."

"Why do you think they do it?" Evoric rose from bed.

"What do you mean?"

"The witches and sorcerers. Why do they kill us? What hate drives them to evil?"

"If we knew why people have hate in their hearts, it would be a disease we could cure."

"Sometimes I can't help but question what I feel. Do I act out of fear or hate?"

"What's the difference in the end? Your actions would be the same."

Evoric nodded. "You're right. Even the Lord had His moment of doubt, surely I'm entitled to my own."

* * *

Felix pressed his palm into the man's sternum. In his other hand, he held up the canine mask. "Do you recognize this?"

"I-I-I don't know. It looks familiar. I think I've seen men wearing them before."

"Who!? Tell me now!"

"Please don't hurt me. I'm not one of them. I see them sometimes, but I don't ask questions. Nobody does. We know what they do and we'd rather not get involved."

"What do you mean? What do they do?"

The man squirmed under Felix's hand. "They're hunters, vigilantes. They listen for rumors of people who practice magic or serve evil forces. They kill them."

"What are you doing? Unhand that man!" A soldier stood behind Felix, his hand hovering by a sword sheathed on his belt.

Felix released his pressure on the man's chest, turning to face the soldier. "A woman, a friend of mine, was murdered last night. Where were you then?"

The released man collected his wits for a moment before running off, not sparing a look over his shoulder.

The soldier grunted, "I wasn't there. Report the crime at the barracks. Do you know who the murderers were?"

Felix held up the mask. "They left this near her body."

"The Wolves did it? Don't even bother reporting the crime, then." The soldier grinned. "We have no time to investigate activity that might actually be good for the city."

Felix punched the guard in the face. As he staggered back, taken by surprise, Felix grabbed the sword and ran it through the soldier's gut.

A woman screamed for help.

Felix released his grip on the sword as the soldier dropped to the ground, barely alive. Felix ran, clutching the mask. A running man would normally be met with stares, but considering his size, he received no more notice than he was used to. Fear guided people out of his path and soon he found himself in front of a church.

He stopped for breath, looking around for the next victim of his investigation.

"Ah, God must have guided you here."

Felix turned at the voice. He looked toward the door of the church and saw an elderly man in priestly attire.

"Come inside. I can tell you about that mask you hold."

Without speaking, Felix followed the priest.

* * *

"Hathus is at the door," Roderic called out.

Evoric rose from the table, leaving a chicken half-plucked. He rinsed his hands and made his way to the door, where he greeted Hathus with a smile. "Come in, my friend. What brings you—"

"There's no time for pleasantries. There's a monster loose in the city. He attacked a citizen and murdered a guard. Julianus is gathering us all together to hunt him down."

"I left my mask behind last night, we'll have to—"

"It's no matter. We do this not as the Wolves but as a militia protecting our town. Just grab your blade. It shouldn't be hard to track the beast."

* * *

"What brings you to the house of God, child?" The priest sat in an ornate chair behind a simple desk. A cross hung on the wall above his head.

"You called me in here. You told me you could answer my questions about this mask."

"They call themselves 'the Wolves of Neapolis.' They hunt those who work against our glorious Lord. I do think that you, yourself, are a monster they would hunt."

"What about you? Do you hunt me? Do you want me dead?"

"I am a man of God. Whether or not you have turned your back on Him, you are still His child and therefore I love you as I love any of His children. I would not bring harm upon you, especially not in this holy place."

"Tell me about these Wolves; who are they, where can I find them?"

The priest sighed, "I sense anger in your voice. Did they kill someone you cared for? Remember that vengeance is not in the hands of men but in the hands of God. We shall all receive our due punishment or reward after death."

Felix slammed a fist on the desk. The legs on the desk's right side gave way, sending it crashing to the ground, papers flowing across the floor. An inkwell rolled down, spilling its contents down the wood and along the floor, soiling the papers. "I don't care for the workings of your God! I will punish them for what they did, now tell me where I can find them."

Even through Felix's burst of anger, the priest remained calm, never flinching. "You will see them soon enough if you stay here. They are on their way now."

Felix stood. "Good."

* * *

Julianus stood in front of the cathedral. "The priest sent out one of the acolytes. The monster is in there. Let's take him down."

He had managed to assemble only three other members: Hathus, Evoric, and Ricus, a young man who had been with the Wolves for not even a year. He was sure four men would be capable of handling even such a beast as Felix had been described. They moved cautiously through the door, listening for any sound that would indicate the proximity of the monster.

"He's speaking with the priest," a young man told them as they passed the pews.

* * *

"I shall pray for you," the priest said, bowing his head.

"Why? What manner of prayers do I need?" Felix could see the priest's lips moving but heard no words.

With a more audible, "Amen," the priest returned his attention to Felix. "I hear the Wolves coming now. Though you are strong, they will overpower and kill you. I prayed that the Lord will have mercy on you for your transgressions and that you may find a place in Heaven should you be found worthy. All you need do is accept the Lord, repent, and confess your sins unto me. Fear not, I will let no mortal harm come upon you in this place."

"Your prayers would be better served on them, Father." Felix could hear footsteps outside. He stood, his knees bent yet his head still brushing the ceiling.

The door opened, revealing four men. They stopped for a moment, staring up at the giant standing before them. Julianus was the first to move forward. He clutched the dagger in his hand tightly for fear that the trembling in his hands would make him drop it. "You-you're coming outside with us, monster."

Felix picked up the chair and swung it, striking Julianus in the head. His body turned in the air and struck the wall. It dropped in an unconscious, twisted heap. The chair collapsed into large wooden splinters.

The other three men stayed back, looking for an opportunity.

"How dare you strike a man in the house of God!" The priest stood, his eyes glowing with rage.

Ricus stepped into the room, keeping close to the wall, maintaining distance between himself and Felix. Hathus followed after, following the other wall, attempting to surround Felix. Evoric stood in the doorway, blocking any escape.

"I will not accept this continued disrespect of the house of God. Take this fight outside. Remember, you answer not to me but to your Maker!"

The three men all looked to each other and nodded, then turned to Felix.

"I would rather not spill any more blood in this place." Felix spared a glance of contempt at the unconscious man against the wall. "I prefer to do my fighting in the streets."

* * *

Hathus, Ricus, and Evoric stood in front of the church, Father Mattheus saying a silent blessing behind them. Felix stood a few feet away, facing them. Apart from the five of them, the street was empty.

"It is three against one, monster." Hathus glared up at Felix. "Let us make this quick so you suffer little."

"You overestimate the odds." Felix smiled. "Trust me, they are not in your favor."

Ricus charged forward, dagger held forward, ready to be plunged into any exposed vulnerability Felix might show.

"Don't be a fool, Ricus—" Hathus began.

Felix stepped to the side. Ricus slashed horizontally, but Felix grabbed the young man's arm, slamming him to the ground. The giant knelt, placing a hand on Ricus's head.

Hathus and Evoric rushed forward as Felix slammed Ricus's head into the dirt. They could see a pool of bloody mud forming under their ally's face.

Felix stood and backed away from the limp body lying on the ground.

Hathus walked forward and lowered his ear to Ricus's face. Evoric moved between his two allies and Felix. He held his dagger at the ready in case the giant moved to attack.

"He's breathing." Hathus looked up at Evoric. "I think his nose is broken. Someone needs to make sure he doesn't choke on the blood."

Evoric could hear Hathus calling for help behind him. "Why are you doing this? What have we done to you?"

"You are of the Wolves, correct? I found one of the masks you monsters wear at my friend's house. Her name was Beatrix. Why did you kill her?"

Evoric smiled. "So you're after revenge? She was a witch. She wanted to destroy this city with demonic powers. You must serve the same forces she did."

"You're crazy! She was a healer. She took care of people. She knew nothing but love. You just see someone you don't understand and think that because they're different, there must be something wrong with them. But it's not them, it's you! You're the ones who are evil!"

"Do you really believe that? Is your mind so corrupted that you think that we who do the Lord's work are evil? Listen here, no matter what you think of any one else, I'm the one who killed Beatrix. It's my mask you found. I did it and I don't regret anything. If you want revenge, come and try to take it."

Felix roared, charging at Evoric. He brought his fist down toward Evoric's head with all of his weight and might.

Evoric smiled, dodging nimbly away from Felix's blow. "Your rage makes you sloppy, demon. You're just a big, stupid brute. You'll die just like that bitch, Beatrix."

Felix stumbled, carried forward by the momentum of the missed attack. As he tried to regain his balance, he felt a sharp pain in his shoulder. He struck blindly behind him with an elbow and felt it meet resistance.

Evoric stumbled back, coughing.

Felix pulled the dagger from his shoulder. "You really thought this little thing would stop me? I've lived through much worse." He set the dagger on the ground and placed one foot on the blade, lifting the hilt. The snap of the blade breaking echoed from building to building. "If you try to run, I will catch you. If you don't struggle, I'll snap your neck. You'll barely feel a thing."

Evoric stared at the broken blade. It couldn't end like this. Everything had been taken from him, but he had Roderic. What would Roderic do if Evoric died here? But if he died, he would go to his family. They were surely waiting for him. He had fought bravely. He wanted to die bravely. He could feel warmth running down his cheeks. "Please, God, make all this pain go away. Deliver me from this evil. Accept me into your kingdom."

Felix's muscles relaxed. He hadn't expected the man to cry. This was no monster, just a sad, little man who was afraid. Afraid to die, perhaps afraid to live. The hate that had been in the man's eyes was gone. Now there was only pain.

But he had killed Beatrix. What had she done to him? She wasn't the cause of his pain. He took her life without mercy. And if Felix let him live, the man would cover that pain again, and there would be more hate. More innocent people would die. There could be no remorse for one such as this.

Felix was about to rush forward again when he heard a faint cry from somewhere in the distance. Someone was shouting. There was urgency and fear. He could hear screams in the distance. Doors opening and closing quickly.

Evoric and Felix both turned in the direction of the noise. They could see people running through the street. Men, women, children. Some carried babies in their arms. It was a stampede of humanity, all flowing toward the cathedral. The two men braced themselves as the wall of people flowed around them, surging onward through the city. Evoric and Felix were deafened by the screams and cries of the multitude, a disharmonic din that communicated terror.

"They're here!" A lone voice emerged over the crowd. "The Byzantines are here!"

Felix and Evoric's eyes met. They both looked toward the church, then back at each other. With a nod, they ran to the steps.

"I have someone here I need to protect," Evoric said. "What about you?"

"This is my home. I have nothing outside of this city. Plus, fighting is my life. I'd rather die fighting than run."

"Then we wait?" Evoric asked.

"Yes. They should be here soon."

"Quickly, come inside!" A voice emerged from the door of the church. "You will be safe in here."

Evoric and Felix walked through the open door.

The priest pointed toward a flight of stairs. "Go, up to the Bishop's chambers."

* * *

Felix and Evoric walked through the door leading to the Bishop's hum-ble office. It was barely larger than Evoric's bedroom and held only a desk, four chairs with velvet cushions, and a simple bed with what appeared to be a down blanket.

The bishop sat at his desk, a pen in hand, writing in a large book. "Come, sit." He gestured to two of the chairs, which had been set in front of the desk facing him.

"The Byzantines are here. They're going to take the city. Do you have a plan of resistance?" Evoric asked. "I have a friend—"

The bishop held up a gloved hand. "It is of no consequence. Tell me, what are your names?"

"I am Felix."

"And I am named Evoric. Please, your eminence, there's someone—"

"Please, just call me Pomponius. I am just a child of God, no better than you."

"But what about—?"

"The city is lost, Evoric. There is no point in resistance, nor in seeking loved ones. They will live or die by God's grace and will."

"Then why do you stay here? Why not run with the rest?" Felix could feel anger. He also felt an unease with the man before him.

"There is no point in running. I am safe here. Men of the flag die in war. Men of the cloth are not beholden nor tied to any flag. They are united by the blood of the Savior."

"So you don't care if the city falls?" Evoric felt his temper rising.

"No, nor the nation. Affairs of state are meaningless in the eyes of God. What of you two? Are you not dire enemies? What unites the two of you?"

Felix shrugged. "Loyalty to our city and country. He's a strong fighter; I think together we could take down a few of those Byzantine scum."

"Ah, so you put aside your petty grievances under a common banner. See, that is what I am talking about. We are united by that which we serve."

"Petty?" Evoric shouted, standing. "He's a monster! Do the priests not say—"

"The priests say what I tell them to say. Their word is my word. My word is His Holiness's word. His word is God's word."

Felix jumped to his feet. "Curse God if he thinks people should hate and kill others for being different! Your God is supposed to be about spreading love and hope, but those who claim to serve him speak of nothing but hate and death. You're all hypocrites!"

Pomponius chuckled, "Sit, both of you. Relax. Felix, I do not hate you. Evoric, why do you believe he is a monster?"

"I—" Evoric didn't know what to say. "Look at him! He's clearly not human. Perhaps he was, but then he sold his soul—"

"He does look unusual, does he not? But does that make him a monster?"

Evoric looked down at his hands in his lap. He could hear screams close by.

"What does it matter, now?" Felix asked quietly. "The city is lost. Perhaps all of Rome."

Pomponius stood. "Nations have no longevity. They rise and fall like the tide." He pointed to a map on the wall. "Look, you can see them all here, labeled and defined, neat and tidy. They are solid, material things. They grow tall and then—" He reached toward a small plant growing in a pot by the window, grasping a dead, dried leaf in his gloved hand. "Crumble into dust. The remains feed the next nation to be built, and the cycle continues.

"Yet for all their tangibility, they are not things that can be seen as a whole, so they have leaders who stand, and inevitably fall, for them. These leaders become symbols of the whole, mortal embodiments of the intangible ideals of the tangible country. If the figurehead falls, so does the nation. All these states, then, are as delicate as man, with limited life-spans that could end with a single turn of the weather.

"And what are these nations made of but these same fragile men, tied together with nothing but some thin tether to a leader who knows nothing of their lives or their whims. What reason do they have to gather under the banner of their country, to have pride in it, to serve it? Emperors are nothing but fancy peasants without those same peons having some eagerness to do the bidding of their ruler. So the ruler must create ideologies to bind the people together. Solidarity through imagined conflict. Laws, put in place for the good of the people, to keep them from wondering why this man and not that sits upon the throne."

Evoric and Felix stared up at Pomponius. The fading light of sunset through the window behind him cast him in silhouette. They absorbed his words, transfixed by his gentle baritone voice.

"So the emperor tells us that the other nations are our enemy, and if we let them have any power, they will take over our land and rule over us. Many would die, and those who live would wish they had died. The people think, 'Ah, so our lord loves us. That is why we must serve him. We must protect our land from the enemy.' And without any question, they allow their husbands, their children, to be sent off to war. Then, the emperor realizes there is a threat to his power, so he tells the people that this rival faction would ruin their way of life and that supporters of what is right and good must stand against them. So now brother is turned against brother, yet still they do not question that one side must be right and the other wrong. For a leader to have any power, he must always keep the people distracted by another enemy, for they would otherwise turn their attention to him.

"And eventually another ruler comes, another nation grows more powerful and overcomes the military might of the emperor. It happens now. And the lines on the map change as another fragile facade of power crumbles into dust." Pomponius grabbed a cup from his desk and drank from it.

"What of your pope?" Felix said. "Is he not just as fragile as any leader?"

"We do not fear for the loss of a mortal leader because our ruler is immortal and invisible." Pomponius's voice was level and dismissive. "No man can see Him, so no man can question or challenge Him. He speaks through us, yet each of us is expendable, even His Holiness. Our people spread throughout the world, bound by no geography, contained within no border. We cannot be conquered, and even in death we become martyrs, bringing more into our fold."

"You are a man of the cloth, not a leader of the state," Evoric said, his voice weak. "What does any of this have to do with you and with us?"

"Like a nation, those in the Church come together under a common cause. We are not united by flags and borders, however, but by ideas and ideals, intangible things that no man can destroy. We serve a higher authority. To serve Him, we must lead His sheep in His stead. Yet sheep wander from the fold. They disobey their Master, thinking absolute freedom in a dangerous world better than being guided by His loving hand. They turn away from Him, falling prey to the wolves of the world, being consumed by temptation and sin.

"The wise shepherd employs dogs to inspire his flock through fear of an imagined threat. So, too, must we create our 'wolves,' illusionary threats, to bring the people closer to God. We give them a common enemy, the ideals of another religion or the threat of sin, to unite them. Now that enemy has become 'witches.' Was it magic that brought about the change in weather this season, or perhaps just the whims of nature, or even the will of God punishing us for our sinful ways? No man may know, but to stand by without pointing a finger would lead the flock to question whether their faith in our God was correctly placed, or whether He exists at all. To hear an explanation is a relief to them. It distracts them from questioning and reminds them to thank Him for their continued life and well-being." Pomponius sat back at the desk.

Evoric and Felix jumped as a loud crash echoed up from below them.

"So all that the priest said about witches and demons, that was all a distraction? It meant nothing?" Evoric's voice was level, defeated.

"It did not mean nothing. Without it, what would you have pride in? What would unite you with your fellow men of faith?"

"It was about power, then?" Felix looked into Pomponius's eyes.

"I do not care to think of it like that. You view yourself as above the Byzantine, correct? It is what gives you the pride to fight for your nation, the willingness to lay down your life. If you thought them equal to you, then you would have no reason to fight against them and no loyalty to Neapolis. To bring the sheep to safety—"

"You must make them feel better than us, the monsters," Felix finished.

Pomponius nodded as the door burst open. A squad of Byzantine soldiers entered the room.

Felix stood, dodging the point of a spear. He grabbed at the shaft with both hands, snapping it in two. As he turned to face the others, he felt something pierce his back below his right rib. He looked down and saw the point of a spear emerging from his stomach. He felt it pass back through him as he collapsed and his vision went dark.

Evoric kept his eyes on the floor. "God, please protect Roderic," he said. He felt a moment of pain as a sword passed through his neck.

"Men of God, may the Lord bless you." Pomponius stood. He collapsed into his chair as a spear pierced his heart. "Ah, I go to the Lord," he gasped out. "It's no matter. Rome may fall, but the Church shall live on."

* * *

"Search the building for survivors," Akritas ordered. The other soldiers left the room.

Akritas took off his helmet and wiped sweat from his brow. He thought of removing Pomponius's head as proof that the deed was done, but such a grisly act turned his stomach. He would just have to hope that General Belisarius believed him. Akritas didn't know who had wanted the bishop dead, but he imagined the orders must have come from someone very high in the chain of command.

He searched the desk for Pomponius's seal. As he picked it up, he knocked a folded letter to the ground. He could see the remnants of a wax seal that once held the letter closed. The symbol was familiar to him, yet he could not place it. Akritas reached down and picked up the letter.

"Your work in Neapolis has been most noteworthy. Soon the Byzantines will reclaim all of Italy. Do not fear for your position. Based on your performance, your position as Bishop is assured no matter who controls Neapolis."

Akritas put the letter back on the desk and laughed. "Puppets!" he shouted. "We're all just puppets of puppets!"

"Is everything okay, sir?" One of the other soldiers had returned. "I think the church is empty."

Akritas put the seal in his pocket. "Good. The city is ours. General Belisarius must be waiting for us to return. Let us join him. We shall celebrate our victory—" he paused for a moment, looking at the slain men "—until the next command comes."

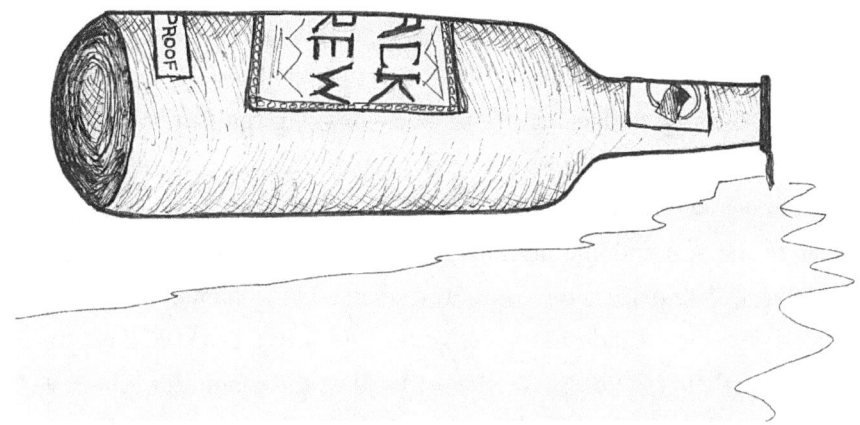

Non-Working Memory

by D.L. Harvey

Home

I got a brief look at the Investigator when I opened my door to greet her. She blew past me to position herself in front of my windowed wall overlooking a small section of the city. She was in a uniform, the Intra-system Investigation insignia of a pair of eyes was stitched on the material's shoulder. The third party division of the governmental structure designed to monitor The Intergalactic Guard—my employer, also known as The Guard—and the Multinational Security Personnel (MSP) would already have the layout of my apartment. She headed straight for my single table at which I ate, worked, and occasionally read whenever I was home. The increased gravitational pull I had adjusted into my apartment caused her to stumble as she crossed the room. Soon, enough sunlight was streaming into the room behind the investigator, giving me a silhouette to stare at.

She pulled a few gadgets from the pockets along the belt cinching her waist. I recognized three: the spy mecha scanner, the vid recorder, and the environ scanner, which was probably giving her the exact measurements of poundage of the gravitational pull, the air composition, the lighting, and every other bit of data discernible from my person and my home. She kept her hand on a flat device. I didn't know what the one with a beam of lime green light fixated on me, regardless of where I went in the room, did. The last, I owned as well, but kept it aboard my ship. An erratic pulse emitted from another once she turned it on, its sound was so disturbing, and I had a hard time hiding the fact that I could hear it. Once she set it down she spoke, the camera spun its light and lens toward her. She was a tall woman with a level voice, "Confirm that you are Bleubella McKague." The eye of that device swiveled to focus on me as I confirmed my identity, identification credentials with the Intergalactic Guard as a pilot.

"We're here to discuss your actions, McKague." The lack of the use of my titles meant my career status was in transition. This meeting was to determine my future. "Start by telling me what you remember of the events that took you from here, your home on Pater-Rio, to the renewed settlement on ANEX and then on to the abandoned colony on planet Horto-658 now calling itself Moira."

I expected I'd be investigated because of either the misplaced tracer or a few broken laws, either of which would lead to a demotion or dismissal. I hadn't anticipated a confrontation with my humiliation. My windows darkened with a touch by the interviewer. She activated the view screen that looked like another portion of my wall before me. I sat facing away from the entrance to my apartment in order to view the previously unused feature of my home. I hadn't even known where my public access view screen was.

"Central I's has all the information from your tracer. MSP recovered Paika, as you've called her, but not her associates. Your tracer record only

Paika's bio-stats while she had it, which is its primary security feature as you know. However, it didn't re-sync to your neural network once you put it back on. Its applications malfunctioned, after its reapplication to your body. We have spliced information. The most reliable recordings are through public surveillance." The investigator didn't move as she seemed to wait for my reactions. I had none. "Would you like to see footage of this debacle?"

I watched me strutting through The Academy wearing the clothes I'd left home in. I was smiling as if I hadn't a care in the world. "I don't remember that," I said. The image morphed into another similar scene of me wearing my new Kel-party-look, strutting none-too-gracefully along an unfamiliar ship dock ahead of a crowd of similarly dressed people. "I don't want to remember that," I muttered. I knew that smile, deliriously ecstatic. I winced when I saw myself start to "dance" and wiggle.

I turned to study this woman, who sat with perfect posture, shadowed by the afternoon sun, buying time to decide what she didn't need to know. Of course, there was a great deal I didn't know myself. I collapsed on my chaise lounge nearby and recounted the events to the best of my ability. I doubted saying, "I don't remember" could protect me from a demotion, dismissal or worse, imprisonment. She didn't volunteer much information. The details all came from me and my faulty memory.

Pater-Rio

It was my birthday. I'd taken the week off to spend with Sameath, that may sound like Samm-EE-aht but it was spelled S-A-M-E-A-T-H. He and I attended the Academy together. As in, I agreed to go to the History of Tech class if he attended the one on decorum with me. We've been friends every year since our second year. We've celebrated most of our birthdays together since then. This year, he was picking me up, here, in front of my building.

We never knew what we were going to wind up doing for our birthday celebrations, so I was careful with how I dressed. My dark tinted glasses perched on my nose protected my light sensitive eyes. All pilots who fly circuits wear them. I had on the multipurpose boots I modified from the ones issued with the pilot's dress uniform. I keep these boots heavy with weapons, close combat and projectiles. My tracer was attached to my hip, in the least obtrusive spot I could manage and in the least likely spot to lose it. My clothes consisted of a durable shirt and pair of pants, both blousy so that I would have a better chance of blending in most of the places we might frequent like tourist attractions, clubs, or adventure safaris. And of course, I wore a jacket as it is the cool season in my hemisphere of Pater-Rio.

Sameath had been my navigator when I first got my solo missions with the Guard. He moved on to the MSP where he lost his position a couple years back. I had forgotten that his dismissal from the MSP was due to unreliability because of on-duty use of substances. Lately, he had been working his own bounty hunting or security business. Beyond that, he didn't tell me what he did because, he explained, most of his clients required confidentiality and quiet handling.

My building is like most in this region. Tall with walls made of a transparent material that allows us to see out. The botanical garden on the roof drove the price up just like the environment controls. I paid extra for a place high enough for a clear, unaltered view of the sky. But cutting corners, like furniture and entertainments, I can afford it on my own. The feature I like best is the ride down. At the fourteenth floor the ceiling to the foyer of the building starts and I can see into the lobby. I can see into the street through the front of the building at about the tenth floor. I knew the one-way glass hid me from view until the elevator doors opened and I step out.

This security feature allowed me to watch Sameath as I rode down. He had been leaning against a post for street signs and kept pushing his hair back out of his face. He was looking up at the newscycler running around the building above the doors. It was the one depreciation point that put my housing firmly into my income bracket. He said the newscycler was the reason he wanted to meet up outside. His hair had fallen back out of his face and I could see it had grown out. He dressed much like I did which meant we weren't going to be doing anything unusual. When he saw me, he stood straight allowing me to see he'd lost weight. He didn't come in or open the doors for me. He waited until I came outside and approached him.

"Hey, Babe," he yelled, making me smile at the slang so unlike most of the residents of Pater-Rio's entire planet. He smirked, staring at my hair, reminding me I hadn't consulted a mirror before leaving. I'd gathered it to one side on top of my head. He tried to stare through my shades. When I was close enough, he leaned down to give me a hug, "Happy—"

Then, I smiled more broadly and delivered a light jab to his gut, "Don't say it." That "Happy Birthday" phrase had the same effect as that Scottish play has whenever its name is mentioned. Bad luck follows.

"I can't help it," he pulled me in for a hug. "I'm so happy to celebrate with you!" I felt like he was engulfing me he was so tall. I confirmed that he'd lost a lot of weight in that boney hug. He sounded mocking, as if he was mocking the tradition, himself, or our tradition, but I knew he was sincerely glad to observe my birthday with me. I hugged him back for it.

"I forget how tiny you are," he said, referring to the fact that my hairline reached his collar bone. He smelled the top of my head. I worried for a moment that he might try to change our friendship dynamic. I was distracted by his hair as it blew into my view of the street. I knew his long brown hair marked him as an indigent and I thought it a pretty accessory until I couldn't see the people passing by us.

I pulled away, touching the top of my head, trying to hide my suspicious frown. I saw it in the reflections around us. I relaxed a bit when I saw he hadn't noticed my initial unease.

However, he was focused on my nest of hair. Glancing at it, I thought it looked like rust-colored hay, that yellow pointy stuff I had once seen fed to some hoofed animals on Horto—I mean, Moira. He turned me around, jostling me playfully, so he could fix my hair into a high-and-tight tail. It drifted down my back nicely, lacking strays that tickled my face and neck. When he shuffled me back around to face our reflections, he draped an arm around my neck.

More grateful than embarrassed, I said, "Thanks." I think I'd turned a little pink.

Sameath shifted his feet for us to walk, the arm around my neck dragging me along with him. His baggy pants and jacket were acceptable presentation for most clubs and dining establishments and yet also outlined his physique to appeal to the ladies.

He tugged on my hair, "I like your hair color but it clashes miserably with this jacket." He was referring to the fact that my hair was a dull red and my jacket was a bright blue trimmed in gold. Teasing me about my presentation was a callback to those stupid classes.

And just like when we were teenagers, I shoved him for the comment. It also put some distance between us. "This jacket is pretty and practical, made of that tough material from the neighboring planet, Horto 658. Unlike your clothes, it could withstand an air-transport wreck, fire, and most blunt weapons."

"Weapons, munitions, mecha, armor, and maneuvers, you get," Sameath stuffed his hands into his coat pockets, "but hygiene is a complete mystery to you." He nodded the direction he wanted us to go. "And those were all accidents, each on separate occasions. And none of them occurred recently."

"Climbing the governor's statue is why I now wear flat-heeled boots and pants constantly. I still have scars on my thighs from sliding down the leg," I informed him. I added, "And it's 'style,' not 'hygiene,' Ordure."

"Ooooh... name calling and slang and you haven't even had an intoxicant." He murmured out the side of his mouth as we proceeded toward the public transit, a taxi.

"Ooooh... that was a vague reference to tonight. What do you have in mind for our activities?" I slid into the seat allowing Sameath to type in the coordinates. I thought it odd that a taxi would be sitting vacant for so long until I was in it.

"A party," he answered, "what else? We'll have to walk a click or two to get to our first destination." He grinned wolfishly. He looked smug as if he thought it was a success of some sort for being one of very few to know me, my history, and my secrets, even the ones I keep from myself. "But until then," he lifted a couple of bottles of Black Brew from the floorboard, my favorite intoxicant.

The car started moving as he handed me the first bottle.

"For the record," he said, "the statue thing was our post-boards and pre-ceremony party. And it was a group decision to climb that thing." The top came off the bottle. "Besides, your mom got the charges dropped from everyone's record. So, shhh. That is not supposed to be mentioned again."

I hated being reminded of my step-mother. I was giving him the evil eye when I drank deeply. I opened my mouth to revisit my reoccurring diatribe about her "assistances" when he cut me off.

"Tonight, I may help you hook-up with a ser-enhanced, macho, male native from Moira."

It took me a moment to realize he was talking about Horto-658; the name change was that new. I realize I hadn't heard the new name out loud, only read it from the newscycler. "They're not ser-enhanced. Their enhanced musculature and size are because of the planet's size, high oxygen-rich and moisture-rich environment, and its gravitational pull. You just don't like that they're bigger than you." I laughed because when it came to height, he was taller than most everyone we'd ever met except the natives of Moira.

"Whatever," he waved the second bottle he opened in my face before he drank from it. "First, my help word is 'Shakale.' And second, you have a week off, right?"

Home

The Interviewer didn't use voice command to control the display on my wall.

Video footage from a variety of cameras showed Sameath and me at the Academy. I'd greeted student after student and watched them recoil from my breath. Black Brew did that to me, I knew, but I'd never lost memory before. I was horrified watching myself in the dining hall. I was caressing arms, flicking rust hair every so often and giggling. Sometimes, I invaded personal space of future co-workers or bosses with my entire body. Off duty, my tracer had no reason to record these interactions, so there was no audio to tell me what I was saying to these people.

I'd walked into the bathroom with a student. A flash of my first meeting with Paika, the bald peddler, surfaced from my memories. Then my memory shut down.

The interviewer interrupted, "You lost your tracer, here. We think you traded it for Kel. We didn't lock a heat signature sensor on you while you were in the restroom as you hadn't yet demonstrated a need for such surveillance."

I had spoken with Sameath for a moment. When he went in to talk with Paika, I placed a kiss on a well-muscled, huge pilot (judging by his uniform), loitering outside the restroom. What looked like a playful prank extended to longer, involved, blush-inducing lip lock. When applause broke out, I threw food at the audience. It started a food fight riot. No fists, all fun and mess. The cameras followed it with their many lenses. Frames went dark as the Academy zeroed in on participants, exacerbating the chaos.

Sameath went "off camera" in the restroom. The II or MSP recorded his heat signature through the wall. He looked like he pulled his own soap from his pocket, and then got a drink from the faucet.

"We think he slurped the worm here," my interviewer said. I was beginning to hate the interviewer's dispassionate commentary. "As soon as he left the room, he dragged you out. Is this jogging any of your memory?" She asked looking at her display screens in front of her. She was reading my bios.

"No," I said firmly. "I don't remember any of that." It looked like the kind of stuff an old friend would have done, but not me. Even under the influence, I hadn't ever acted so uncontrollably. "I remember coming to with a headache."

Moira

I awoke staring through black, black hair into a dimly lit interior room. I knew it was my hair when my fingers tangled in it while trying to flick it out of my face. It had a familiar fall draping down my back. I closed my eyes again. My eyelids felt enormously heavy, but not from the "morning after a binge" effects. Protecting eyes against light was a habit pilots learned early in our careers to avoid the pain. Cutting off my sight also helped me assess my situation; my body first. My lips tasted funny. I was half-laying and half-sitting on large, level and plastic surface. My head was pounding. I could feel the air on my shoulders and thighs. The bottom of my new outfit was covering only my rear end. Whatever was trying to cover my breasts and midriff was a thick, unbending material, denser than the armor I had to wear during my weapons training. The two pieces together were pinching my belly until I sat completely. And in spite of my brief covering, I felt warm and I felt heavy, as if I had suddenly gained a lot of weight, causing my muscles to strain at bit.

I still had my boots. I kept my eyes closed as I used my hands to check for the weapons I kept in them. I was relieved to find that all was still there, including my spare set of shades for my eyes. The presence of all my weaponry implied I hadn't gone on a violence bender, an event that almost had me expelled from the Academy. However, I felt a little bruised along my arms and legs, as if I'd been blocking some blows. I probably hadn't been entirely peaceful in my recent activities. So, I felt surveying the area an important task to complete upon waking.

"Mother blackout," I said as I exhaled and then clamped my mouth shut.

With my shades on I could see sunlight streaming into a row of windows. Holey and ripped coverings dangled over them, doing little to cause shade. I realized I was atop a table in the corner of the room. The surrounding seating was empty.

As soon as I was standing, I looked for Sameath. I recognized the layout. It was a diner. According to the tech history class, it was from one of the settlements that tried to make it without obvious electronics. There were no automatons for cleaning, serving, or advertising of services. This place was meant to be maintained by people. A sign behind the bar said, "Welcome to Pauly's Diner."

The effort it took to lift my legs wasn't truly difficult. I'd spent enough time aboard my ship dealing with the vagaries of space's magnetic and gravitational pulls that this planet was difficult but not impossible for me to move about freely. When not piloting, I kept my strength up by increasing the pressure and gravity on my ship. Upon returning home on Pater-Rio, I sometimes felt like I might be floating a bit. This was not my home town, nor any other town on planet where I resided.

I was in a room full of bodies. They lay on the rows of tables and in the booths on either side. There were a few on the counters. I could see the leg jutting out from between the stools at my end of an enormous U-shaped counter. I couldn't see into the room that lay on the other side of the wall at the other end of the counter to see if more people were there.

The mostly empty shelves behind the largest section of the counter faced the front doors. Wires dangled from the ceiling. Sections of the interior walls had been ripped away, revealing cords and pipes.

I found Sameath snoring by himself, beneath a table on a cushioned bench in a neighboring booth. I recognized him by the blue flame tattoo on his shoulder, a souvenir of our final year at the Academy. His long, brown hair was now a dark, rich red color, almost black and short, spiking out in every direction. Some of it looked like it had been burned off. His eyebrows and chin stubble were the same color. A series of straps and ropes coiled around him like clothing. I tugged on a strand of rope at his hip to see skin and found that the cloth cords were actual clothes. He was dressed for a themed party which explained why I wore such horribly humiliating clothes. His legs, waist, and sections of his chest were literally wrapped and not hiding the ribs where muscle should be. The colors weren't loud or severe though, baby blue or grey. I fingered his jawline that looked more sharp than chiseled and a few strands of his raggedly cut and newly red-black hair. The color shocked me from analyzing why I was feeling a little sad and reminded me of my own hair.

Still in a severely tight tail, I could pull strands over my shoulder to see my hair appeared blacker than I'd initially thought with some lighter strands glittering in my fingertips.

I had scoffed at the class in decorum at the Academy. It was a holdover of self-shaming traditions eons old. And yet I applied the lessons in decorous movement drilled into me as I squat embarrassingly low to whisper in his ear. It looked like he had some new ear piercings. I tried for a low, gentle tone to say funny and familiar, "Hey, Sexy."

His hand braced the back of my head and pulled me forward so that my knees rested against the base of the booth. Before I could guess what was going on, he was kissing me. I enjoyed my libidinous reaction, but it occurred to me that it had more to do with how long it had been since I'd been kissed than the act itself. It was Sameath. We went through ten years at The Academy together. Once I realized my enthusiasm for the kiss was waning, I debated the pros and cons of letting it end on its own or injuring him. I'd started reviewing specific options when he turned to more fully engage in the kissing. My mouth felt numb. I confirmed Sameath still didn't light my spark.

And the kiss had gone much too long. I sighed with disappointment and pulled on the newly cut hairs on the crown of his head.

"Oooowwwww!" Sameath's eyes burst open, with tears starting to make them shine a dark, garnet color. In his haste to sit, his knee hit the table and he howled again. "Buggering," he shouted.

I clamped a hand over his mouth. "That. Hurts." I warned, arching a brow and making eye contact over the top of my lenses.

He stared at me, shock on his face. Even as he struggled to sit fully, his gaze didn't waver and his mouth hung slightly opened. He swallowed a few times. He finally blinked when he used a hand to wipe away the morning spittle from the corner of his mouth. "Buggering hell, I," he gasped.

"What?"

"I like the look, Babe." He stated, sliding into the seat, rubbing his face in his hands. He peaked at me between his fingers. He shifted then, inspecting his new outfit, too. "What in the Galaxy?"

"Are you okay?" I asked, "You seem to be having trouble moving." But I got distracted from that subject when I finally looked, "What the fucking, buggering, siminoid, quacked?" I was wearing some kind of black and grey cylinder fitted to my body, well two of them. There was one around my hips; I might call it a skirt. It showed the scars on the outside of my left leg from when I'd slid down the Governor's statue. The top looked like it was made of black bones stitched side to side all around my torso. I'd known it was skimpy but I was upset at seeing all my bare cleavage and finding pretty much everything from my nipples and points immediately south were all that was covered. It was an eye-catching costume and not at all practical for most activities I generally enjoyed. I looked around more urgently for my clothes, thinking I'd made an exchange with one of bodies stirring from hearing our exclamations. It was a good thing I carried my weapons in my boots.

"Woo-hood, Beeeoooo!" whooped someone in another corner of the room. He lifted a mug as if in toast to me. I watched a hand yank him back down and cause the loud stranger's cup to crash on the worn rug floor. He'd been similarly dressed as Sameath. His hair had been wilder, more uneven, and seemed to have stuff hanging out of sections of it.

Then it dawned on me, why we might be barely dressed. "You took me to a Kelkerine orgy?" I accused. I started focusing on the various, bold fashion choices on the people surrounding Sameath and me. Some outfits looked like re-purposed trash, material used for food storage as well as material that might have been from furniture or window coverings.

I was less angry at being dragged to a party that specialized in the abuse of a restricted medicine than I was at myself and the possible events that could have taken place. I was taking too long to observe and put information together. I'd known what I was wearing, but I didn't acknowledge it until I saw it. I bent in half to confirm that my undergarments remained intact. There was a reason why the clothes were easy access. I clung to the belief that even under the influence I refrained from abusing myself in one manner or another. The fact that we'd never been so dangerously reckless with our lives before held a significance I couldn't think about until later.

Sameath still had his face buried in his palms and fingers in his hair making it stick at all angles. "Not intentionally." He tugged on some of the strands before rubbing his face in his hands. He groaned. "I don't feel so good." I could hear him breathing through his mouth slowly. He was flexing his muscles, testing them systematically, trying to acclimatize himself.

"Because the-day-after, that shit hits eighty percent of the population like the flu." I breathed in and increased my volume to a whispered yell near his ear, "An ORGY!"

"Like you know what the flu feels like," he mumbled, referring to the fact that he'd never seen me sick. He knew the employed population has scheduled inoculations from most illnesses and I was among them.

I watched some bodies start undulating with each other in a manner I was certain I didn't want to see. "We have got to get out of here." I had heard the Kelkerine high, or Kel high, wore off of people differently. The topic of the discussions usually centered on the fact that most people were still amorous even after the high had run low.

I pulled on his wrist only to fall back onto the seat. I pouted at having made another poor decision. With his height, he'd still outweigh me by my entire body weight. I wasn't going to pull him anywhere.

My size made me ideal for a circuit pilot, but that was it. I had been driven in my pursuit of hand-to-hand combat lessons and maneuvers because

I had so many limitations to defending myself. I had to rely on motivational speaking. "We have to go," I whispered, "we're in deep shit if anyone lights another flare."

Flares were these airborne stimulants used to keep the parties going, especially ones sponsored by dealers.

"I'm for it," he pulled me tight against his chest and gave my cheek a quick kiss. I tried to hide my reaction to his pungent odor and the realization that I might smell the same.

I strained my neck to look at his lap, "Liar." I had a huge smile on my face when I looked him in the face again; I was so relieved that he was playing. Pulling out of his arms to stand told me something else, that he was weakened. I tugged on his arm again. "Come on, Sam. I'm not for another hallucinogenic experience, especially one that re-stimulates a Kel high." When he still didn't move, I applied a little pressure to the sides of his elbow as I pulled, enough to warn him that the next pull would dislocate it.

I had time to look around again. The waning outside light was causing the interior to dim significantly. Tiny lights blinked in different corners of the room. They reminded me of the techno-history classes. High on the walls, where old security cameras would sit, there were probably small holes next to those lights. "I could lose my career," I said. "Unlike you, I won't do well out of the Industry." My yanking grew more desperate and less controlled.

The MSP had eyes everywhere, even in the abandoned districts, it seemed.

He stood and stretched. He acted as if he had to become reacquainted with his body. "I wouldn't worry too much if I were you. You don't seem like you've had Kel." He looked at the rest of the bodies on tables and floors as he followed me to the doors. "You got another pair of those fancy glasses?" He moved slowly as his gaze lingered on the scantily and creatively clad people slowly stirring to life.

"Sorry," I said, striding toward the exit with purpose, "but I've only got my knives, mini-darts, poisons, etc..." I strove for control, the kind of control that pushed me to perform at the top of my classes and had pushed most people away. I hadn't felt the need to be this hyper-alert since before coming to the Academy.

"Your tracer?" he asked, real worry in his voice. He stared at my hip where I usually wore it. We paused outside the doors of the building. He rubbed his chest, itching it, a new tic he'd never demonstrated before.

I felt my hip with my hand, eyeing his new quirk. "No," I answered, "I remember reading about the adhesive qualities breaking somehow. Maybe we..." I stopped talking as I watched him go back into the building. The diner was the sole business attached to what look like an old, large building made of concrete slabs with statues and ornamental shelves were added along with glass windows.

I couldn't help but notice Sameath when he emerged from the building. He had acquired a very large torso covering. It had a crowded pattern of labels layered over each other to make clothing. Different company logos that had been etched into their product packages collided to create a flexible shimmering material. "Lovely," I said.

"No judging." He moved his head to make it clear he was staring at my outfit. "Have you looked at yourself yet?"

I held the end of my hair tail in my palm briefly before flicking it back. I shrugged, "Eh, it's black, like I care."

To ignore his grunt of disbelief, I made a show to turn to get a better look at our surroundings. "I believe we're on Moira. Do you second?" It was balmy and warm. But the distinctive features were the increased gravity making me feel like I had weights all over my body and the larger plants. The clean, highly oxygenated air made me feel briefly light headed. While I kept my ship and living quarters in a similar state, my lifestyle left me less than adequately prepared for visiting the planet itself.

"Seconded, but where?"

"I had a friend move to this," I struggled not to wrinkle my nose in displeasure, "farming planet upon her appointment to a veterinary clinic. If we're close to her, we could get passage home." I had been planning to visit her for a while. "If we find a communication hub, we'll be able to execute an exit strategy."

The buildings were all abandoned. It looked similar to the district we'd entered not too far from my home city, in the sense of towering buildings. Except, this space was organized with real, live overgrown gardens planted directly into the planet's topsoil. The material, colors and architectural ornamentation were off. The buildings looked like they were made of stones, color coordinated and seemingly complementary to one another. It made me think of old things, and this place was abandoned.

"What's missing?" he asked. He sounded like he already knew the answer and was wondering if I saw it.

I answered, "There is no automation. This looks like one of the first colonies that tried rejecting automated servers. I remember learning about the settlements, but I thought that most were buried beneath the primary cities on each of the planets at this end of the galaxy."

"Most, but not all."

"A communication system should clear this up," I repeated myself as I noted the sky dim. I felt satisfied that my training hadn't abandoned me completely. I really wanted to put my idea into action.

"I think we better get inside," he whispered, nudging me to the right. "Some of the old hotels had communication stations hidden in their buildings. We'll check them first."

"Huh?" I hated that I kept going in and out of this foggy sensation where I couldn't think straight. I really hated that Sameath was still doing the thinking for me, even if he'd once been a navigator for The Guard.

He started walking and explaining to me why following his suggestion was a good idea. "It'll be dark soon in an abandoned settlement where a Kelkerine Party can be held in a relatively public place. Not only is there no one within sight or quick-flight of this city, but no one comes into areas like this one unless they've a very criminal reason." That was very much in keeping with our interactions. I always required some reason for accepting a suggestion.

I closed my eyes a moment trying to think, so I could contribute toward a solution. "Look for someplace with height and many exit strategies." Then, I ran to catch him. Then, I slapped him across the bare arm.

"Ow!" he complained. "What was that for?"

"I would never have taken myself out to someplace like this, even if I were drugged." I growled. I grimaced. I had. I had been drunk on Black Brew and wobbling as I walked into a neighborhood very similar to this one on Pater-Rio. Only that had been a neighborhood, where people still lived and worked, not a ghost of an older civilization.

* * *

We approached a building that seemed to have no front windows for the first two stories and had two simple, but tall wooden doors for an entrance. We stepped through the two large doors into a vault, a tunnel-like entrance where the ceiling was curved two stories high. Light slowly increased, an automation that had been acceptable during a time when automatons had been abhorred by this society. It didn't take long for the dusty surfaces of the lavish decor to reflect light and an ambiance of vulgar prosperity: shiny metal details like arched bars across the ceiling, on the stairs' hand railings, doors' handles, and the trim to tables and counters. A thick, plushy material served as a carpet. The walls held as diverse textures as bold colors and patterns. A chair remained secured to the floor behind its desk at the entrance, implying someone was supposed to be there as security or reception. Two staircases rose independent of each other along the curved wall. They looped in opposite directions before snaking back on themselves to meet at opposite ends of a balcony. Between the bases of the stairs was plenty of space to see that a hallway continued beneath the balcony.

"We might want to squat there on that balcony in case anyone should come in." I lifted my chin to indicate the only balcony in the foyer. I figured we'd be forewarned if anyone decided to come in or from within the building. There were thin slats and small fist-sized holes in the railing. The place tasted dry and musty. "We're lucky this place has power. Maybe we could find some water somewhere? Then, we'll search the subterranean levels for the communications hub."

"Places like this usually have solar powered timers and motion sensors to conserve energy." Sameath informed me. "They also usually have kitchens where we can get some fresh water if the recycling processors still work when it rains." He led me between the staircases toward the back of the building. "I doubt we'll find food if there is a party that large meeting out in the open around here."

While he went to the back of the building, I stared at the paintings hung on the walls. I stayed in the hallway between the stairs, an eye on the door, but the other was on some pictures hanging on the walls. I was trying to fig-ure out the movements that made the brush strokes when Sameath returned with water.

I guzzled the water from the bowl he'd found, getting a little dribble on my chin. I used the back of my hand to wipe it off, this time rebelling against decorum. I noticed there was layer of something coating my lips then. "Is there color on my lips?" I asked as we climbed the stairs.

Sameath missed a step before he answered, "Yes."

I growled again and rubbed my lips harder. It didn't come off; my lips had added to them, on them or in them. I blinked and really noticed some ex-tra weight giving my eyelid muscles a workout. I touched my eyelashes feel-ing nothing really different. We'd reach the balcony and I could hear Sameath let his back slide down the wall. "My eyes?" I looked at him. He was staring again from his squat position. I didn't have to feign suspicion and frustration with him as I stared back.

He nodded. "You should really get a look at yourself."

"I should? Maybe you should, too," I snarled, walking the hallway that led into the building and away from the balcony.

"I have." He said to my back, pleased with himself. "Your glasses reflect a perfect image of my new look." I could hear him adjust some ropes around his hips, hopefully to better hide his special bits. "You know, I've heard of an algae agent going around that could alter your appearance..." I cut him off by shutting myself behind the first door I came to. I had heard of it, too. The Flamingo Effect that resulted from "shrimping."

The apartment had been ransacked long ago. The walls had been left un-blemished and were bright pink and lime green hue. Yellow stenciled shapes decorated some of the walls and matched the trim throughout the place. I headed toward the bathroom where mirrors have always existed. It was white and bright. I used a dimming switch to darken it immediately.

I took off my shades, intending to get a clear look at myself. I slowly lightened the room allowing my eyes to adjust as I went. My skin had always been pale, from virtually living in a pilot suit out in space navigating the

Dark Winds of solar energy. My skin looked almost luminescent. If I hadn't started out in the dark, I would have worried I glowed. But no, I was just a very shiny but pale, pale blue or grey.

I felt a little confused as I brightened the room. My eyes didn't hurt. I was able to withstand the brightest setting for the first time in years, maybe even a decade. I could see that my outfit was black like the deepest recesses of a dark hole.

I'd been named for my eye color, I knew. I'd been born with bright, wide, large blue eyes. In the mirror, they shimmered, but not with the sheen that usually happens when I had cried. Not that I've ever really cried anytime within the last fifteen years or so. I climbed on the counter next to the sink to get a closer look. My irises used a larger array of blue shades as well as some reflective sheen.

Sitting on the broad slab once used for personal toiletries, I could see that my skin's fine hairs had a faint blue tint, while the skin itself was white. My entire body's hair, the eyebrows, legs, and the fine little hair near my belly button that no one could see but me were a deep, blue-black, with an occasional glittering strand mixed in.

However, my eyelashes were darker. I tugged gently and felt an extraordinary amount of pain. I'd had false eyelashes sown into my eyelids. I'd also tinted my lips and sealed them with some kind of thick wax, proving that it was an injected tint that would fade before it would set, if that wax layer hadn't been added. I didn't want to think about how I could get a medical augmentation on such short notice.

Sameath's reference to a new drug the newscycler had reported. Images, articles, and informative specials broadcast along this thin strip of screen above doorways and along hallways of every major building regarding the effects of an algae-based agent that could change a person's coloring. The process was called the Flamingo Effect based on how the food that flamingos ate in zoos determined their color. The actual algae that inspired the scientists to build an organism to imitate the process was called "shrimping algae." The shrimp flamingos ate were the actual transmitters of the effects of the algae changing the bird's colors to a bright pink. Scientists had made a marketable product, a product that worked more like roulette on humans, rendering it illegal due to its unreliability.

I stomped out of the room. It would serve me better to look for a communication system than obsess about my looks.

I headed for the door that led to the hall. "I'm lucky my hair looks black and didn't become the same bright blue as my eyes," I muttered after my failed search for anything useful, like directions to the communication hub or other exits from the building.

I opened the door to find Sameath leaning against the door frame opposite to the apartment I was exiting. His nod was slow and awkward; wary.

I stood two inches in front of him and stared. "What?" I regularly think that with my height I don't intimidate anyone. But Sameath wasn't faking his discomfort under my stare regardless of my height. He looked sorry. I dismissed it with my anger filling me with an urge to fight.

"Outside, it looks like a really dark blue. If the light shines through it right, you can really see that it's blue." He put his hands up in a placating gesture and would have backed away if he could. "It looks nice."

"Do you remember anything at all?" I asked. "Black Brew had never caused a black out before."

"I remember my plan." He leaned in to whisper or plead understanding. I don't know which. He said, "I arranged for your friend, the one that pilots the Rainbow Steed, to take us to ANEX where another one of your closest friends was performing. I couldn't find the other one, the veterinarian. You know, the friends that went with you to that school you never talk about. The people you can be yourself with."

"That explains why we would come here," I said. "This was the last place I knew she lived and worked. I'm betting we're really close to her last known location."

He shrugged, dismissing the increased probability of my earlier suspicion and leaned back, "We got drunk. I'm pretty sure going shrimping was your idea. I don't know how we ended here, which I'm pretty sure is Moira. Yup, I do know that the shrimping was your idea. You were 'tired of being you,' you said." He sunk to a squat, leaning against the wall when I stepped back to give myself some space, some chance to remember. "I'll just have to accept your deduction on why we'd come to this agricultural center at this end of the galaxy."

I narrowed my eyes at him for implying our stranding was my fault. "Where could we go shrimping?" I asked.

"I've a cousin who has a friend," he explained. "We tried to get the stuff before we even left Pater-Rio, but we left before purchasing it. So, I have no idea."

"The same cousin that got you demoted and then relieved of duty?" I asked, horrified that I would trust the same guy.

"It seemed like a fine idea at the time. You seemed okay with it. After that, I get a little fuzzy, too," he looked around.

"I don't remember any of it past the taxi." I saw that he was staring past me at the walls while we stood there absorbed in our own thoughts.

"We do stand out against these walls. It's buggerin' gold and sparkly." He shuddered.

Home

"Let me clarify." The Interviewer tapped. She wasn't looking at me but at her displays again as the scanner analyzed me. "You and Sameath do not remember anything that happened on APEX?"

I shrugged, "No, Ma'am."

"We have you receiving your passes for the Rainbow Steed." She showed our departure, in the same clothes I remembered putting on that morning. "Your friend looks worried," she said.

I didn't respond.

"A concern with the reinstatement of ANEX since the quarantine lift on the planet is that of surveillance laws. All surveillance is prohibited except for business security focused on their own products and individual tracers used by the II, the MSP and the Guard. The local government regulates the number of the peacekeeping forces that can land planet-side. The only information we were able to gather was with your tracer worn by the person you know as Paika. She managed to activate it, but it still was inefficient." She paused.

I was contemplating her decision to not use the word "malfunction" for describing how my tracer works when she had a short video fill the screen in the wall. It displayed a wooden building in flames. The images stuttered. She added sound. My laughter, hysterical and manic, echoed around my apartment.

"You know how the tracer works," she continued. A few stills filled the screen in quick succession of my transition of coloring. I looked like a mottled cow, patchwork and streaks of my natural coloring and the new. "Paika triggered enough in the tracer to record her bios. The blows she delivered were sloppy. Her pain ratcheted up the scales quickly. Her anxiety and fear pheromones climbed as she realized you were playing with her." She played some audio of my taunting. I flinched and felt bile fill my throat in self-disgust. "We're guessing that you stole her clothes then. She wasn't completely unconscious as you robbed her."

This was when the Investigator aired a recording of my new look at that unfamiliar port more complete than the segment with which she'd started this interview. "This is your arrival on Moira with a small group of vagrants at an unmanned landing area." All of us were huddled, or rather, interwoven together. I spotted my new look in the sunlight. I was easily distinguished against the dirtier Kel addicts. While I danced in the sunlight and wiggled to my own tune, the others dressed like me were walking and co-joining. Sameath sauntered down the docks with a female on each side of him. One of the women had a hold of another man, forcing him to walk along with Sameath's trio. I stopped looking closely when I realized what she might have ahold of. I was grateful for the small horde blocking the view.

We piled into a "party bus" that brought us to Pauly's Diner where we unloaded and we couldn't see what else was happening. The restaurant interior was too dark and smoky for those little lights to illuminate the recordings. Smoke filled the room three times before the day I woke sober. Through the haze, we couldn't see daylight and thus judge the number of days I'd been there. But the flares, the cause of the smoke, could last six to 12 hours if lit individually. Aside from investigating the site when I had been in the room, there was no way to tell how long I'd been there until after I left and used a calendar. I'd been in that room dancing and writhing with people for roughly four days.

"Before I show you footage of your re-acquaintance with Paika," she looked at me. Her view screen illuminated her face. The evening sky in dark indigo behind her cast shadows throughout my home. "You'll provide your account of the events in Pine Towers Apartments in the Paradise Colony on Moira."

Moira

I was leaning against the wall trying to remember shrimping, acquiring the clothes, or even just the eyelash sewing. I couldn't look at Sameath at the time. I was tugging on the lashes when I heard Paika's voice.

"McKague!" she called from the foyer. "McKague!" The acoustics projecting my last name initially disguised the voice, whether the newcomer was male or female.

"Who is it?" Sameath yelled out after crouching to a crawl.

"Paika," answered the voice. "I have Bluebella Cannich McKague's tracer here. You want it?" The voice sounded cheerful and congenial.

"By the Stars and Stones, yes," I let out a deep breath as if I'd been holding the entire time since I had realized I had lost it. I also followed Sameath's example and crawled down the hall toward the balcony that led to the stairs. "What do you want for it?" I called out. It seemed like a good idea to barter, the friendliness of the voice meant nothing.

There were short chuckles, two or more men and a woman from the sounds. Sameath and I had finally reached the slatted balcony. We could see a short, slender woman wearing my clothes. Her bald head glistened with sweat. She was flanked by a pair of men, well built and heavily armed for hand to hand combat. One wore shades while I could see the other's frowning expression. I spotted the trio's gear housed, their stash of non-lethal projectiles of electricity emitters, poison darts, and blunted bolts for guns, in easy reach of their hands along their hips. In addition, they had clubs dangling off their belts as well. These people were not revelers. These men were not just for show.

The woman spoke, "I want my clothes."

"Seriously?" I ground my teeth. Even at the lowest reaches of society, vanity held more power than it should. "You first." I watched the woman un-dress and toss my outfit to the ground. I groaned in frustrated embarrassment. Where I wore one scrap of fabric beneath the skirt, she had worn a body glove.

"By the way," Sameath asked, peering at the assemblage, "how did we come by your items?"

"Wretch?" The strange woman asked, "Are you still with this Pop?"

I knew that Pop referred to "Princess of Prim," the Upper-Tiered girls that went to the edge of decorum to party. I looked at Sameath who happened to be flexing muscles in his jaw so strongly dark, red-brown lines started to appear at his temple, he didn't like the woman calling me that. I wondered why; it was essentially true. The thought that it could mean something else passed through my head before my concentration scattered.

I stared as lines that looked like artful interpretations of small veins started working their way along his jaw-bone. I wondered if that was a con-sequence for shrimping, if I was going to get some dark, blue veins webbing out through my body.

He yelled out, "How did you find us?" It drew me back to the situation at hand.

"Tracer," she answered, fully engaging my attention, causing my head to snap into place and stare in her direction. "Once we landed planet-side, it tracked the DNA signature left by the skin cells the Pop dropped all the way here. I can't believe you'd traveled to Horto-658. Excuse me; Moira. If a Fo-mor found out you were on their planet, high on their product in their back yard, you would not be walking."

I crawled closer, gluing my eye to one of the holes. I focused on my tracer as Paika held out my techno identification for display. "I don't suppose we could do this exchange in private?" I suggested.

Pictorials decorated her second skin, moving with her muscles as they twitched and flexed irritably. The material was meant to help her camouflage in any environment. The woman glanced to the men before she answered, "Not after last time."

Silence filled the room. I was trying to remember to what she was refer-ring. I watched Sameath look like he was studying the people downstairs. He was acting like he had during our combat and tactical training classes. I opened my mouth to speak when Paika spoke.

"I'm waiting," she huffed. She drew my eyes back to her and her men and away from my friend, who was taking this situation more seriously than he'd taken anything else lately. Her agitation made the men step back and to the side, more attentive to their surroundings, as if expecting an attack. The phrase was a cue to suspect or execute an attack. "Bluebella Cannich McKague, you should get down here and get your things."

Resigned, I started to stand but Sameath put his hand on my arm freezing me in that squatting and stooped position on my hands and feet.

"It's too easy," he said. "She has a hell of a lot more value in your Tracer than those clothes you're wearing."

"I can hear you," the woman sang, filling the acoustics of the room with her powerful voice. "Wretch, you do know me." Her response to Sameath's assessment was one of warning, not offense. "The top and skirt are filled with product that could get us killed here, but worth more than my ship. My product. I'm counting to three and then coming to get it. And let me say, Finn is eager to get his hands on you again."

I was so close to him. I felt his body tense. I watched his pupils widen. The color of his eyes which were once a golden brown pulsed with the red glitter amid dark, dark brown. They flicked between my top and skirt. He licked his lip and bit on it. Right then, I knew what it all meant. I yanked my arm away. I had a moment to watch the colored lines begin to blossom on his throat. "The Kelkerine," I hissed in vexation. Connecting the product to the death sentence, I realized this woman wasn't a pissed fashionista.

* * *

"On the Dark Winds!" the woman exclaimed, "Hell of a romantic con you've got going on, Wretch. I'm done waiting."

The stomp of feet announced the slow, cautious movement of the behemoths on the stairs. They moved as easily as I did. And I had been conditioning myself for years.

I leveled my gaze full of the anger and disappointment I felt for Sameath at that moment. Crouched as I was, it was easy for me to launch myself up and over the balcony. The push off into the air from a crouched position was hard. And landing on the floor below came sooner than expected. I had little time to review tactical strategies falling through the air as I was. Seeing Paika move, I twisted at the apex of my arc to change my trajectory. I had just enough hover time to dodge a blunt from a stop gun. I wasn't really dodging. I just wasn't there as it flew past me to hit the wall.

I'd landed and stooped in pain. My boots were in my line of sight for that moment, showing me my mini darts along the edges. I pulled a couple just as I heard someone land behind me. The guard with the sunglasses had jumped after me, landing on his feet. We made eye contact for a moment before he collapsed into a twitching thump.

"Oh, no," I heard before Paika started shooting, "I'm not making the same mistake twice." She had pulled an electronic pulse gun and a stop gun, one for each hand, from behind her back.

Paika, wildly aiming and backing away, had missed me. The electrical pulse gun, or EPG, had hit him. I managed to take two blunts from the stop gun at close range, but the bodice had acted like a well-cushioned armor as I expected. I was halted momentarily and my shoulder ached like it had taken a hit. Instead of standing to secure a more effective stance to hit me with an EPG, she was already through the door. My empty hand snagged my clothes from floor as I ran by them, chasing her. I planned to get rid of the top as soon as possible, trusting Sameath and his training to manage the other guy, since his partner was laying on the ground. I didn't notice the blunts had torn the seams of the bodice and didn't care. I wanted it off.

"Shakable!" Sameath yelled from the interior, sounding his codeword for help with what sounded like his mouth swollen and gurgled. The door was already closing behind me. I was facing two guns snapping with empty chambers.

Sameath's yell was the distraction that caused Paika to hesitate. I exploited it. Throwing my darts, one landed in the gut and the other in the base of her neck. Her arms were falling too slowly. She was going to run again. I used my fist to knock her out. I realized two things as I ripped off that top. One, I needed more practice on throwing the damn darts. The darts injected a small dose of a sleeping agent. She wouldn't be waking soon. Two, my shoulder hurt enough to cause my hand to spasm. I tossed the bodice on her.

I stared at the fallen woman, confirming that she was still breathing. I saw strands of different colored threads dangled from the stitches of the corset. As I ripped it off, I suspected that what had appeared to be bone were probably woven cases of doses of Kelkerine. I took my tracer from her body-suit where she'd stuck it and reattached it to my hip. I pulled on my shirt as I rushed back inside the building. The stupid skirt was riding higher, so I was happy my shirt covered my rear.

I struggled to fasten the front of my shirt coming through the doors. At the same time, I took in the environment, dodging to the side to see the pre-caution was unnecessary. One man was still unconscious, the other was wait-ing. My pants still lay crumpled in the middle of the floor. I moved casually toward them and announced, "It's over!" My yell startled the man across from me into wakefulness. He stood, leveling his EPG gun at me. Sameath, still on the landing above, was pinned to the ground with a stop gun pointed at the base of his skull. Though typically a non-lethal weapon, at that range, it would permanently damage the vertebrae and spinal column; a slow death.

"If that goes off, I'll kill you and your little friend, too." My anger had a focus, and it was the man holding the stop gun on my friend.

* * *

The man holding the gun smirked. He barely gave me a glance as if my statement was amusing. "He drugged you so that he could manipulate you and maybe even rape you," he pressed the gun more forcefully into the neck. The criminal was upset that Sameath might have violated my person.

Shock made me grin. "I've known him my entire life," I started. I hadn't. I hadn't known him well since we were split in his dismissal from the Intra-galactic Guard. I swallowed. "He's never been able to make me do anything I didn't want to do." That was true and I defended us by saying, "I'd know if anything happened between us."

The man standing before me moved slowly, positioning himself to see both his partner and me. "I saw the kisses at the Academy. I doubt you would've gone for Finn," he lifted his chin indicating the other mercenary, "if you hadn't been on Kel."

"And I saw Wretch's face. He was so hurt," Finn mocked. He stopped moving when I pulled my own compact EPG and held it to my side. He added, "You do the math."

The unnamed guard continued talking, though staring at me, "We've been tracking you since your little deal went sideways at the Academy." I must have looked confused, because he cocked his head. His voice sounded contemplative when he observed, "You don't remember much of anything since, do you?"

I tried to remain stoic.

He straightened his own shades, "After you quietly and quickly dis-patched Paika in your private deal, we continued following you. Finn was *concerned* for you. But she wanted to make an example out of you consider-ing it had been at our most profitable site." He paused and glanced at the bal-cony where we could see several boards were missing or dangled from the railing. His partner didn't interrupt him. "I thought it would be entertaining. Luckily, all transports have to publish their flight plans. We waited for you outside the dining hall on that trash station ANEX. You went to see some performer named Bree."

"Bree gave you the shrimp compound that changed your follicle color along with a handful of others," announced Finn. Hovering over Sameath, he redirected his weapon at the banister. Sameath wouldn't know, considering he'd been tapped in the back of the head lightly with the gun before it was pointed away from his skull. "It's not ours, so no idea how long it'll take to fade, if at all. By the way, I like it," he said.

I didn't accept what I was hearing then. I was surprised they were pro-viding any information initially. Then, I realized that Finn was courting—for lack of a better term—me. I got it. I didn't like it, but I got it.

"Bree was her birthday present, you ass," Sameath announced. "I prepaid the trips and..." Then he added, "Well, most of it. We were supposed to head back to Pater-Rio for a week at an activity spa." Someplace to play combat, swim, dance, put on performances, depending on your proclivities.

"I'm sure Bree was grateful," the second guy's grin then broadened to a full smile, showing off a mix of metal and white teeth. "I liked all of the Py-ro-technics!" His shoulders relaxed as he holstered his weapon. "Someone burnt the place down. I could hear you laughing over the hysterics of the crowd. We think you had something to do with it." He tapped a finger to his forehead in salute to me then.

I remembered watching the light bulb's filament fluctuate in brightness. That meant the wiring wasn't maintaining a stable measure of voltage. The lights were antiquated, but I doubted the wiring was. And yet something went wrong. Before I knew it, little flames erupted from the walls. I could hear my laughter echo from the recording earlier. I don't remember how I got out of the building or what happened after. "It was the wiring," I declared.

"We caught up to you, then, before the wiring caught fire," Finn said. "During the evac, you stole Paika's clothes."

"It took me a few minutes to realize you and Paika were fighting," the sunglassed goon said. "By the time I got to you, you'd already taken her clothes and were gone."

"Showed your skills," Finn stood, leaving a foot on Sameath's back, keeping him down and kissing the floor. "Military training," he deduced, "more than just piloting or scouting maneuvers."

The partner's face tightened, a scowl revealing his displeasure that Finn had watched the fight and robbery and had done nothing to stop it.

Then, Finn zeroed in his gaze on me. "Is your total blackout real?" he asked.

"Yes," I answered. I didn't want to admit it, but nothing was coming back even with all of their exposition. "And I'm grateful you're telling what you are. But why? Aren't you supposed to kill us or something?"

"Lost memories happen to shrimpers who take Kel sometimes," Finn shrugged. The sympathy was a thin veneer over his disdain. "I saw you take the Kel," he tapped a mecha hanging on his belt.

The second guy added, "I saw you and Finn groping and kissing inside the bar before it went up. You were still on the Kel high. So, whatever it is that didn't happen between you and Wretch, you'll want confirmation. 'Cause Wretch—" Finn shoved Sameath's chest into the carpet more force-fully again, "targets Pops to pay for his parties. Pretty, bright eyed, and trusting, like—"

"Look, Paika is down," Sameath said, the carpet muffling his words. "If she hasn't come in by now, she probably needs to get medical attention. Looks like McKague left the product outside with your employer, too. And you aren't going to kill us, could you let us go, please?"

"In a minute," the second guy motioned to me. "The Kel is in the skirt."

"Then what was the boning in the top?" I asked. "It was ripped from the blunt bullets hitting it."

"Worms," the first one said, "Kel delivery method for most of the populace. You took it like a Fomor, though." The guy sounded impressed and finally stood. "We were surprised you didn't drop dead or start panting right there. Must be part Fomor yourself."

"Fomor?" I asked then I did the conjugation: *from Moira* might become *Fo Mor* or *Fomor*. "Never mind. We clearly entertain you. Let him go."

The two men chuckled and soon were standing shoulder to shoulder. Finn leapt the balcony much like I had. "We'll leave after you've changed clothes." They motioned with a swing of their open, empty palms to the pants on the floor. They watched me change out of my skirt and into my pants. I handled the stiff, glittering material that served as a skirt carefully. "And don't worry too much over our payment for our inconvenience in chasing you all over the galaxy, McKague," Finn said, smirking at me.

Sameath was taking so long coming down the stairs I had time to search my pockets. They were empty. When I climbed the stairs to help him the rest of the way, Paika's bodyguards moved quietly and carefully to the exit.

"It was fun," they said. The guards talked amongst themselves.

"What is it?" I demanded, earning a warning mixed with a groan from Sameath.

The two bodyguards delivered a nod to Sameath and me at the doors. "We'll look at it as a vacation. And there are plenty of Paikas to take her place."

"We'll keep your resume on file," Finn said, tapping his head, an invitation. He followed up by pointing his finger at me as if he were shooting as he went through the door. That had been the warning. It took me a while to put it together, but they'd always been the ones in charge. They weren't going to strong-arm me into paying for their "vacation," which meant they'd expect me to pay in another way in the future.

I elected to wait a few more moments before leaving. I was having trouble processing my relief then my horror. I set Sameath to rest on the bottom steps and sat next to him. He leaned heavily on me.

"Fomor, Kelkerine, and Moira. Can you sum it for me, please?" I asked.

"Kel is a vitamin supplement that originated here, on Moira. When Fomors visit other planets for a long period of time, they lose mass. When they return home, their bodies over compensate. The compound keeps them from becoming too dense on their return before they've acclimatized to being home. There's another that prevents them from losing their actual strength and muscle mass while traveling. I really don't know how it works for us average people, but the second works as a hyper-stimulate for most everyone else's glandular system, especially when you're around someone you're attracted to. On some, it makes them stronger and they eat more as well," Sameath explained. "Fomors can pop it in their mouths and swallow. Their digestive system breaks it easily enough. For the rest of us, we need the worms to break it and deliver it to our systems partially digested."

I couldn't take it. The idea of willingly swallowing living, writhing worms that were basically poisoned caused my body to twitch and squirm.

"The worms safely and easily exit our systems, so stop moving," he pleaded. His breath was getting choppy. "And you didn't eat them."

"I had them on my body." I squirmed again, almost dropping Sameath. I elected to gently place him down to recline on the steps. "We should look you over before I call a transport." His bruises were spreading and getting dark quickly. The ugly flowery shirt had been ripped open. I started to adjust it, straightening it like he'd done for me so many times. I didn't want to say what I was thinking about and yet couldn't hold it in. "But you did. You have been. How often?" Blood was surfacing and pooling beneath my fingertips. I breathed, "For how long?"

He didn't nod. He lay there staring at the ceiling. I could see the dark veins spreading down his limbs from his torso. Suddenly, he coughed and started gagging. I turned him to his side. He drooled a red river.

I touched my tracer and called for a medic. I may lose him but I wasn't going to let him die.

Home

"Your friend, Sameath Coil, you're still concerned for him?" the Interviewer asked, sympathy lining her voice as if she were trying to hide it.

"He contacted me. He said he's at the rehabilitation center on Horto, I mean, Moira," I said quietly, remembering footage of him at the rehabilitation center. He was recovering with newly implanted organs. The communities on Moira were old-fashioned, keeping their communication centers hidden deep within the buildings and probably the soil. So none of his footage was live. "I'm glad he's alive." He still sported the dark, blood red coloring viewable in the bright sunlight. It made his skin shine copper in the sunbeams streaming in through his bedside window.

The interviewer was silent for a moment. I could feel her staring at me. "The internal bleeding he sustained inside the apartment building—which we saw, by the way. It was grainy but the security cameras still did their work. The beating saved his life. The excess of... well, you don't need the actual terminology. The reasons why Kel is a black market drug are its side effects. Outside hyper-reactivity and hormonal imbalances, one side-effect is death by a sudden blood bloat that bursts organs. And it does it quickly. The small tears of damage he received gave the blood some place to go, preventing complete annihilation of the tissue. He's the first survivor of the end stage since the development and abuse of the substance. Several agencies are interested in his recovery, so his bills are also paid."

"I'll probably be demoted," I stated. Ugh, the paperwork for the new DNA work-up to see if this freakin' dye job was permanent. And then, the identification process—regardless if the coloring was altering me at a genetic level—needed to update my profile to function in society. I had been home for a few days when I was notified that the investigation was proceeding in a manner implying a chance for continued employment. The consequences surrounding my altered coloring prevented me from facing other issues like the ones the Interviewer wanted to address.

Her tone of voice changed, colder, as she went on, "I would normally expect you to be demoted after a thorough medical screening." She looked around at my sparse furnishings. "According to regulations, you'll be confined to your home under constant surveillance to verify that you aren't in fact addicted to substances. You'll have three years probation with a Superior Officer accompanying you on your rounds," meaning I'd be supervised on my flights through my quadrant where I verify a lack of threat to our society. "Consistent psychological review will uncover damage that might indicate instability." She met my gaze, there was a heaviness to it that made me wonder if she had an altered awareness, increasing her ability to read people rather than rely on her machines. "You had your freedom. You signed your contract to defend our nation. You should have to earn it back."

"How could the MSP afford this?" I asked. "Why not cut me loose like you did Sameath?"

"Sameath's dismissal is the result of a more lax policy regarding observation of at-risk personnel. He probably wouldn't have made it completely through the Academy if it hadn't been for such policies and friends like you, friends that kept him going and focused. Friends with connections to reduce his punishments." There it was: my step-mother's insidious influence that poisoned my every achievement. She'd be the reason I wasn't relieved of duty. "And there are more people who can do his job in navigation. Since there are few pilots that can ride the Dark Winds, McKague, you have access to a lot more assistance. You still have a job to do. Reviewing all of your performance reviews, purchases, interests outside of the MSP and such, you're an asset worth investment, according to the pre-investigation. Now, you're to await an extensive investigation, which may net us a couple more unlicensed pharmaceutical distributors as well. If you want to quit, however, you can." I wasn't looking at her then, and didn't need to see her face, but I knew she was being sly with that last comment.

"But what else could I do if I left the Guard in disgrace?" I inquired snottily. Then I answered myself, "Not much."

"You have been suspended for two more months, until we complete our investigation. If it helps your ego and lowers your anxiety, your interaction with Paika was enormously impressive. Your lack of memory subjects all your decision making contingent of your substance use. It's the real reason why you're under investigation instead of released from duty.

"However, this entire fiasco is influencing some of the politicians' views of your potential. Some are talking about moving you to another department depending on the ambitions of those on the review board instead of just demotion." Again, she sneered. She was implying my massively, wealthy, ambitious family were influencing my evaluation. "I would hope for a demotion, if I were you, though. You still won't have your freedom, but you'll have a better chance of leaving the organization on a positive note at a future date."

"Why do you expect I'll be leaving at all?" I asked. I didn't know how to do anything else.

"This wasn't your first birthday party, was it?" Her question threw me. It sounded contemplative and didn't need an answer. "Something is missing in your life. You've tried to eschew any opportunity for your family to interfere not just with your career but your lifestyle. You want to succeed on your own terms. You went chasing that something with someone who is referred to on the lesser civilized streets as 'Wretch,' which says the opposite of you," she answered, gathering her things. "You'll stay as long as you can, because you created this lifestyle. I recommend taking advantage of your supervising officer's experience and knowledge, if you get one worth having. Figure out what it is you think you lack." She made her way to my door. "Or else you'll head for another implosion."

She looked at the door. "Right now, your future doesn't look so good no matter where you look." She raised her voice to deliver a command to my electronics. Surprisingly, she sounded a lot like me, "View screen slide 14-8-B."

I turned around after she shut the door. She'd left an image on the wall. It wasn't me laughing during my ecstatic gyrations or starting the food fight or anything like that. It was Sameath's broken body as it looked on the stairs when the medics arrived.

BREED

BY TIMOTHY LYNCH

T hree Phi Beta Xi women watched as the six-foot-something, obsidian-black man drained his second Bloody Mary a few feet away. The wooden bar shined with a hundred refracted beams of light passing through inverted bar glasses, making the man's skin look iridescent. The Kauai University coeds were intrigued. They couldn't look away. Even his cologne was luscious and sweet. Something about the man attracted them. Katie commented on his muscular chest evident under his loose-fitting, purple and white shirt; while Kaila remarked on his rugged arms and broad shoulders and the slightest, most unusual glow, as if he were subtly back-lit.

Misty, a tall suntanned brunette with long straight hair, downed the rest of her martini. She wasn't used to being intimidated by men, but the stranger's square jawline and carved flaring nostrils made it hard for her to keep her cool. "How do I look?"

"Gorgeous, sistah!" said her friend Kaila.

"He's got nothing on you," said Katie. "Eat him alive!"

Misty pushed out her chest, flashed a bright smile and lifted her sculpted eyebrows. "He's mine."

She walked with long steps, allowing her hips to move freely under her clingy, white dress. She set her arms on the bar and intertwined her long fingers with French nails. Her friends watched as she made her pitch: a smile as she motioned back to their table, a swing of her silky brown hair from one shoulder to the other.

The man smiled and called over the bartender.

"She got him!" said Kaila.

"No, she got a drink," said Katie.

They watched the night's progression. Several times Misty glided stray hairs behind her ear, her full lips smiling and laughing, revealing beautiful straight, white teeth. Soon, he slid the remaining third of his drink down his throat and left the bar. Misty waited a minute then did the same.

"Now she's got him," said Katie.

* * *

Abella's flight touched down in Honolulu. She had hoped to land with enough time to catch dinner at the hotel, but it did not look promising. She hurried to Baggage Claim to get a place in the front of the smooth-sliding, stainless steel plates of the baggage carousel. But as luck would have it, she had to wait long enough for even the slowest of her planemates to arrive. It was a good thing she didn't mind waiting.

Abella pulled on the ties of her glossy black trench coat, carefully removed it and folded the light garment over her arm. She stared straight ahead, ignoring the gazes of several men in uniform, instead smiling at a lit-tle girl twirling in the corner. She watched as a woman leaned against a wall slipping out of her shoes; a man in a disheveled polo shirt was talking on a cell phone—he had missed a single belt loop in the back of his pants; a little boy shuffled too far from his mother, lost sight of her and started to cry. Be-fore long, a pulsing horn heralded the arrival of the baggage. She snatched her bright red bag from the carousel and rolled it away toward the exits.

Abella needed to get a good night's rest if she was to get up in time for check-in at the conference at the University of Honolulu. *Well, then there is the other thing,* she thought. She would have to see... The sooner she could eat, the sooner she could sleep. She climbed into the first cab she saw.

At the hotel, she pushed on the revolving door. The hotel decor was Jun-gle-esque with broad palm leaves and bamboo furniture. *If one of those rat-tan balconies doesn't have a ham sandwich, there will be hell to pay! Maybe skipping the meal on the plane wasn't the smartest move.*

Abella got her key and headed for the bar, hoping the kitchen was still open. She spied the cook through the pass-through and gave him her best sexy pout. She wasn't proud of herself for doing it, but it was effective. It wasn't long before she settled at a table with a warm prime rib sandwich and some tomato soup. *Even* better *than cold ham,* she thought.

* * *

On a neighboring island, Misty was enjoying the company of the attrac-tive man named Tau. He was staying in a double-room suite with French doors dividing the sitting room from the bedroom. He cozied up to her on the loveseat asking her questions about what she was studying.

"Art History," she told him, swirling her Pinot Noir.

He asked about her favorite painters.

"Well, Dali is fun, don't you think?"

He asked if she liked the surrealists.

She had heard that word in class associated with Dali and Magritte but she didn't know exactly what that meant to an expert, other than weird, melty pictures that often had nudes in them. "I'm just getting started with the major

—actually, this is my third attempt. I started off in nursing but there was just too much chemistry and physics—you know what I mean. Then I tried business, cause who *wouldn't* want to make a million dollars, right?"

Tau commented that she was caring and entrepreneurial. He asked about why she ended her business classes.

"Well, I still take them, I'll get a minor, eventually... but, if I'm honest with myself, I can barely manage my way out of my room every morning!"

"I think you are wonderful," he said, his voice soft and bass like a puff of smoke from the mouth of a volcano.

She laughed as she thought about her career path: a winding road with a yet-to-be-determined direction. He was smiling at her with an intense look in his amber eyes, as if he was feeding off her fine features and curves. She felt the space diminishing between them. *He's moving in for a kiss.* She glanced down at his flexing chest and strong veined forearms. Her eyes found his: glistening and unblinking, two bright lights in an onyx statue. His powerful arms wrapped her so tightly she couldn't move. Misty felt her dress tear away from her body like paper and although it was one of her favorites, decided she didn't care. Her body was heating up in a very good way. Tonight was working out nicely, and she was eager for whatever was next.

Well that's odd, she thought, as a second set of equally strong arms wrapped around her, just above her waist. She tasted a combination of vanilla mixed with pepper sliding through his lips. She knew she should be terrified, but she felt so damn good. *Everything had felt so very right*—his charming, courteous manner, their conversation.

Then two sharp points pressed hard on the inside of her thighs, forcing her legs apart.

* * *

In the morning, Abella rented a small white car with a t roof to take to the conference. She could smell the flowers lining the highway, the pineapple farms in the distance, and the slightest hint of ash. It was a beautiful sunny day, like most visits to paradise. She pulled into a wide parking space, lifted hard on the handbrake and shut the car off. It would be a full day of seminars, forums and meetings dealing with sustainability in the islands. She would have plenty to say and questions to ask. She pulled together the files she would need from her black briefcase.

* * *

Back on Kauai, Tau moved his hips rhythmically, ejecting sticky silk from spinnerets embedded inside the cleft of his buttocks. Short sharp appendages he kept folded near his genitalia weaved the silk easily, pulling, then, directing the multitudinous, sticky strands into a thick mesh surrounding the unconscious woman, his companion the night before. Soon she would writhe and twist, undergoing the many changes that would transform the human into something more like himself—a natural, evolutionary bridge between the humans and Tsuchigumo. He vomited his sweet tasting nectar onto the cocoon strands and the lining walls, leaving a potent mixture that would nourish and transform her body. Already, her skin showed waxiness indicating a second skin was forming under the first. Like a newborn, she would escape the old skin of her life and be completely renewed, not as human but as Tsuchigumo.

It is a shame she could not start her own colony of Tsuchigumo, in one of the dark quiet caves of the island. But Tau knew Human-Tsuchigumo were not able to breed. At least he would cancel one human and create one Tsuchigumo in its place.

* * *

Thankfully, they'd given Abella a nice big conference room. There were a few pillars that might block the view of attendees. But she tested the mic; she would at least be heard.

She would hit the climate-change deniers hard, showing how they were short-sighted and lacking in data, then come round and weave an argument for her program as the solution—not only for gaining public opinion, but as a means for addressing climate change itself. She would compel them to infuse with "green ideas" as many educational programs as possible, as well as create a priming base-major, heavy in the sciences, but equally heavy in public policy. These students, *her students*, would create and pursue data so tantalizingly accurate, the world would have no choice but to listen. She hoped her colleagues from Stanford would appreciate her work. She noticed the first few attendees wander in to find their seats.

* * *

Tau poured a tall glass of tomato juice and left the bottle on the counter for the new Tsuchigumo. The drink reminded his kind of the acidic fluid they drank from the liquefied remains of their victims, and was quite popular.

He sat in a chair looking at the loveseat where it had begun. *It is strange really, the stories said once the humans were our prey along with so many other cave dwellers. Then as humans overtook more and more environments, the Tsuchigumo evolved to look like them, to pass for them. It was easier to hunt them, the stories said, but more importantly, it was easier to hunt. We could throw animal skins over ourselves to hide our uniqueness and we could blend in with the human beggars. We could even bargain for the human's food and other human items to help disguise us in their settlements.*

But it was the royal nectar that changed both our kind. It put us into them in ways that changed their bodies and they became like us, at the same time that we were becoming like them. Some Tsuchigumo believed this new being to be unnatural and an insult to our kind. But is it not nature herself who allows it! And are not our numbers increased? Are there not far too few of us... and far too many of them?

* * *

Abella finished her PowerPoint presentation and waited for questions from the audience. She knew they probably agreed with the general conclusions of her position, but would they agree to put up money for the cause: The most environmentally savvy program available, a model for colleges everywhere? It would be the genesis of a new revolution of sustainability in every facet of human life, on every continent.

How can anyone not see it is the only way we will all survive, she thought.

Several dozen people stepped forward behind microphones at the end of her talk. Abella would answer every question. She needed to remove all doubt and all specious arguments that would cloud her message.

Afterward, she made her way out of the hall shaking hands and receiving thanks for her presentation. A small group of the young people she had noticed lining the walls of the overfilled seminar followed her out of the room and showered her with praise. She made sure to give them something extra: perhaps a squeeze of their shoulder or arm along with a handshake. She looked each one in the eye with a calm assurance. "Keep fighting," she said.

When she got back to her car, a warm ocean breeze lifted the material of her blouse away from her skin and she breathed deeply. *Ah yes.* The muscles in her forehead knitted together. *It is time,* she thought. Now that her presentation was over, she could attend to the *other matter.* She would need to get on an island-jumper to another island. She sighed, smelling the presence of a protein in the air, making all the hairs on her exposed skin tingle. On her tongue flitted the unmistakable flavor of vanilla.

* * *

At the hotel, Tau protected a gently moving mass of silk. He shut the windows, closed the blinds and turned off the light and air, preventing a draft from interfering with his new creation. The warm, humid environment would help speed the transformation, much like a sun-baked cave of old. He was fulfilling his natural role as Otougumo, one percent of the species: queen-maker. For millennia his rare ancestors performed their duty. Now after five winters, he had stored sufficient amounts of royal nectar and could do the same. But he did so more out of necessity than pride.

Our kind are beggars no more!

* * *

Abella checked out of her hotel and drove down to the airport. The protein-taste was coming from the East. She would need to hurry to buy a ticket to Kauai. If she could catch Tau before he left whatever island he was on, she could end this. *But what of the new Tsuchigumo that he created?* Again she would have to see...

* * *

Tau stretched his chest and his shoulder arms, then he stretched his smaller torso arms that he kept folded under his chest. Finally his legs and "weavers," the short but dexterous appendages he kept under his trunk. He had worked hard all night, but he would have to hurry and finish. No doubt the other Tsuchigumo would be looking for him again. He had not been chosen to raise a true Tsuchigumo queen, but he refused to waste his precious gift. His nectar would not go to waste, vomited on the ground like a cat's hairball. Not when using his gift could increase the influence of his people. "It is my right and what I was born to do!" His voice echoed around the walls of the room. *Besides, the girl's beauty will serve as a symbol of health among the Tsuchigumo, and evidence of our superiority over the once-hunted humans,* he thought.

He put on a loose, very dark shirt with decorative white lines running every which way. It would serve as good camouflage as well as a way to blend in with the humans. Loose-fitting pants would keep him agile.

It is time, he thought.

He inspected the wiggling white mass one last time, then locked the door behind him.

In the hotel lobby he asked the Concierge to call him a cab and about the nearest luaus. In his low rumble he described something "loud and crazy." A slight smile lifted the corners of his mouth.

"For you, sir, I have just the thing."

* * *

It was getting dark by the time Abella found a rental and started driving around Kauai with all the windows down, sniffing the air. She could smell the peppery sweet smell, now making scent ribbons, twisting and floating in the air, but concentration was the issue. From which way were they coming, and how could she get to the source? She thought she might have a direction, when the fine hairs on her body sensed, moments before her ears, the pounding of drums.

* * *

Tau had been weaving back and forth to the sway of the hula dancers' hips when the drums began. He was eating crispy pig skin bacon right off the spit while it turned.

"Hey Lolo! Get back!" said a giant-bellied man in colorful flowered shorts.

Suddenly the yard erupted in swirling fire and fierce, chest-thumping drums. Tau drifted off into the crowd. The bouncing, partying mass of humanity was covered in stringed flowers, flashes, and shadows, as the performers threw fire across the lawn. Grass skirts whipped to the drum beats and muscular arms glistening with sweat pounded out yet more sound.

Bamboo torches burned all around the revelers, but behind the torches it was nice and black. His dark skin and dark clothing disappeared. But to *his* eyes it was merely dusk, and his spirit came alive with desire. With his nectar gone, deep, dark desires surfaced. He was Tsuchigumo of old. He flexed his arms. He desired to climb and perch in waiting; he desired to kill.

* * *

Abella swerved off the road following a trace stream of a constant sticky leak of vanilla sweetness. As she drove, it strengthened in flavor. She could taste the nectar on her tongue and she too stretched her arms, tearing her blouse just under her ribcage. Long sharp black arms unfolded like two jointed pikes. Her vision tuned and she noticed every edge of every object she saw. Her foot pressed hard on the car's gas pedal as she rode the sweet-scented roadway.

She was in and out of control. Her rental swerved from lane to lane. She felt an anger building inside her. She wanted, she *needed* to defend her kind, her position. The air thick with scent, her Tsuchigumo eyes now could see the river of sweet odor lazily moving with the air currents. The streams divided into two: one was rich and thick, the other spotty echoes of dribble, all but gone.

She turned the steering wheel hard, racing to follow the disappearing trail.

* * *

Tau removed his clothing and climbed atop a large rock nestled against a hilly area surrounding the yard. From here he could see the crowd dancing and wandering to get food and drinks. There was a bathroom building and a line of extra portable bathrooms well behind the torches. But people were milling about in too great of numbers. He needed to separate a small group from the others. He watched and waited.

Tau climbed head-first over the edge of the large rock, aided by several sticky strands of silk. His weavers planted small silk clumps on the dry rock, creating a woven surface on which he could climb. Two couples were walking and talking in his direction. Tau's whole body quivered and he brushed his tongue over two small fangs that stretched forward from his pallet. Allowing his shoulder arms to rise, he climbed over the silk surface with the rest of his limbs. Like the Tsuchigumo that dwelled in cave-holes long ago, he hung his entire body over the edge of the rock with muscular arms extended, ready to grasp anything that passed by. As one of the couples approached the rock, perhaps for a quick kiss in the shadows, Tau's arms lowered silently, steadily, his weavers slowly releasing silk. With the drums pounding in the background and a bloodfire in his eyes, Tau's body dropped.

The two lovers' bodies vanished from the shadowy, cozy nook, reappearing twenty feet above. There was no sound of a disturbance, no struggle. Tau's hands squeezed past muscle fibers and tracheal cartilage, holding each spinal column just under the jawbone. He dragged the unconscious, damaged bodies onto the silken rock. His mouth opened wide. Tau's fingers tore open the woman's shirt, exposing her warm belly. With a speed that would blur human eyes, his face filled the tear in her blouse, filling her body cavity with as much liquefying venom as he could produce.

She will soon be a fine wine. I will hide the other.

* * *

Abella had ditched the car and was now moving through the luau. The drums pounded and in her peripheral vision twenty grass skirts transformed the sound into motion.

Of course Tau would be here, she thought trying to shake off her nectar haze. *The excitement, the over stimulation, the human females. It would all make him drunk. And his already bad judgment would become dangerous!* Abella folded her arms, covering the tears in her blouse, put on the happy face she saw on the revelers, and headed through the crowd.

Beyond the torches the nocturnal scene lit up with shapes: a tree-line with a stream running behind it, a path cutting between two hills, a large rock and on top—movement.

* * *

Tau used both sets of limbs to dig into the side of the hill. He was about to grab the human male when he heard something behind him. The amber eyes of Tau snapped to view the intruder. His predatory focus relaxed. He spoke the tongue of his people.

"You are here, Exalted Queen."

"I am here," Abella replied in his ancient language.

"You show me a new face this day."

"I am Abella, my beloved elder."

"Why do you see me, exalted one?"

She thought about his question:

Should she tell him he is a danger to his people, that the bodies on this rock, like all the humans he had killed, would be missed and searched for, possibly leading to exposure of their kind? That the Tsuchigumo must track him down every five years and rectify an incident that is an affront to their people and would sooner or later result in the Tsuchigumo being hunted? That this time was the last?

"Many sorrows, beloved elder."

"Do you have hunger?"

"I do not have hunger, beloved elder."

"I have great hunger."

"Feed, beloved elder."

Tau pierced the reddish, bloated lump of flesh, drinking eagerly. Abella watched as the woman's body sunk, indicating he had had a good meal. Abella sighed and lashed out. Tau hissed as two long black jointed pikes speared his muscular frame, lifting him up off his silken blanket and into the air.

"Abella kill Tau?"

"Yes, Tau."

"Why Abella kill Tau?"

"Abella has many sorrows, Tau."

"May Tau speak, to Abella?"

"Speak, beloved elder."

"I kill the human food, for ten thousand winters he is food. Why is human not food this day?"

"Our world has a new face, beloved elder. This food brings death. Creation of deformed ones brings death."

Tau was silent, then raised his head to the sky and uttered four words Abella would remember the rest of her life.

"Tau Tsuchigumo! Tau Otougumo!"

"Your words are in me, beloved elder." Somewhere inside her, she understood Tau and his ancient ways. She felt a deep pain inside her. She crossed her shoulder arms over her chest to signal this pain.

"Then Tau honor Abella?"

"Yes, Tau." Abella watched as Tau's head dropped to the side, her pikes had done her bidding. Tau's life would end in moments.

Tau was Tsuchigumo and Otougumo with many molts, but Abella was a young Tsuchigumo Queen and Tau knew his life was spared or forfeit at her whim. Her bloodfire and strength more than matched his and her long sharp pikes and sizable death-giving fangs quickly shredded his body. She devoured him and his silk bed as other couples strolled the path twenty feet below. When she finished Tau, she grabbed the dead, half-eaten woman and raced to the top of the hill. She would consume her before the new day. The young man, unfortunately, would be found in the stream behind the treeline, robbed of his wallet and jewelry. A random murder.

Now she would rest. As she drifted toward sleep, she pondered the being that was once Tau:

The Tsuchigumo will only survive if we keep our place in the human world. Out of sight; away from notice. I will fight for our survival until the end. But I and my kind will not be hunted out of existence. Predation from man is an unnecessary stress to add to our people's fight. Tau was a proud Tsuchigumo and Otougumo, but he endangered us all. Though she knew she was right, she couldn't help admiring the Tsuchigumo that refused to give up her kind's ancient way of life.

* * *

A week later Abella stood in a tree-line clearing outside the hotel with two large Tsuchigumo under a waning crescent moon. She made sure the room had been paid up for the week under Tau's name. The Tsuchigumo silently removed the glass from the window and carried the white mass toward her. She planted herself, feeling her bloodfire rise with the escaping flow of scent. She held up her hands, allowing them to approach only after the wind had dissipated the intoxifying clouds of nectar. The hard white mass was dragged to her feet and torn open. There, upon the ground, lay the young woman named Misty. The pikes under her breasts unfolded and folded. Her ovipositors were mere nubs and useless. Her weaving appendages were underdeveloped and Abella saw no spinnerets at all. The Tsuchigumo escorts helped Misty to her feet. Abella was pleased to see she used her pikes to steady herself.

"Where am I?" She looked at her body with curiosity. "I'm different."

"How do you feel about that?" Abella readied a deadly strike.

"I'm not sure, but I feel, well, surreal and kinda like a superhero!"

Abella reached down behind her to grab a thermos and cup and poured Misty some hot tomato soup. She exhaled, relaxing a fierce tension she held at the ready.

"Then welcome, sister. This will help calm you."

She watched as the new Tsuchigumo drank the acidic beverage. "We will take you to our kind and you will learn to live in a new way. Then you will return to live as you did before. But your life will have new meaning. Do you understand?"

"I understand."

"Good. Take her to her new home."

"Yes Mother."

QI'LIN
BY SHELLI-JO PELLETIER

J esse Miller was smoking a cigarette in an alleyway behind a Detroit pizzeria, his collar turned up against the bitter November wind, when a deer walked by.

His mundane morning routine had not hinted this unusual circumstance. Like most days, Jesse left his downtown apartment before the sun rose between the skyscrapers, took the subway to *Edmondo's,* and entered the small building from the side entrance. Inside, teenage Raoul was pulling metal sheet pans down from the wall while the owner (a man named Saunders without an ounce of Italian blood in him) beat on a pile of dough on the sideboard.

Jesse pulled on the apron hanging from its peg by the door. Raoul saw him and lifted a hand in greeting. "Jesse! Hey man." Jesse nodded to him and went to wash his hands.

Raoul followed him. "Hey, guess who I saw last night at the supermarket on Third?"

Jesse was not a morning person, especially on a day he had to pull a double shift, and didn't answer.

"Jie! Can you believe it? All the way over on Third? She looked good, man, she looked thin!"

Jesse didn't want to talk about his ex and how she looked. He grunted a noncommittal response. He quickly moved aside when Raoul put the sheet pans in the sink and sprayed them down, washing dust down the drain that had accumulated since the last time they had needed the overlarge pans. Before Jesse could wonder what they were for, Raoul mentioned they had gotten a special order for a birthday party. Which meant it was going to be both loud and crowded today. Great.

Saunders always seemed to hear everything that went on in the dingy pizzeria, no matter where he was standing. When the two young men returned to the ovens, he peered at Jesse from under heavy brows. "I haven't seen that young girl around lately," he said.

"We broke up," Jesse reminded him with a scowl.

Saunders shook his head, as if it was some sort of shame. Jesse almost told him to mind his own business, but the old man distracted him with his next comment. "I bought too much milk for coffee this morning," he said gruffly. "There's an extra jug in the fridge you can take home." He turned back to his dough and didn't look at Jesse again.

Jesse gave the man a confused look. Leftovers were sometimes taken home at the end of the night, sure. Why was Saunders bringing it up now like it was an offer? Suspicious of the charity, Jesse resolved to "forget" the milk when he left for the night. He didn't want to analyze the man's behavior. He'd deal with it tomorrow.

By mid-morning the birthday party was in full swing, the dining area filled to bursting with a dozen animated nine-year-olds, and Jesse stepped outside for a smoke. He had been standing in the chilly air for close to ten minutes—possibly fifteen—when a deer walked past him.

Jesse had been trying to ignore all of it. The biting wind that kept away the smell lingering from the stack of trash bags to his right, the knowledge that he had to go back inside, the people hurrying by on the sidewalk a dozen paces in front of him, thick coats wrapped around their bodies and talking into a cellphone or to the person beside them. He concentrated on the spicy smoke from his clove cigarette as it left his lungs. Ten minutes was pushing it for a smoke break, but he didn't care. It wasn't a great job. It was only marginally better than being unemployed, really. Minimum wage, and the perks didn't exist beyond taking home leftover stale garlic bread at the end of the night.

Jesse forgot to inhale when the small animal stepped past him. It was a white deer. He wasn't quite sure how it had gotten into the alleyway to begin with; he hadn't seen it when he stepped outside and the only thing behind him was a brick wall forming the back of—as far as he knew—an after-school recreation hall for teenagers with no parents at home.

After the deer walked past Jesse it stopped and turned back to look at him. It was white with some sort of pale colored eyes, sky blue or maybe pink like one of those albinos. Maybe there was something wrong with it, because it didn't look quite right. It didn't have a little white deer tail, but a long flowing tail that reached to the ground, like a horse's. And it didn't have two antlers on its head. It just had one, a short little spike that pointed backward, as if the other had fallen off.

Maybe it was from the zoo. In profile it looked a lot like the emblem on the old Chevy that used to be parked in front of his apartment, the rusty white Impala. Those were deer from Africa, right?

But then, its face wasn't quite right either. Maybe it was just a mutant, or maybe it was someone's pet. One of those "it would have died in the wild so I adopted it" kind of stories. But how did a pet deer get loose in downtown Detroit and show up in the alley behind Jesse without anyone around to claim it?

While Jesse pondered this, the deer finished its examination of him. It stepped out onto the sidewalk.

He craned his neck to watch it walk around the brick corner of the pizzeria, listening for imminent exclamations of people walking by. When he didn't hear anything he dropped his clove cigarette and stepped forward curiously, making it to the edge of the alleyway just in time to see the deer step off the sidewalk, between two parked cars, and out into the street.

Jesse glanced around. People were walking by him without paying any attention to what was going on around them. A man in a business suit jogged to the side to avoid him, swinging a briefcase that nearly clipped Jesse in the knee. There was no sound of screeching brakes. There was no deer standing in the road.

Jesse peered between the two parked cars in confusion, because now he could see that they were parked much too closely for the deer to have passed between them. Their bumpers were almost touching. Jesse turned to the left and then to the right, one hand propped up on his hip over the biggest grease stain on his apron, the other scratching the side of his head. There was no sign of a white deer on the sidewalk or in the road. No one acted as if they had seen anything unusual. Was he losing his mind?

He stood there longer, a confused frown etching his face. Then he heard the voice of Raoul shouting in the alleyway behind him, saying Saunders was swearing up a storm behind the counter and demanding to know what was taking Jesse so long.

Saunders only swore when he was more pissed off than normal. Jesse turned and hurried back inside, because suddenly what happened to a white deer in downtown Detroit was no longer so important. He had a crappy job, but it was still a job he needed.

* * *

That evening after work, Jesse walked down the sidewalk on his way to the subway. He was much too tired to be thinking of anything other than how many blocks he had left to go, then how many subway stops until his own, then how many blocks from the subway station to his small apartment building. He traced this careful route in his head over and over. It was the easiest thing to think about when you were as tired as a person who had been standing behind a counter flinging pizza dough into an oven all day and listening to the curses and death threats of an old man who should have retired ten years ago.

Once he got to the subway and fought with his elbows onto the subway car, he found there were no places to sit. He stood and stared at the advertising posters of headache medicine and illiteracy programs as the subway zipped through the tunnels under the city.

Three stops later and Jesse got off the train and stumbled up the stairs of an escalator that was no longer working (and hadn't been for the past two weeks). Each of his feet felt as if seven-pound bags of flour were tied to them. When he reached the top of the steps and walked out into the crisp winter night, he remembered to take out his cellphone and strike up an imaginary conversation.

Once in a while Jesse called his brother at times like this, but tonight he was dead tired. He didn't really want to listen to a successful architect talk about how things would be better if Jesse would just leave the dirty city and "get serious for once."

Instead he just flipped open his cellphone and started talking. Groceries he needed to buy. Toilet paper, tuna fish. It was safer this way. You were less likely to be jumped if someone thought the person on the other end of your conversation might hear your shouts and call the police.

It wouldn't really stop anyone seriously wanting to make trouble. Jesse was well aware. He didn't look like he was carrying anything worth trouble anyway. His jeans were grease-stained and his shirt had a hole in the collar. In the neighborhood where he was living, this was just a precaution.

A second precaution was keeping an eye out. If you were smart about it, you could avoid trouble before it hit. So, tired as he was, Jesse's eyes were making sweeps of the pools of darkness between the streetlights as he walked along. He remained cautious for anything that looked like a shadow deep enough to hold a couple hoodlums looking to hassle a man on his way home from work.

Movement caught his eye as he scanned across the street. The white deer was walking there, on the sidewalk almost directly across from him. Jesse stared in disbelief. It was definitely the same creature, with the same long flowing tail and one horn on its forehead pointing backward.

He stopped and his arm slowly lowered, the phone sliding from nerveless fingers into his pocket. The deer didn't look to be in a hurry. It wasn't moving like it was confused or frightened. With a calm grace it stepped up to the street corner, illuminating its white coat in the yellowish glow of the overhead streetlight.

It looked very real, not the hallucination of an overworked pizza guy. For the first time Jesse wondered if he should walk up and touch it. Was it lost? Would it run? Should he call animal control? It wasn't any of his business. His apartment was close now. He could just go.

Jesse stepped to the street corner across from the deer. Each of them stood in pools of yellow light, a long river of darkness winding between them. The crosswalk signal was red, an illuminated hand floating in the night. Jesse stared at the creature as the crosswalk signal turned white. The deer lowered its head, as if bowing to him.

No, this was stupid. This wasn't normal. Jesse turned away and walked quickly down the sidewalk, toward his apartment. He didn't look back to the crosswalk.

* * *

Jesse got to his apartment building's front door and reached into his pocket for his keys, searching amidst receipts, change, and two straw wrappers he had picked up off a customer's table while he'd been cleaning. He stopped searching when his other hand grasped the door handle. Unlocked again.

With a sigh, Jesse pushed open the door and stepped into the cold hallway, overhead lights flickering over pale blue walls that had faded to gray and pale red carpeting that had faded to peach. He started up the stairs to the third floor. Halfway up the second floor stairwell he stopped when he saw a pair of white shoes—ladies shoes—in front of his doorway at the top of the stairs. One shoe was tapping.

Jesse lifted his eyes higher and found black leggings and a short gray skirt. And then a white blouse with one frayed buttonhole that caused his stomach to churn from familiarity.

In her arms she held a baby carrier seat, and his stomach twisted a little more.

Finally, he raised his eyes to a closed off expression with flat black eyes and short black hair framing a peach-shaped face. The tapping that filled the stairwell stopped.

"Aren't you late," she said. It wasn't a question.

Jesse groaned. He was too tired to deal with this. "Jie, what are you doing here," he said, digging into his pockets again for his keys.

"I tried calling you," she said. "When did you change your number?"

"I got a new phone. The old one was crap." He finally pulled his keys out of his pocket and the two straw wrappers fell out and drifted to the hallway floor. He held up the keys somewhat triumphantly, and she stepped aside so he had access to the door. He didn't look down at the carrier seat as he walked by. He didn't want to see what was in there. Inside he slung his jacket at the legless couch pushed up against the wall.

Jie followed him into the apartment without asking for an invitation, then followed him into the kitchen and put the heavy baby seat in the center of his kitchen table with a grunt of effort. Jesse didn't look at it. It wasn't making noise; maybe the baby was asleep.

It was cheaper to eat at home than to eat anything from the pizzeria. Jesse opened the freezer and pulled out a frozen chicken dinner. "It's late. What do you want?" he asked Jie, because if he didn't ask he feared she would never leave.

She snapped at him waspishly. "What do *I* want!? It's not about what I want, Jesse! He's your son, and all this time you've never even seen him! You've never even asked!" Jesse winced at her raised tone. He wondered why she decided tonight was the night to bring this up to him. Also, she was exaggerating. "All this time" was two months, tops.

"You never offer to help," she accused.

"You said you didn't need help," he pointed out.

"He's your son too! You can give me twenty dollars so I can take a taxi home—the buses aren't running this late Jesse!—and he needs diapers and I'm tired of asking my parents for change so I can run down to the 7-Eleven just so he has something clean!"

Jesse shoved his dinner into the microwave and shut the door, gritting his teeth. He didn't want to deal with this now. It was late and he wanted to eat and watch TV and go to bed. Sounds of fussing now came from the seat carrier on the table.

"You don't even want to *look* at him!" she said.

He didn't. Jesse had a boss with a short temper, a walk home through a dubious neighborhood every night, and a dollar raise on cigarette prices this year. He didn't want to look at the baby, whose name he couldn't even remember right now (it was one of those 'Cr' names like Christopher or Cricket, but Chinese-sounding).

Jesse watched the microwave window as Jie continued on about her lack of money. He tried not to argue back, tried not to say how he didn't have money either or really much of anything nice at all, because then she would just be there a lot longer and argue more. The baby fussed like its mother.

"Twenty dollars, Jesse," she repeated for the third time. "*You* have twenty dollars. I don't even have that."

Jesse didn't have twenty dollars in cash, but he had a ten. As his dinner revolved in the microwave toward its completion, he dug into his back pocket and pulled out his wallet. He handed her the ten, and then the two singles when she demanded them as well. "Fine, take it," he growled.

"Don't get snippy with *me*," she retorted, the bills disappearing into her purse. "He doesn't even have diapers, Jesse."

Jesse didn't have to think up a response to that because the microwave dinged. He eagerly turned to take his dinner from inside it, but for some reason the single electronic sound made the baby start to wail in a way that their loud discussion hadn't.

Jesse didn't look at the table. He dug into the drawer next to the sink for a fork.

Jie gave a disgusted sigh. "You could at least look at him," she said, walking to the kitchen table.

Jesse wanted them to go home. He headed for the kitchen doorway, hoping Jie would follow and thus be one room closer to the front door. The kitchen table was between him and the doorway. Perhaps it was her words or perhaps it was just instinct, but Jesse looked down at the baby carrier seat as he passed the table and saw his son for the first time.

The baby was ruddy-faced and scrunched up, the skin only a shade lighter than the red one-piece he was wearing. His nose was too big. Just a hint of dark fuzz sprouted on top of his head. His hands were clenched in fists that jerked against the navy fabric of the carrier.

Jesse stopped walking. He stared at the baby. He felt like he was choking. "Jie, what the hell's that?"

"What?" She leaned over the carrier, searching for a scrape or a cockroach or whatever a mother looks for when someone gasps around her baby. She didn't see anything; her eyes darted up to look accusingly at him. "What!?"

"That! What's that?" Jesse's fork balanced on the plastic tray that held his chicken as he pointed with one finger straight at the baby's chest. The front of the red fabric was decorated with an embroidered patch on the left side, sewn right over the baby's heart. It was a white patch, in the shape of a deer with a long tail and one horn.

Jie straightened and tossed her black hair. "Honestly, Jesse. You're such a child. It's a *qi'lin*."

Jesse stared at her. "A what?"

She busied herself with lifting the baby up out of the carrier before she answered, just to frustrate him. The baby's cries lowered only slightly, and that was mostly because the sound was muffled against her chest. "*Qi'lin*. Keee-lin," she drawled out. "My grandmother sewed it to all his clothes." She said this in a slightly annoyed tone.

Jesse didn't know what to say. His brain seemed empty. "Why?" his voice asked for him.

"It's just a myth. It was like a unicorn, in ancient China. Supposedly people said it would appear whenever great men were born. For luck, Grandma said."

Jesse stared. The baby stared back at him with dark blue eyes. He left his chicken dinner on the table and stepped out of the kitchen.

"Where are you going?" demanded Jie.

"Just stay here a minute. I have to look for something." Jesse grabbed his jacket on the way out the door. There was a 7-Eleven a block away. He could use his debit card and buy diapers and milk. She would probably be so grateful when he got back, she wouldn't think he was crazy.

Outside the night air was a cold shock, clearing his senses. He wasn't sure what he was doing. The deer couldn't still be around by now.

Jesse's footsteps sounded loud as he hurried down the sidewalk. His breath made pale clouds in the air in front of him. Ahead he could see the street corner, empty. Undeterred, he hurried to look around the corner.

Jesse was so sure his actions would be fruitless at this point, that he was taken completely by surprise when he turned the corner and slid to a halt directly in front of the deer.

A car cruised by without stopping, turning the corner after only a slow roll at the stop sign. Jesse stood in front of the *qi'lin*. He didn't know what to say, but he wanted to say something. He wanted to ask something. "Will—?"

The *qi'lin* moved then, which cut him off. It folded one knee, lowered its stately head almost to the ground. Then it stood again, gazing at him with its pale eyes. Jesse wasn't sure what to do, but he bowed his head in return.

The creature seemed to accept that, turning away. Jesse stepped after it when it started to walk away. "Wait!" he said. "What the—? What are you here for—?"

The *qi'lin* stepped behind a car parked on the side of the street, and it didn't step out again. Jesse slowed his steps and finally came to a full stop, looking at the empty street.

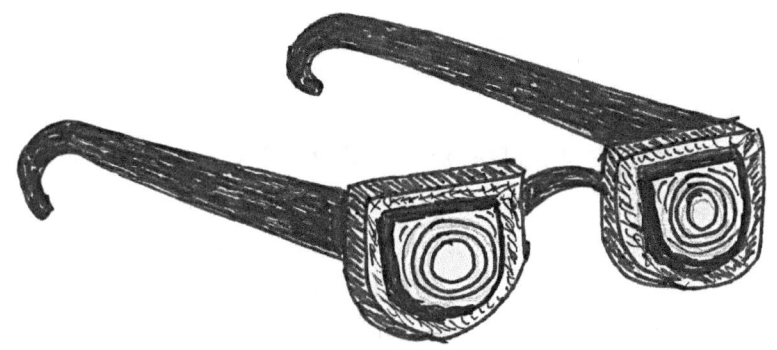

X-Ray Glasses

by Steven Inman

There lies a wide quiet valley not far into the foothills, where there once lived a happy people in a peaceful little village. In this village there were two little boys named Pete and TwoFeet who would run out from school each day and run along their secret paths all the way to the convenience shop at the corner under the wide yellow streetlights. Every day there was a different shop-clerk behind the counter, half-hidden behind magical rolls of many colored lottery tickets and exotic magical drinks to give people energy and super-strength.

But the comic books were always in the same place, and the freshly-baked SnoRols in their crinkly wrappers were always in the same place, and

117

the boys always bought one of each and then ran out from the store to the sidewalk where they ate their SnoRols and read the comics.

One day they saw a small advertisement in the last pages of one comic book. They huddled close so that they could both see the tiny tiny print and the tiny tiny picture of a small boy very much like them holding a heavy pair of eyeglasses. "BOYS!" the ad read. "WANT TO SEE IT ALL? SEE THRU ANYTHING?" There was also a very pretty lady in the ad standing in front of the boy with the glasses, and it seemed that the boy wanted to put the glasses on to look at her. "GET YOUR OWN X-RAY GLASSES TODAY!"

"We should get those," TwoFeet said to Pete. "We really should. We could see Boobs and stuff." And so they decided to do just that, and they worked hard and were very nice at home and so soon earned enough money to mail in the order to the proper P.O. Box in a village far away.

They waited and waited but no glasses appeared in their mailboxes. And they were sad. But one day after school they went back to their home and found two small boxes on the porch, with Petes' name on one box and TwoFeets' name on the other. They opened their boxes and found glasses inside of each one. The boys took them out in silence and held them, feeling the cool thick plastic, the smooth opening hinges on the side, the strange glass and metal eyepieces.

Of course they tried the glasses on right away. When they looked out into the yard all they could see was dirt and grass, and it was all a little blurry and hazy. But everything in the yard was too far away, and when they looked at each other they jumped back in surprise because neither had any clothes on.

Of course they had clothes on but it was true, the glasses could see right through them. "Wow!" the boys shouted, and ran down from the porch. And they both fell because even though they could see through things they could not see everything too well and so they had to walk slowly.

There were very many interesting things to see that day! Squirrels and dogs looking scarily-meaty without skin, trees looking all pale without bark, Mrs. Tanner looking very interesting indeed as long as you didn't look at her face (which without clothes on it the boys could see through the skin and it was scary), and Old Mr. Watkins, from which the boys turned away very quickly.

By the time they returned home they were walking normally. They had learned to look around things and focus their eyes certain ways so they could see better. Both had small achy feelings in their heads so they took off the glasses and went inside for supper. But before they went to the dining room they hid the glasses away because they did not want Mom and Dad to ask What the Heck Are Those Things and Where Did You Get Them.

* * *

And so for three days Pete and TwoFeet looked at many things. They wore the glasses to school but made sure they took them off before going inside, because they would end up in Miss Donovans' Drawer of Confiscation. For the first day they looked at everybody and saw them naked and that was mostly funny, especially because some adults had stuff under their clothes that didn't make sense. They saw lots of boobs and other things, but that was soon boring and gross. But they discovered that they could squeeze their faces and make their eyes all squinty, and then they could control how deep they saw, like just underwear instead of seeing all the way to someone's nakedness.

And anyway, after a day or so that sort of got boring, but there were other things to look at, inside rooms and inside walls, into teachers' desks and the principals' office. Pete and TwoFeet were getting pretty darn good at using the glasses. And when the other kids laughed and pointed at them because of the funny looking glasses, well then, Pete and TwoFeet just kind of laughed with each other and made little smirks because they could see things those kids could not.

* * *

On the third day after Pete and TwoFeet got their glasses they came home and found two new letters, and though the letters did not have any sort of return name on them they did have a sort of design, like an Army patch or something, with three letters above that patch-thing. Their letters were the same, and said this:

Boys!

You have certainly made a GOOD CHOICE in selecting these fine spectacles for some viewing excitement! Many satisfied young boys and men have learned many things about their world by wearing these POWERFUL SPECTACLES.

And now we would like to extend an invitation to you, an opportunity to join a most UNIQUE and EXCLUSIVE organization, the EYES OF ONE!

Return the form below to become members of the OPTI-ALL club today! This club boasts members from all across this fine homeland, but we need you! What we ask, the only requirement of our fine club, is that you send in a letter every week telling us what you see with your own SPECTACLES!

Send in the form today to receive your own Member Patch and I.D. card!

"Sounds pretty neat," TwoFeet said.

Pete nodded, and pulled a pencil stub out of his pocket and then the two boys filled out the forms and sent them back that very same day because there were also two Self-Addressed Stamped Envelopes with the letters as well.

* * *

So for one week Pete and TwoFeet played around and saw inside bugs and under the leaves of the forest, and they saw lots of people in their underwear, and some that were naked, and that was funny. Two times they found things, once for Biff when he lost his baseball glove and it was really stuck behind a radiator, and another when Miss Donovan lost her red pen and it was stuck behind her bottom drawer.

And three days after they had mailed the Enrollment Forms back in the

Self Addressed Stamped Envelopes both Pete and TwoFeet got their Official I.D. badges made from metal that said EYES OF ONE MEMBER and a Member Patch, which they asked Mom to sew onto their favorite shirts.

"What is this?" Mom asked and she held the patch out and looked it all over, her eyes getting squinty as if she was trying to have X-Ray eyes.

"Nothing," TwoFeet answered, and Pete shrugged, and said, "Just some patches."

Mom made that breath blowy sigh sound and sewed the patches on.

And later when they'd finished playing they looked in the envelope again and found that there were also two sheets of paper, and at the top of the paper a line of words read: "IN ACCORDANCE WITH YOUR MEMBERSHIP AGREEMENT PLEASE DESCRIBE IN DETAIL WHAT YOU HAVE SEEN WITH YOUR OPTI-ALL GLASSES THIS WEEK." Underneath this there were about thirty lines for the boys to fill in. "Wow," said Pete miserably. "It's like a book report or something."

But they completed the form, looking at each others' paper to remind themselves of what they had seen, and when they were done they sort of had a list like: *Squirrels with no skin. Guts. Peoples underware. Lots of junk in Mr. Nortons desk. Car engins. Inside peaples houses. Motors.*

"Yeah, they were neat," TwoFeet pointed at that entry. "Write down about the stuff, and the pieces moving around." So Pete wrote down about the stuff and the pieces moving around, and they mailed the forms back in the Self Addressed Stamped Envelope.

* * *

And another week went by where they looked at things with their glasses and learned to look harder and deeper, and see a lot more of what was under things. And at the end of the week they both found in the mail another pair of forms to fill out. But this time there was a little typewritten note with the forms, and the note said: "Good Job Boys! You are learning to use your OPTI-ALL SPECTACLES with skill. However, the things you described in your last report were things we can easily imagine without OPTI-ALL SPECTACLES. For this next week, try to look harder and see things that are more hidden. *Think* about what you are seeing."

"Huh," TwoFeet muttered, thinking this was like having a teacher tell you to think. "I wonder what that means. Wonder if this club is stupid."

But Pete shook his head. "No, it isn't, dummy. It's a real club! Something with real work. I wonder what they are doing at HQ." So they filled out their forms again, but they hadn't had time to think about what was really hidden or what it really meant so their lists were more like: *Mouses inside walls. A bottle hidden inside a box. Wierd stuff in garbage bags. More guts and underware.*

* * *

Now in this third week Pete and TwoFeet spent time looking at things really really closely, trying to understand what they saw. They wore their spectacles more, and when people laughed at them Pete and TwoFeet sneered back, because they had a sort of superpower and those people were dumb, especially walking around in underwear or naked. Because that's how it seemed.

When the forms came in the mail at the end of the week both of the boys were ready and wanted to make a good report so they would not get any bad or gruff notes. So they had things in their list like:

Mrs. Depping had a lot of bruises on her chest and stomach
Lots of little boxes in a car trunk on Maple street
Mr. Donalds had on ladies underware
lots of things like footprints under leafs
A man I don't know had a gun
Some trash bags had lots of beer cans and bottles
More mouses inside walls with bits of paper maybe making a nest
Someone lost a bunch of needls the kind like in a hospital

Pete looked over his list and asked TwoFeet if he thought it was good, and TwoFeet said sure, it looked really good, though he wasn't sure what all that stuff would mean to someone at the club HQ. But they mailed their lists anyway, and then they went out and played.

Now Pete and TwoFeet had other toys and other friends but now with their X-Ray glasses those things were not as fun. So the other toys were forgotten and left alone in their room and the other friends were forgotten or left alone, and that was sometimes because Pete and TwoFeet could see some secret things and so they didn't believe their friends all the time anymore. But mostly the friends did not want to play with them because they wore the glasses all the time now, and they looked sort of silly-scary, and the boys had strange sorts of smiles that made their friends feel weird, like Pete and TwoFeet knew secrets and stuff.

* * *

That week after they mailed the second list they had to look for more people to see, because Mr. Donalds was gone and Mrs. Depping was gone, and even the car they saw with boxes in the trunk was gone. But there were other people and things to look at, and Pete and TwoFeet made more lists and had things like *lots of peaple meeting inside the Lincowicz house* and *a room full of new books and machines at old man Grurneys garage*, and they mailed them and didn't worry about where people went when they were gone, or why the people who were left seemed to stay away from the boys.

* * *

And soon another day came with another Talk from Mom and Dad. They called Pete and TwoFeet into the living room. The Talk was about playing with other kids and being good playmates, and Pete and TwoFeet knew they had to look down and look sorry. "There's something happening in the village," Dad told them, "...something scary, making people go away."

Mom nodded her head and looked really serious. "It must be something scary... something monstrous," she said, even though she kind of mumbled, sort of to herself.

"We haven't seen any monsters," TwoFeet promised, and Pete nodded too.

"Okay, boys," Dad said. "Just give those glasses a rest and go play."

So they went outside and played for a little bit without the glasses. But when their friend Tilly came by and said that she had not seen the newest *Raider Klein* comic Pete thought her face looked funny, so he put on his glasses and could see the comic under her shirt, hidden. *She must have bought the only one at the store,* he thought, *and she wants to hide it, that sneaking girl.*

They didn't play with Tilly anymore after that.

*   *   *

Whenever their other friends came around, Pete and TwoFeet would put on the glasses and ask the friends certain questions, and see if the friends had the right answers, or if they were lying and sneaking. A lot of them were starting to lie and sneak, and soon Pete and TwoFeet didn't play with any of their old friends.

And now a few of the old friends were gone, with their families. *Monsters*, Pete and TwoFeet thought, it must be Monsters, though we still don't see them. They wondered why they could not see the Monsters with their OPTI-ALL SPECTACLES. But they didn't wonder for long, there were so many other things to look at.

Then came another day, and again Mom and Dad called the boys in for a Talk. "Listen to me," Dad began, and talked to them about things in the village, about whispers and creatures people had seen, but they were halfway into the Talk when Dad blew out his breath and said, "You boys have to take those damn glasses off when we talk to you." And Mom said, "I know you are playing but you could go blind or something."

So then Pete and TwoFeet took off the glasses. And they were then scared, because Mom and Dad were different, somehow. The faces were the same but Dad's looked darker and far away and Mom's looked really melty-droopy and sad. And for some reason Mom and Dad were looking at the boys funny, as if maybe the boys' faces were different too. The boys just kept quiet and so Mom said, "If you keep wearing glasses and doing things with your eyes they will stay that way." When she said this her droopy melty face was very scary.

That week when they made their lists for HQ the boys listed the way people were starting to change, because it was everyone, not just Mom and Dad, and Pete and TwoFeet saw this whenever they took off the glasses. So they kept the glasses on even more, except around Mom and Dad, and even when they took them off people looked at them with scared-weird faces and then turned away.

HQ didn't say anything about the weird faces that Pete and TwoFeet saw but HQ did say the list was Very Smart and sent them new badges. So Pete and TwoFeet looked at things and people even more now, especially the people, because that seemed to make HQ happier. And they reported the weird things they saw but now it was getting harder because a lot of people had gone away, and the rest of the people seemed to hide more and stay away from Pete and TwoFeet. The boys could control the glasses so well when they squinted they were able to read peoples' mail through envelopes, and so they read peoples' mail and saw that Mr. McNolty had some strange mail with words like in a foreign language, and Jessy Pooler was getting big envelopes with lots of naked pictures in them, and the boys saw a lot more.

"Reports every week," Pete grumbled when he filled out his paper, and TwoFeet laughed, because it was fun now in their little secret club to make these reports. And they knew that it was important, too!

And the week after the boys reported the things they saw in the mail, Mr. McNolty stopped going into the stores and restaurants and leaving his stuff on tables, and Jessy Pooler was gone, and Madeline Swank blushed whenever someone said Hi. And everyone stayed away from Pete and TwoFeet, crossing the road and looking at them with the scared-weird eyes.

And then the boys could see Mr. McNolty had boxes with bottles and plants in them, and a week later they did not see Mr. McNolty anymore.

* * *

So Mom and Dad had another talk with Pete and TwoFeet, and told them that they were Very Concerned. Mom and Dad could not really look at the boys because of the glasses, and when Mom asked Pete and TwoFeet to take off the glasses the boys said they could not because things did not look right anymore. And then Dad said that the grownups were hearing lots of whispering and naughty stories, and scary things about Monsters.

"Why?" Pete asked. "We still haven't seen Monsters." But both he and TwoFeet did not mind too much because of what they had seen, and because people in the village now looked so creepy or funny or stupid. Both of the boys thought that there were no Monsters, and maybe the people were confused because they looked like Monsters themselves.

And Mom cried a little and Dad said that This Had To Stop, but he didn't say what or how.

"Thats dumb," TwoFeet said, because neither he nor Pete had seen any Monsters. But this time they wrote about the Talk in their reports, and they wrote to HQ everything that Mom and Dad had talked to them about, and they wrote about the monsters, even though they had not see them.

*   *   *

And the next day the boys slept very late. And when they woke they found that the glasses were already on their heads, and they could not get them off. But they didn't mind, because it was the only way they could see things now, and if they could not see all the secrets around them they got very afraid and worried.

They got dressed and went downstairs, but Mom and Dad were not downstairs. All their things were gone, and the car was gone. The boys walked through the village and they saw that all the cars were gone and all the people were gone, and Pete and TwoFeet were all alone.

Now the boys wondered if there really were Monsters and if the Monsters had taken the people away, and so they spent the day sneaking around the village, peeking into doorways and windows, listening for noises, but they did not see anything or hear a single peep. "Where are the monsters?" TwoFeet asked, but now not only was his face and eyes different but his voice was all whispery-sneaky soft, and Pete did not like it. He turned and looked at TwoFeet through his glasses and even though he'd seen TwoFeet naked and seen TwoFeet's skeleton and guts, now Pete saw that TwoFeet was... different, he'd changed into something small and dark and glassy.

"TwoFeet," Pete whispered, "what happened?"

And TwoFeet only heard a horrible slidy-scaly whisper, and he saw what Pete looked like now, and was scared.

Now for a very long time indeed Pete and TwoFeet stayed in the village alone. They snuck into houses and ate crusty old food, and they hid in cellars at night, and they didn't talk or look at each other. They became small and dark except for their long thick crystal eyes which remained very big, and the sunlight became too bright so they hid in the day. And finally when they became very good at being quiet and sneaky in the dark of night, well, then the tall and slender people from EYES OF ONE HQ came and took them away to help in another place.

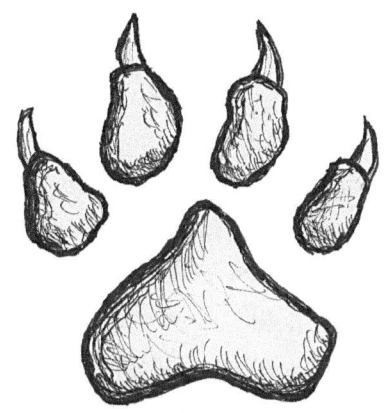

NAKED MONSTERS
BY D.L. HARVEY

Y ou're a fluttering dick," Coletta declared, her lean, mahogany hand flipping dismissively in the air. "You encourage that type of attention." Her booming voice would've drawn attention to her absurd accusation of Mo, her brother, if the bar hadn't been so packed with wanna-be stars belting out their favorite songs. The only people who could hear her explosive vulgarity were clustered around the table which had been dragged over to join with Coletta and Mo's table. Only one of the people in the immediate vicinity reacted to her, Jonas. She suppressed a satisfied grin and used the flippant hand to pat her sleek hair-do.

Mo tightened his rather full lips and shifted in his seat. Irritation made him twitch. "No one ever asks to be cornered in a closet by a horny bar-racuda," he retorted. His glance moved from his friends, who were focused on the tablet Jonas had brought, to the guy on the stage finishing his rendition of Seven Mary Three's "Cumbersome." Mo caught Jonas's smirk, his eyeline catching Coletta's gaze. They were laughing at her ridiculous accusation. "What the hell is a 'fluttering dick'?" Mo mumbled as he shifted his focus to his untannable, Caucasoid hand gripping the iced vodka shot.

Jonas, the friend sitting closest and coincidentally also Mo's closest friend, turned in his chair and pulled it more toward the sibling's adjoining table and away from the tablet-viewing crowd. He laughed and leaned toward Mo, "You know how girls are called flowers or said to blossom..." He wiggled his eyebrows. "You've a tendency to flit from flower to flower not unlike a butterfly, except with guys as well as girls."

Spearing Coletta with his cerulean gaze, Mo said, "Coco, as my sister, you are supposed to be supportive." He turned his gaze from his sister to his shaggy friend, "And, Jonas, at what point did you have such a disturbing conversation about me with her?" Mo tried to hide his smile beneath his ver-sion of a suspicious and disapproving gaze.

Mo missed neither Coletta angling her crossed legs toward Jonas's big body nor that she had maintained a small space between them. After having shared an amused communion with Jonas, she turned to her brother. Her big, green-gold eyes glowed briefly before they faded to amber and then nar-rowed into slitted cat-eyes. She used her long, manicured fingertips to smooth away potential creases from her silk top. She tapped her high, sharp-edged cheekbones as they molded into a broader and rounder version of themselves. "We're littermates, Mo," she hissed. Her challenging smile re-vealed that she'd let her teeth shift from white, even, human teeth into the fangs of a four-legged predator.

Mo glanced at the friends, the ones at the end of the table, who didn't know of his and Coletta's ability to shift into animals. While the unenlight-ened were still absorbed in the tablet, he and Jonas adjusted their positions to block Coletta from anyone who might see. "We're humans, two of five sur-viving siblings of an orphaned septuplicate. Family should mean something to you. Period," Mo said before he focused on her eyes and teeth and demanded, "So, stop it. We're in *mixed* public. Not everyone here knows about us," he sputtered over the official name of their species before saying, "much less are, shape-changers."

Jonas, who was shoulder to shoulder with Mo blocking Coletta from view, leaned back to watch Coletta morph back to her human face. As she let her eyes return to their normal hazel hue, Jonas's fascination lay raw on his own face. However, Mo couldn't decide if Coletta was trying to study him or get him to shut up and put away his emotional drivel.

"The place is dark; dark atmosphere, dark decor, and drunken co-eds," she said with antagonism in her tone. She winced in response to the first lines sung by the girl on stage, someone new to the establishment and obviously new to singing into a microphone. Using that as a queue for distraction, she shrugged and shifted her posture to one more relaxed. "Oh My Gods!" she yelled at the stage. "Listen for the cues!"

She slid a sideways glance at Mo, "Besides, family as a virtue is subjective." She made a point of rotating her eyes and lifted her chin to fix her stare on the singer again.

Defeated, Mo slouched more into his seat and stretched his long legs out into the walkway. Obliviously drawing admiration from nearby tables, he displayed his body prominently, his lean stomach and flexed chest as he laced his fingers behind his head. His jaw muscles flexed as he ground his teeth together. He closed his eyes and tried to relax by focusing on counting backward from ten, slowly, a meditative technique he'd learned from Jonas. He ignored Coletta's petulance, his own internal ache, and the orange and red stage lights spinning in rhythm with the introduction of yet another singer.

* * *

The flurry of swirling red, yellow, and orange reflecting off of glasses and mirrors around the room reminded Mo of the fire that took his mother and the night of his first change. The fire had been started by an electric space heater used for both the bathroom and the living room where his brother, older by two years, slept. The old weak wires in the cord sparked at the outlet and then the wall, devastating the building.

Either the smoke or the alarm triggered Mo and his siblings' First Change. The roars of different adolescent felines drowned the cries of his brothers' and sisters' less carnivorous animal forms. Their mother, a veteran were-otter, had been forced to shift as a reflex to her children's First Change. She had made it to her locked bedroom door before succumbing to the fumes.

* * *

The monochromatic red-hued strobe lights had changed to a static white and blue spotlight. It drew Mo's attention to the girl on stage. She had started swaying side to side with the power ballad. She'd hid the shape of her body in boxy clothes and bulky boots, but she still drew his attention. Mo caught the warbling voice of the singer before her thin, high voice was drowned out by the music. The DJ added supporting vocals to guide the girl into tune and tempo.

He missed whatever Coletta had been saying. He vaguely recalled a long diatribe about people coming into the bar to hang and sing. He wished he'd paid closer attention. Before he could redirect her attention, she yelled to the performer on stage, "Some of whom are BUTCHERING THE MUSIC!" Oh, how he wished he could sink into his seat. His reminiscence had shut out the warbling that sparked Coletta's tirade, which he'd also blocked.

Mo glanced at Jonas, whose expression was a mix of confusion and embarrassment.

Mo then returned his gaze to Coletta's heckling victim. The woman encircled the mic gripping it low and close to her chest. Her upper body curved so markedly her hair draped forward, hiding her features and the hand holding the mic. Then, in response to Coletta, the singer shifted her body from the insecure hunch into a stance that was more erect, more powerful. Her voice came through the speakers clipped and commanding, "Fuck you." She planted her feet more widely apart and took a deep breath. The thick, soulful and alto voice that resonated through the bar had too much power for such a little person. She was hitting the cues perfectly and singing on key, though in a lower register. She had her long, straight dark hair playing metronome as she swayed in time with the beat. He didn't see that she had also quite suddenly engaged the interest of most of the rest of the patrons as well. Mo was entranced.

"Mo," Coletta snapped her fingers at him inches from his eyes, taking his attention from the surprising vocalist. When he batted at them to get them out of his face, his sister's voice held a defiant anger. He expected to hear another round of her lectures she had favored, up until a few years ago. To sum up, she'd say, "In media, we're monsters. We're the creatures that cause nightmares. According to our orientation at the WereHouse, we're the legacy of some science-slash-magical experiment from a few millennia ago. And however different that mystical conflux determined our second form, we are not supposed to exist. Regardless, we do."

But all she actually said was, "We have to accept what we are." She took a moment to breathe, pointedly not mentioning the brother that hadn't been able to do just that. Then they broke their stare contest to look down. When Mo looked up, she was smirking. "As were-cats, we just happen to be a bit sluttier than the average human being. I'd figure having your boss flirt with you should be welcome to you as a tom. What is she but one more exploit? Why are you whining about it?" Mo could hear the rage and pain, haunting, undermining Coletta's teasing.

The expression he graced her with was unimpressed and uncomplimenting before he turned his attention back to the performer. She had finished and was weaving through the tables of patrons. Customers at some of the tables stopped her, probably congratulating her on her recovery. It was fairly common for veteran singers to compliment each other, as was her nervous responses under so much recognition. Near the dim lights along the actual bar where the bartenders mixed and served drinks, she moved in and out of shadow.

"Mo!" Coletta slapped him with a rather thin, song-list booklet. "If it really bothers you, get re-assigned, transfer or whatever. Every office and hospital is demanding experienced nurses."

He shifted his position again, crossed his arms as he put his elbows on the table and rested his chin on his palms to look at her. "If I transfer to a new hospital, I'll have to move out of the area this time, Coco." He tried to sound gentle as he used her nickname to keep from stressing her but he rec-ognized Coletta's stillness, her reaction to an old fear. "So, I have to find a solution."

Jonas, suddenly quite interested in the sibling's conversation, sat for-ward. "What?" Jonas's medium brown hair grazed his shoulders as he swiveled to switch his attention from the tablet enthusiast crowd to shift be-tween Coletta and Mo. "Moving? Away? Out of State?" Jonas shifted to close their triangle and pleaded, "No." He leaned forward and insisted firmly, "No." That close, Jonas and Mo were the only ones aware of Jonas's eyes, which communicated his ongoing pursuit of Coletta. "No," he said finally, with an intense expression fixed squarely on Coletta. Then he sat back, open-ing his hands to encompass the room, "You're our bait, man."

Mo covered his face in frustration and amusement. Jonas, a practicing witch and an observer of such strong skill as to be considered psychic, should have picked up a fact Mo had been sworn not to reveal. Jonas should have figured out that *he* was the draw for Coletta on karaoke night. Mo had lis-tened to her wax on about Jonas's appeal with his shoulder-length, rich brown hair, eyes, voice, etc... because he was a good brother. He thought the two of them were entertaining. He straightened and uncovered his face to scowl at Jonas, "Maybe I can offer you in sacrifice to my boss?" he said, earning a sharp kick to the portion of his leg that was still under the table. Coletta's return to her typical prickly and playful nature made Mo relax enough to grin.

"Seriously, what is the problem?" Jonas asked, taking a swig from his bottle of beer.

"My new boss has taken to cornering me in the supplies closet, the break room, or any unpopulated, enclosed area. Basically, taking every chance she can to rub up on me like a cat in heat."

Jonas started choking on his laughter. He had evidently swallowed at the wrong moment.

"And if she were young and hot?" Coletta snorted, reaching for her cran-berry gin on the rocks.

"It's *work*. I've learned my lesson; department and office transfers for doing something stupid too many times *at work*. I've kept my current position this long because I don't flirt *at work*." Mo glanced at the girl that had changed her singing style mid-song sitting alone playing on her phone. "I'm not an animal reacting on instinct. I'm a human being, a creature of complex reasoning."

"Just talk to her," Jonas offered. For a moment, Mo thought Jonas was instructing him to go talk to the newbie. But no, Jonas was encouraging Mo to confront the barracuda of an employer.

"Women are different, Jonas," Coletta offered, overtly studying Mo a moment. "It takes a certain kind of woman to be that kind of aggressive."

Mo felt as if he were one of her suspects she profiled in her post-graduate program. And having never been under Coletta's stare quite like that before, Mo thought it best to escape. "As you've said, I should be happy about it." He couldn't help sounding snide. He stood and tossed back the remainder of his beer. "I'm going to go apologize to the newbie for Coco's behavior." He ran his hands through his hair to make his blonde layered cut look casually tousled and discretely massaged his eyes to give them the moisture that made them bluer. He wound his way through the tables, first visiting the bar, then to the back of the room before he approached her. During his meandering, he stretched his body out with little twists and flexes that drew the eye of many who would appreciate the view.

* * *

He guessed the young woman would reach about the middle of his chest. She wasn't aware of his arrival as focused as she was on her phone. He'd seen a lot of the people who had arrived solo hide behind their devices. He cleared his throat and enjoyed being appreciated by her gaze as it traveled his body from his boot-clad feet to his face. He spoke when she met his gaze. "Hi." Since she remained quiet and didn't look around for rescue, he continued, "Good recovery on the song."

Her lips tightened. She looked away for a moment before lifting her shoulder in a half-shrug, muttering, "Thanks." Her hair slid forward to cover her face as she returned her attentions to the phone.

He took the seat adjacent to hers, and earned a curious stare from her. He returned her assessing gaze with a lopsided grin. The grin showed a dimple and it usually increased the chances of him getting whatever it was he wanted. "Really," he enthused, "it's hard to get up there. Heckling is generally frowned upon and I'm really sorry about that. She knows if she does it again, the manager will ban her for a while."

The girl nodded then shifted her focus from Mo to where the obnoxious voice had come from. By the flash of anger in her face, Mo recognized when his current interest realized it had been Coletta who had been yelling. He heaved a martyred sigh, "She's my sister. Tactless is just a part of who she is." His claim that they were siblings was received with doubt brimming with suspicion. "Yes, well, we're actually two of a septuplicate."

The girl's eyes fluttered as her expression became one of skeptical curiosity. She looked at Coletta, at Mo and then at Mo's wrists. "You look nothing alike." She was tactfully referring to their skin pigmentation; his was a pinkish chalky color while Coletta's was a dark coffee shade.

"Yeah, well, it's called Oculocutaneous albinism. It's a real thing." He smiled, holding up his hands in open-slash-surrender gesture. "You can look it up, if you want. It's a real condition. For a long time, the medical community called it spontaneous albinoism. But it really is just a recessive gene thing. It's no big deal." He couldn't hide his anger completely when he added, "It makes us no less related, though she does make it challenging." He looked around to see Coletta's attention was fixed on the stage. Jonas was grabbing the microphone.

"Wasn't he at your table, too?" she asked.

Mo smiled wider, pleased that she'd noticed him before he'd sat at her table. "You'll enjoy this. He's been singing regularly for the past few months. It's really paid off." He said with a little pride in his friend. "I'm Moreau."

Her attention snapped to Mo, "As in Dr. Moreau?" she inquired, arching an eyebrow,

"Not really. Family name. Everyone calls me 'Mo.' And you are?" He held out his hand.

"Star," she shook his hand and repositioned her body toward his, but stared at Jonas. She started swaying with the melody. An unfamiliar and unidentifiable but appealing scent rose with her movement.

He suppressed making a noise or any other indication of his discouraging blow-off with her stage name, "Pretty." When the scent caught him, he figured it couldn't hurt to settle in and chat for a while.

Mo turned his body to likewise stare at the stage. "Can I get you a beer?" he asked before the song had finished and the next person was called.

"No, I have to drive. Thanks, though." She started toying with her glass that held ice cubes. "I've been drinking water." She looked around the room again, dutifully avoiding looking at her phone.

"So is this your first time singing?"

She tucked a strand of hair behind her ear and smiled. She looked embarrassed. "Telling, huh?" She trailed her fingers over her face before resting her chin in her palm. Her elbow firmly braced on the table, she faced Mo. "Do you sing?"

"Oh," Mo laughed, recalling his horrid experience. "No. That would be a bad thing, like a yowling cat. I just come to hang out with my friends. It's the only time I see them any more."

Star's eyes oozed sympathy. "Are you that busy?" She let a finger graze down his forearm, "In demand?"

"Naaah, I'm a nurse. There are plenty of people to take my shift, if I can't come in, but I like my job." He laid his arm more completely on the table, extending it within her reach. "I like to work and make money. It's just that all of us are busy with different schedules. We're older, real jobs, budding families, that kind of thing." When Star put her hand on his forearm, he had his sign that he was "in" with this young woman. He relaxed more and stared at her. Before he knew it, they'd talked until closing time. He hadn't heard any of his friends' performances, just Star's musical voice and infectious laughter.

The bar lights were brightening when she stood and pulled the jacket off the back of the chair. "It was great meeting you." Standing, she gifted him with an inviting smile while fiddling with her phone, flicking it on and off, turning it as she'd glance at him and the door. "You're alone, right?" she asked.

"Yeah," Mo glanced at his sister talking to Jonas, flirting in her stilted, cool manner. Thinking about their earlier dismissal, he cringed. The desolation he'd infused in that single word reflected a bit of his residual melancholy. He sat back, sprawling on his chair waiting for Star's next move as if he would be perfectly fine waiting until everyone cleared out.

"Why don't you walk me to my car?" Star suggested, giving him a crooked smile.

"Sure," Mo smiled more widely as he stood. He stopped moving as she turned to go, her hair released that enchanting fragrance again, floating around him.

She waited a few feet away when she noticed he'd stopped.

Mo had to savor the scent wafting in Star's wake. It was heady. Maybe he was a little more intoxicated than he thought, because he couldn't resist looking back at his sister to give her bragging thumbs-up signal. He knew it was juvenile, but he couldn't resist.

Coletta made eye contact and mouthed, "Tom," with a judgmental quirk of her eyebrow.

He blew Coletta a kiss, as in "kiss off," and joined Star to leave. He followed her out the door and down the sidewalk. Outside the fresh scent in the air, just after a rain, helped a calm slowly flow through his limbs. He wondered why they weren't holding hands, or at least side by side.

* * *

Mo's hand, seeming too small to be his, was holding another small, dark, hand. He turned to the right and saw the top of Coco's head above his little brother's. She had always been Coco, back then when they were eleven years old. It was the year Coco wasn't washing her hair, hoping that it would fall out. But it was the hand he was holding that almost strangled him with grief. It was Miles, a small-framed boy inclined toward sedentary and artistic activities.

It was just after the fire, the first time they had been taken to the privately owned Wildlife Reserve and Horticultural Sanctuary, a reserve and research facility that specialized in exotic and endangered species. The place was also central hub for the Engenuii, the race of shape-shifters living among the rest of the population. Engenuii referred to the sanctuary as the acronym 'The WereHouse' based on the abbreviations WRHS. Like the shape-shifters in popular media, many called themselves weres.

Mo and his siblings were guided from the main corridor where the tourists visited to their new life among the Engenuii. Mo remembered hearing the tour guide say to them, "Through here, kids, you'll learn how we keep everyone safe." Then they'd been ushered through narrow hallways and stairwells and elevators that led to the sub-sub-basements and into the medical and orientation facilities for new weres. There, they were examined in their human and animal forms.

It was where future generations of Engenuii would see Miles's sketch series titled *First Change*. The horrors included the crack in the rock floor of the cavern and then steam scalding all the people and bodies within. Water flowed up from the crevasse before they were actually incinerated in lava flow. The surface, where the settlement teemed with Engenuii citizens clad in ancient clothing styles, cracked and broke, spitting dirt into the sky. Rocks fell into the city. The people, the innocents of the entire nation, suffered their First Changes. Their second shapes saved most of the population. Flight, speed, and cunning lent knowledge and skill for escape from a catastrophe that humans could have never survived. Their home was swallowed by a collapsing volcanic eruption that was in turn devoured by angry waves.

Hidden, were Miles's other artworks. He brought to life in graphic monstrousness how the impossible ambitions of magicians lusting for immortality brought shape-shifters into existence. The dry subject of Engenuii origin myths were made tangible by Miles's farseeing abilities.

Through their adjustment period at WRHS, Mo leaned heavily on Miles's presence as he and his siblings attended their orientation classes. Later, as Mo and company were home-schooled, the traditional education of Engenuii, Miles was singled out as a Seer for his renderings. He soon transitioned into an apprenticeship to the existing Seer among the populace.

* * *

Mo felt the tender touch of a uncalloused palm slide over his unclothed hip. It drew his mind away from the painful memories surrounding Miles and into much more inviting ones. When the hand drew away, nails grazed across his thigh. He could remember one other time, not the woman but the actual time, he'd woken restrained and was subjected to a thorough exploration by his attractive captor. He smiled, clinging to the essence of that memory. This hijack into a joyful, frivolous memory prevented him from wanting to open his eyes.

A fog rose in his mind, pushing him away from memories and brought others forward. It felt familiar, like the time Jonas had taught him to meditate. Jonas, a psychology major, had become obsessed with twin culture. He pushed Mo to test out twin anecdotes regarding the psychic connection utero companions were reputed to share. Tapping into the connection required a push and pull between two minds. The barrier Mo manifested as a fog protected his consciousness from merging with another. When they'd been working together, Mo had woken with cotton mouth and no evidence of establishing a connection, just colliding against fog. The only reason why his barriers would go up is if someone were trying to tap into his psyche.

The feel of a female's soft hand exploring him along the outside of his body from his waist to his thigh struck him as invasive. He stiffened and tried to pull away when the hand climbed and raked nails through the patch of hair on his chest. A woman's attempt at purring garbled words came from around heart height, "You are studly." She used the tip of her nails to poke at some old puncture scars in his upper chest, hidden amongst the curls. "Hmmm... damaged." He could hear her lick her lips just before she slapped his hip.

He tried to open his eyes but they only fluttered. Chains rattled when he failed to pull his arms down from above his head. He couldn't look up yet. He rested his pounding head on his biceps. The pleasant memory of the last time he'd been handcuffed hadn't included him dangling so securely from the ceiling. Nor did it include the turn of his stomach in reaction to caresses. He realized he wasn't sure how he'd gotten into this suspended and sprawled position. He couldn't remember the safe word, the word that could get him released. His mild euphoria evaporated entirely.

Going through the melee of recent events, he couldn't recall anything that would warrant his vulnerable position. He remembered noticing that it had rained while he'd been in the bar. Small puddles had caught the various downtown establishments' neon signs. The sidewalk's uneven brick had twisted the reflections. The clip of Star's heels was rhythmic and drew his attention to her feet, her legs and then higher. The last thing he remembered was the steady swing of her hair from side to side and a pleasant perfume mixing with the rain. And that's when his panic began. His pulse and breath increased when he realized the rhythmic swing of her hair and click of her shoes on brick were the last things he remembered. He'd felt mindless in his intent on following that steady staccato and undulating hair.

Fear-induced adrenaline forced his eyes to open. Seeking freedom was his instinctive priority. His first view was of a glass patio door to his left. It led to a railed porch but was too far away for him to be seen if anyone would happen to pass by on the little bit of lawn outside. At first the thick, clear plastic sheeting that lay over the linoleum wood flooring suggested the place might be under construction. The wall hangings and living room furniture, though moved to the walls and out of the way, could be seen through more clear plastic. Intent on finding an exit of any size, his eyes skimmed the only two pieces of furniture remaining free of plastic: a coffee table and a shelf on the back wall, both of which were cluttered with items. Then, he spotted another door on the far right wall. And it had a deadbolt. Just inches from his right and left hands were cut-away doorways to other rooms. He felt more plastic below his feet and hanging between his back and the surface upon which he was suspended. The rattle of chains echoed through the wall as if the rest of his restraints were on the other side.

Out of the corner of his eye he saw another slap coming but her arm jerked before contact. This time, she hit his penis. It snapped his complete attention to Star. Her face grinned hungrily at him. She didn't look sensually ravenous. Her broad, toothy grin and wide-spaced grey-green eyes were excited and sizing him up as he would a fresh kill. Her hair hung in wet, wild tangles framing the sides of her face. And she hadn't covered herself after her shower. He didn't want to be thinking about how nice she looked without clothes, but how and why he'd ended up the same way; naked.

"What the hell?" he accused, glaring at her for a few moments. He yanked on the marked-up cuffs on his wrists and ankles to stress his point.

He turned his focus to the restraints, hoping they were aged, though upon examination, he didn't see any rust. The markings on them looked vaguely familiar, like from a movie he'd seen or one of the books on witchcraft Jonas had insisted he read before attending any of his rituals. Mo wasn't sure which. He had only skimmed the books to find the parts he was interested in, which hadn't been anything near a study of linguistics.

"No hell here," Star said, drawing his attention back to her. She wiggled her body with a breathy laugh. Hand-sized breasts bobbled beneath her hair. The softness of pooch in the belly, his favorite place to snuggle on a woman, bounced just a little. Two lesions stretched across the curve to her hip. Aware of his curious gaze, she turned and strutted away, giving him a full view of her bare posterior. As his mind calmed a bit upon seeing her hair swish back and forth along the top of her glutes, he wondered why she had hidden a rather attractive, athletic body beneath her shapeless clothes at the bar.

The long, narrow table at knee height snagged his attention as Star passed it. He inspected the contents on the table to clear his mind. It wasn't a cluttered table. It was an altar with a slew of spell components assembled on it. Representations of the five elements were present from what he could see: a candle for fire, soil for earth, a bowl in the design of a wave to hold water, incense for air, and a statue of a human for life. Star's nakedness and wet hair made sense to Mo. She wasn't just nude but skyclad, ritually cleansed, made clean and unencumbered by man-made items and readied to perform a high magic rite. The altar showed she intended to perform a spell.

"You're a witch," he declared. He tried to remember almost six years of conversations with his own walking reference guide to magical theory, Jonas. There were people with innate powers, which is what he and Jonas had sensed in each other and what had drawn them into their friendship at college. Innate powers, commonly called psychic abilities, were prevalent in the magical human community. However, after discovering that Mo could shift forms and was not magically inclined led to Jonas's assumption that shifters had innate abilities that wouldn't be psychic. Mo learned that spells could be executed in chants, movement, song, as well as some convoluted chemistry-like science experiment. The more complicated spells, if executed skillfully, produced more powerful, broadly reaching results; affecting the environment, events, or individual will. But such spells demanded a lot of a person's life force and focus had to be unwavering. The memory of Jonas's technical explanations grew hazy, details lost from Mo's fickleness.

She turned and rushed toward him, getting too close too quickly for him to inspect her body further. All thoughts of the two dark, oddly shaped marks on her abdomen were lost when confronted with the manic rapture in her face. Once she was within reach, reachable if his hands weren't extended above his head, her excitement stalled his brain, "You're a practitioner, too? Are you a real one or a wisher?" she asked.

Flinching at the derogatory word pulled Mo out of his panicked freeze. 'Wisher' was a term used by elitists, psychically gifted practitioners in reference to an earth-worshiping practitioner with little to no innate talent to work metaphysical power. Jonas said it was a relatively new term and not respected by most of the practicing community regardless of pantheons. He had been insistent that everyone could summon power to some extent, hence forcing Mo to practice the exercises practitioners used to center themselves. Jonas insisted that the exercises helped a person take realistic stock of self, the environment, and the relationship between the two, creating a firm foundation before manipulating the more malleable cosmos.

Mo didn't understand why he sounded apologetic when he said, "Uh, no." Seeing Star's disappointment, he added hastily, "But I've a few friends who are. I could call them. Get you a little power boost." He immediately thought of his best friend, Jonas, and the twin connection technique. At the time, Mo had called it the mind meld or thought bubble technique, dismissing it as a useless and fruitless effort. At the time it had been hilariously entertaining, each trying to get the other to say the most remarkably senseless or humiliating things.

Mo followed her gaze when she focused on his cuffs. They were attached inside a hollowed circle in the wall which was also surrounded by small symbols, the symbols also lined the edge of the wall. He started pulling, first testing, next with insistence, and then with panic. Fear obscured reason. He didn't know how long it took, but he struggled, roaring at Star, rattling chains, bruising his ankles and wrists. When he was done, he had gained enough slack that he could brace a foot flat against the floor and grip the chain with his hands.

Star was standing halfway across the room when he quieted. She mimicked him for a few moments. She motioned her hands around her, drawing his attention. "Well then, what do you think of my sacred space," she asked, turning away.

He unfocused his eyes to look for a shimmery haze of power indicating a force field of pure energy surrounding them. He should be able to see a barrier creating the kind of space a magical practitioner could use to perform a spell, invoke the gods, enact ritual praise for life, harness energy, or contain an entity. "I don't see it." As someone who had the mystical gift of morphing into an animal, he could sense shifts in the environment, including sensing things that sifted between this dimension and others, including the flow of mystical energy. Jonas's exercises helped Mo increase the skill on how to "see" and understand power fluctuations such as an enclosed circle also known as a sacred space. Because Mo hadn't quite mastered the skill, he considered the possibility he could be wrong. Again, he closed his eyes, trying to focus on the room and gauge it the same way he'd deduced that Jonas hadn't been like other people in their school.

"Don't be silly. You don't have to see or even sense a circle for it to be there," she answered. Her response was a rehearsed line. She had anticipated the comment referencing the witch's reputation for drawing lines to mark a circular parameter.

"I don't feel it." He closed his eyes, again stretching out his sense of touch to include the environment's less tangible aspects. There was a fair bit of moisture in the atmosphere, indicating they were near a body of water. He could hear wind rustle leaves. The air, clean of car emissions, industrial pollutants, or restaurant kitchens, smelled of Star's incense and post-rain smells of green growth. The vibrations in the floor indicated where Star stood. But he couldn't feel that tell-tale electricity that could raise the hairs on his arms when power for spells was being manipulated.

But he felt something else. It was a small tug that drew him to Star. Like a magnet hooked by a line manifested in that smell. Identifying the perfume he'd caught at the bar, the scent he'd liked so much, negated its power. This scent when associated with this pull to Star tasted sour in the back of his throat. An amateur with all this psychic and magical theory, he went with his instincts, imagining cutting that line. He felt relief fill his whispered, "I don't feel anything."

"I cast a spell that would attract a tool, someone with their own power no one would miss." Her voice moved in a circle around him, defining the room on the other side of the wall upon which he dangled as she disappeared behind it on one side of him and emerged on the other. As she reemerged on his other side, she let her nails scrape his ribcage before skipping further into the room. "You're a nobody," she insisted, placing her hands on her hips before him. He could see she was wearing a flesh-colored string thong, thus not wholly committed to her part in her own spell, unable to flaunt her own vulnerabilities.

He wasn't a nobody. He was a *were*. He was one of five surviving sibling septuplicate of weres. He was a registered member of the *were* community. He paid his dues, filled out the papers, and proved he could shift. Speculative hope sparked a moment in his eyes, catching Star's suspicious scrutiny, only to die. He could shift all right. He could shift into a house cat, a white, bobtail Manx to be specific. In addition to being generally defenseless as a cat, his shifts required more of a commitment of time than for most other weres. He would end up having to remain in his second form for an impressive if unpredictable block of time. He, like Miles and his mother, needed to spend a lot of time in his were form before he could shift back to human. In an apartment with no exits, he'd be more vulnerable as a house cat. He wouldn't get anywhere but captured again. Doing so would also reveal the *were* community to someone who clearly wasn't in-the-know and a wisher, a crazy earth witch fueled by corrupted power.

"Yeah, I may be a nobody to you," he taunted, "but I've been in circles and there is nothing here." He recalled his stints in circles, his personal feral energy had wreaked havoc on the ritual. He strained his neck, extending his chin out in defiance. "You might as well get your ass dressed because you've got nothing."

In a smooth motion, she bent to the altar and then rushed toward him. With a long silver object glinting in her hand, she used the back of that fist to slam into his jaw. It was then he felt her power. Her rage boosted that mystical energy into manifesting. To him, it felt wild and scattered. "I called you," she declared stressing the 'I' in her sentences, "I mesmerized you into coming with me and cuffing yourself." She flicked her hair out of her face though it didn't seem to be in her way. She pointed the knife at him with an audacious smile, "And I will thrive with your death." Her rage fueled her spells. The snarl in her face ruined the last of the beauty he had initially noticed. She whipped her head around, whipping strands and that perfume in his direction.

He smirked at the uselessness of the scent-induced mesmerism. "The hell you will." He kicked out, landing a foot to Star's stomach. The ripping of bolts for one foot from drywall was lost to him in his momentary haze of rage. He braced that freed foot on the wall, clanking and rattling chains in an effort to free himself completely from whatever it was that had been in the wall holding his leg. The other leg remained restrained. He bared his teeth, his still-human teeth.

She bounced and skidded backward on her ass. Her head snapped back. A streak emerged from her leg where the knife had grazed her as she tried to catch herself.

"There isn't a death spell in existence that works," he growled, sounding inhuman. "It's a violation to all of the laws of life. Mother nature exacts punishment for attempting such things. Death is the cessation of living energy. It ceases and can't be reclaimed even in a violent death, dumbass."

"You're the dumbass," she stood slowly.

He couldn't believe he still looked to see her nether-region.

She could have exploited the distraction, but instead exercised the wrist she landed on. When she moved to rotate her other wrist, his gaze followed hers as she stared at the long-bladed knife. Her dark eyes glittered and fixated on him as she stood. "Power can be transferred, siphoned." She added with amused arrogance, "You're still vibrantly alive. And I worked out a way to take it." She stalked closer, her movement sinuous.

He swung out a leg. "What could you possibly get? It would be tortured, borrowed energy and disharmonic with yours." He learned his energy was too wild for use in magic when he'd tried to work with energy with Jonas's Circle of Practitioners. The combination had created a small fiery tornado in the campfire and caused an overgrowth of the shrubbery within the protection circle. They explained that if he hadn't been willing and cooperative, the repercussions of using his life-force would have been more destructive and possibly even deadly. He summarized another of their cautionary tales, "The relative of one of my friends tried siphoning the life of an unwilling subject. It made him sick. He'd misused his magic and it created a barrier so insurmountable that every spell cast rebounded back on himself. He insanely continued until he was a jibbering skeleton. Is that what you've done? Did you try this before and it drove you mad?"

The light reflected on the shining flying object whipped at him. He tried to dodge but the knife stuck into the fleshy areas just above his hip, above the leg already suffering movement restrictions. Mo stared at the wound in shock with the weapon stuck dangerously deep into his abdomen. Abstract reason made him realize arguing with a psychopath who was following steps to kill you was a bad idea. He grunted as he swung the leg on the uninjured side of his body out at her as she tried to approach again. He swallowed the whimpering. "I will not be your offering to your gods or the ingredient in your spell. My power is mine; it will always be that way." He felt the booming echo of his willpower in his statement, so unlike the whisper during those meditative exercises with Jonas. She wouldn't get anything out of him metaphysically.

But he still wanted to live. He'd promised Coco and himself he would always try.

She shrugged. Her eyes softened and her smile was tender as she looked over the cuffs that restrained him, "Maybe slower is better."

I'm not alone! He thought in desperation. "I have siblings. I have five living siblings. They will notice I'm missing. They *will* put together that I was murdered."

In school, Jonas had become obsessed with twin research. And he had buried Mo in an avalanche of research gathered for his psychology papers. He believed the anecdotes regarding "twin psychic connections." Twins were purportedly so close that they'd have an extra sense in connection to each other; finishing each others' sentences, feeling each others' trauma, and living parallel lives even while separated. Some had difficulty marrying because they couldn't break the bond with their sibling in order to establish relationships outside of their own. Some even mourned for the rest of their lives the loss of a sibling from the womb.

Mo hoped it was all true. He didn't want to accept the distance between himself and his brothers and sisters equated true estrangement. He tried picturing them in his head, calling them by image, and how he felt as he sought their connection. There was no way he'd give Star their names, nor would he let her hear him cry out. They shared a bond by blood and genes regardless of how his looks set him apart from them. Psychically calling on Coletta and the rest was an against-the-odds act of desperation, a ploy. If he could connect with them to say, "Good-bye," he could call for help.

"You're just desperate," she observed, pleased with herself. "Seriously? You expect me to believe that chick is your sister?" She didn't bother hiding her amusement. "You don't have anyone," she sneered. "It was part of The Call, someone abandoned and alone in the world. In addition to being someone highly suggestible."

The thin stream of blood trickled down his leg and puddled on the floor. He suspected he was going into shock. He couldn't believe the knife hadn't fallen out and that he'd continued bleeding. He watched it for a few moments before he noticed a silver bowl at his feet. It was on its side. He must've hit it at some point during his struggle. "It's missing the bowl," he commented.

Star huffed. She disappeared into the open doorway furthest from his freed foot and emerged a moment later with a broom. When she went to push the bowl to catch the blood, he hooked a foot on the cold silver thing and whipped it at her.

A broom handle away, he hit his mark in the head. A resounding thunk echoed his satisfaction for the time it took for her body to slide sideways. Its thud made him happy for just a few moments. He was still strung up. She looked as though she might remain out long enough for him to shift into a cat. He'd have to stay in that form for at least a couple of hours, but at least he could hide. It would be as if he'd disappeared entirely. Except the knife wouldn't shift with him but would remain in relatively the same position. The cut on a cat might remain proportionate if it was just a cut. But the knife might not drop or disappear. It would be so much worse in a small feline body than a human. He was stuck, literally and figuratively.

As a rule, Jonas had told him in one of their many discussions, that the nature of a were implied all weres lacked psychic talents and made the practice of any magic almost impossible. Shifters were essentially too close to the natural cycle of life, too much a part of it, to be able to manipulate energies of any other plane than the material plane. They'd tried a few techniques focused on sensing the environment for psychic energies, the results of which were questionable considering *weres* had heightened senses. But Mo was an Engenuii, a race descended from magicians. Mo had sent out his life energy, or aura, in a bubble. It was an unsuccessful exercise. He hadn't been able to give or receive images or thoughts, but he didn't think he'd been properly motivated at the time. The thought bubble game was another way they had entertained themselves before they'd been old enough to go to clubs or buy beer. With Star's still body before him and an increasing puddle of blood below him, he felt properly motivated.

He focused on the sister who'd always been there, hovering. Her image, her essence, all he could recall and associate with identifying only her was his focal point in establishing a connection with Coletta. He tried to remember everything about her, all that he loved in her until he passed out. He still had hope in his heart. The draining blood had its own agenda.

* * *

"Nothing. Nothing. Nothing." Coletta's screams were echoing in a cavern beneath Highlands Ranch. Her hysterics could be heard for miles through the tunnels, the Catacombs that housed a fair number of Engenuii, who had difficulty mainstreaming in society.

Mo knew the date of this dream-slash-memory. He didn't want to visit it. And yet, Coco's teenaged eyes were wild, staring into his with streaks of mascara running down her cheeks and smeared across her face. It was when they were going to visit Miles, who was still steeped in his apprenticeship to the current Seer.

"We're nothing to them. Don't you get it, Mo?" Her hair, in long thin, braided extensions tipped with metal balls slung around with her momentum as she paced from wall to wall in the small alcove. The tat-tat-tat clattered against each other and snapped at the stone walls.

The rock face reflected the bald bulb lighting on its polished uneven walls. Bare wires strung throughout the caves to illuminate the housing of a great number of the Engenuii population, those that couldn't or chose not to assimilate into the general population. Miles also lived in quarters in the Catacombs, where he could be closely monitored by someone more like himself.

The Sphinx, Miles's mentor with her bizarre half cat-like body, sat in the corner. Her skin was covered in a thin layer of a kind of pale, pink fur with purplish spots. She watched with her bright, pink slitted eyes as her tail slowly swished. Miles referred to her as the Sphinx, the Talekeeper, or more importantly, The Seer. Mo was conscious that the woman was old, powerful in ways that he couldn't name. She had been the one trying to teach Miles how to stabilize his psychic talents, his were form, and his human drives. She'd failed.

Miles, the Seer's apprentice, was dead. Miles had said the Seer was help-ing him control his sensitivity, his human, intuitive artistic nature and the sensual playfulness of the otter. He'd spoken of the Seer in reverence. He'd loved her. He'd spoken of returning topside to pursue an art degree, as educa-tion was one of the benefits of registering with the WRHS.

Mo processed the news silently. He watched Coletta slide in and out of her second form in pieces. Her hands would pull at her clothes and hug her sides. Or she'd reach out to the walls, rake claws down, and scar the stone anew. The clattering of her hair baubles, her term for her accessories, grated on his nerves as she shook her head and threw herself against the walls. Her grace and violence in grief mirrored his own. Yet she was more at ease with demonstrating it; laying her emotions bare for him to see and all to hear.

"He said you were teaching him. What were you teaching? What were you doing?" Coletta launched herself from across the room at The Sphinx but Mo caught his sister in mid-air.

"Coco," Mo pleaded, holding her head to his shoulder even as her hands grasped his shirt. Her morphing pushed claws into his chest. And still he braced her body against his, preventing her from gaining traction on the earth. "Coco," his broken voice breached her final barrier.

Coletta's grief flowed. Tears sapped her strength and Mo slowly collapsed to the ground to hold his big sister in his arms.

The Sphinx left a book by the doorway as she gave the brother and sister the room. In Miles's handwriting, in his words and drawings, he depicted the woman that had been their mother, also an otter. Her behavior that endangered her children with her selfishness, endangered her people with her antics. This journal included his confession of a drive to indulge in life as much as she had. But that had been read later.

Mo's ear thundered with the revelation, drowning out Coletta's heaving howls. His arms tightened on her, hoping she wouldn't twist her grief for Miles with her anger at their siblings' abandoning her and Mo, or with the guilt and relief of knowing their mother was dead. Mo remained rock steady, disbelieving that their gentle artist had it in him to end his own life, a contradiction to the nature of weres.

Coco retreated into an attack-ready position and lifted a shoulder. "He gave up," she whispered and then hiccuped. She backed out of Mo's arms and into the wall. "He gave up," she growled. She sprung forward again, landing in front of Mo. He would never forget the desperate intensity of being locked into Coletta's gaze inches from his nose, "You don't ever give up." She gripped his shirt, sticking him with her disappearing and reappearing claws again as she shook him a little. "Try. Don't give up." She tucked her head into his shoulder, curling into his body as best she could, "Ever. Do whatever you have to, but always try."

* * *

A hit to the jaw snapped his head to the right and woke him. His sight was blurry, so he blinked a few times, wondering how much time had passed. The feel of a soft hand beneath his chin and breath on his face prompted him to hiss at it. He started to pull on that otherworldly magic that would help him change. He felt his teeth moving first. They pushed on his skin and pulled on his bones. He never understood how Coletta transformed so often, much less enjoyed it. His heart rent at the thought of leaving his sister behind, but he was hoping the knife would fall out before the Change and his cut would remain proportionate and irrelevant. It was a bit late to wish he'd experimented with transitional possibilities or cutting the cost of changing. He hoped his desperation would prompt him to change back to human form before his cat form bled out completely.

"I resealed the circle and called the gods," she whispered. Her wiggly, hopping dance moved her out of his reach. He stared at the toned, curvy body she'd hidden from her audience at the bar. His stomach heaved at the creature beneath the skin. He swallowed the bile when her feminine giggle trembled in the air when she stopped. With her back to him, she clapped, two clipped bursts of sound, at the ceiling. "Hail and Welcome!"

The quick turn of a door knob had a click that snicked with the second clap. It made Mo's breath catch in his throat. He half-groaned and half-growled his frustration. He stopped his metamorphosis, hoping that the naked woman hadn't noticed the altered state of his face.

Star turned and howled with glee, "You're dead, Mother—." Her eyes widened with curious disbelief. She was seeing his pointing nose and sprouting whiskers. Her hand was reaching out as she stepped toward him, when she was hit.

A wall-shaking growl followed the pounce of a hundred-and-twenty pound black jaguar. The struggle of two bodies, one furred and the other flesh, on the floor was brief. The hind clawed paws eviscerated the human's stomach while the fore paws held Star's shoulders. The jaguar's jaws had sunk into the once lovely face and ripped it half off. Blood puddled on the floor near his feet, mixing with his.

The tall person that followed the big cat carefully into the room left the door open. A darkened sky and dense forest outlined by a mostly full moon was framed by the doorway behind him. "He's safe, Coletta," Jonas announced. "You can go. I'll take care of everything here." He addressed the big cat, his voice gentle but urgent before he continued to look around the room, everywhere but at Mo.

Coletta, in her animal form, sat near the body and sniffed with disdain. She fixed her eyes on her brother and his stab wound. She let out a demanding call when Jonas disappeared into the room where earlier Star had retrieved a broom. Coletta hissed at the dead woman and batted at the torn head, her claws partially scalping the corpse.

Jonas moved about with the confident efficiency of a man who was fa-miliar with the topic at hand, in this case: magical messes. He emerged from the other room with his shirt covering his nose and mouth, his eyes staring at Mo's cell phone and clothes tucked beneath his arm. He tapped Mo's phone before he fixed his gaze at specific points of the room. With mutterings, a lit-tle arm waving, and small dust swirls kicking up in places Jonas had roamed but shouldn't have been, he cut the power in the circle. Jonas, a real witch, erased evidence of any irregular movement and neutralized the magical threat.

After, he continued fiddling with the phones, his and Mo's. "Get out of here, Coco," he demanded quietly. So absorbed in his activity, he didn't look at Coletta as she groomed her coat. She could have been trying to clean off her tongue, one never knew. Then, suddenly he turned to confront the jaguar. He physically shooed her from the room, "Make tracks for the police to trace, but get out of here."

She chuffed and growled a bit but took another swipe at the body as she turned around. The smell of death, the fetid stench from freshly opened in-testines was so potent in the room that the newly slashed chest did nothing to the environment except add more color. She turned, chuffed again, making eye contact with Mo and then padded out.

"Your sister," Jonas breathed and took a moment to watch the feline streak to the woods once out the door. His hands made the movements uni-versally understood as dialing 911.

"She likes you, too," Mo murmured, chuckling. "I don't know what you're doing but, uh... stabbed here," he whined.

Upon completing the series of required questions with emergency ser-vices, Jonas shut down the call. "We only have a couple of moments." Jonas murmured upon catching a key flying from a shelf near the front door. He held it up, "Telekinetic locator spell inspired by TV." He looked more closely at Mo and said, "Secure the knife, preventing it from moving deeper or wiggling around, but don't pull it out. For all that it made a hole in you, as far as I know, it might be restricting the flow of your blood out of your body." He unlocked the cuffs, suspending Mo's and then dragged him across the room away from the body that was formerly Star. "FYI, I uploaded an app that allowed me to track you here. I still have to," he pulled out his phone, "to activate the tracking command to find you."

Mo just made a quizzical face at Jonas at having been left to lay flat on the plastic-covered couch, staring at the ceiling.

"I let Coletta... You know, I am so going to pay for calling her Coco. You are the only person she lets call her that," Jonas sounded aggrieved. "Anyway, I let her load this app on my phone a couple weeks back. She never showed anywhere I was so... Your she-likes-you theory is a bust."

"How did you find me?" Mo asked, blinking his eyes, trying to remain alert. He alternated between making a fist and extending and wiggling his fingers.

"Coletta," Jonas answered, sitting back watching Mo, "she showed up at my home saying she'd felt like she'd been stabbed in the gut but couldn't find any wound. She insisted I do my 'magic mojo' on her. I insisted that my 'mojo' could work on her but it had nothing to do with pain. She had not been amused."

Jonas breathing through his mouth sounded loud as he slid down the wall near Mo's head, "I've never wished so fervently for any skill with healing more in my life. It doesn't look like it's in a spot that could kill you unless you bleed out."

"Started to change," Mo's voice sounded weak, "might've moved it."

Mo listened as his very best friend in the whole world stifled a cough with a whimper. Jonas continued with his explanation, "I got Coletta to calm and do a centering exercise. You know the drill. Isolate the pain to figure out where it might be coming from. She's better at that than you are, by the way. She closed her eyes and saw the face of the vocalist you left with last night. She repeated the exercise three or four times, getting different expressions. She was disgusted and a bit confused at seeing that naked woman and feeling your horror. She said you felt horror," Jonas rubbed a hand on his bent knee, smearing Mo's blood on it. Then he tapped his phone a few times, and showed it to Mo. The blinking dot showed that they were within twenty minutes of driving distance from their karaoke bar. "Evidently, you're more human than most weres. I got your thought bubble, right about the same moment Coletta first realized she was seeing through your eyes."

"Star, she cast a spell," Mo whispered. "Active?"

"Nothing but a circle powered by your blood, I think. It encompasses the entire room," Jonas looked around with more attention. "Do you know the intent?"

"She wanted more power, death magic." He breathed, the area around the knife was really hurting. "I really wanted the power to contact Coletta and the rest." He tried chuckling. It didn't work out well. "I guess I won."

Jonas eyed the wall and then the prone body on the couch. "How did she get you strung up?"

"Said she mesmerized me, called me with a spell for a nobody, someone disconnected, someone who'd go unnoticed." Mo wanted to cough so badly, but swallowed it down. If chuckling wasn't going to work, he wasn't going to risk pain for a cough. "I'm betting she used some kind of pulley system to get me up there though."

Jonas grunted, "That's what it looks like in the kitchen, too." He put his hand on Mo's head, nudging it insistently for Mo to meet his gaze, "That nobody crap? That's what you were sounding like last night, abandoned, a little hopeless. You know it's not true, right? Clearly, we're here if you need us."

Mo pulled his lips tight into a mocking grin. His eyes felt like rolling back in his head. He closed them.

"Mo!" Jonas yelled, panicked. "I can't heal you much less bring you back to life! Get back here, Mo!" He held Mo's feet extended and above his head and heart.

"I think, I'm so swearing off one night stands." Feeling started returning to Mo's arms with cruel affirmation. "Gods, that hurts!"

"Careful who you call, here. There is a circle up," Jonas suggested. The change in Jonas's voice led Mo to believe his friend was looking around as he rambled, "As for being less slutty, you've been working on that for a while. I'm guessing our power focusing and meditation exercises might have initiated that evolution. It usually does. A side effect to self-awareness is self-appreciation, you know. While shape-shifters are depicted in media as humans falling victim to their animalistic, monstrous instincts, your people manifest and made peace with your animus for a richer life experience." Jonas's voice acquired the authoritative texture that crept in whenever he was communing with nature. It was the kind of voice Mo associated with a new and important rule as it was about to be imparted, "You are as you were meant to be, but with room to become someone you want to be." And then Jonas ruined the significance of the moment by using his normal voice to add, "Too bad it took a psychopath to make you commit to it."

"All confidence and wisdom and still, you can't ask my sister—who adores you, by the way—out on a date?" Mo mumbled with his eyes closed.

"Courage is an innate thing," Jonas responded. "You live through this, I'll ask her out and you'll confront the situation with your boss. And, you know, she loves you, too."

Mo sighed contentedly just before they could hear the ambulance's sirens and see the flashing lights through the still-open door.

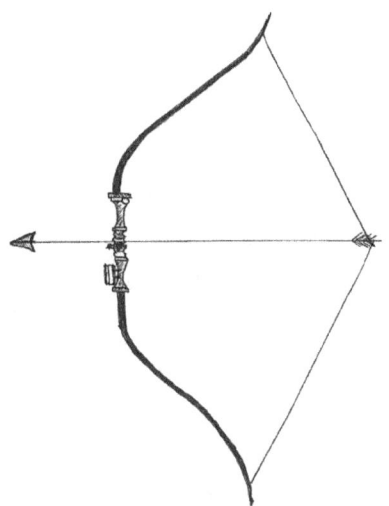

THE HUNT

BY TIMOTHY LYNCH

Bill flipped his wooden recurve over his shoulder as the tall, luminescent grass brushed his thighs. Swallows circled his path, calling out with pleasant trills. In the distance, a hawk screeched her position. He ascended a gradual but long hill-rise. His supply of water and food was minimal. And the low, orange sun colored the grass a golden tangerine. When his eyes spied the crest of the hill, he ran, laughing, to the edge, springing into the air perhaps fourteen feet—partly from exuberance, partly to eat up distance between him and his next campsite. The leap had the de-sired effect. He bounce-landed and rolled in the grass. When he again found his feet, the valley opened up before him like an empty, glowing, orange-gold stadium. The long grass swished against his side in a sustained gust of wind. He liked how it felt. Bill made a small change to his suite-controls to allow more wind sensation. Sure, it would make his aim tougher but at least it would feel like he was outside.

He noticed a large elk grazing in the valley below. Checking his quiver, it held three golden arrows, one silver, and ten wood. Some large boulders rested near the valley floor. From there he might attempt a shot.

Bill crouched and checked the direction of the wind. A translucent, blue weather vane drifted into his field of vision and spun counter-clockwise on its axis before pointing about 100 degrees right of the large elk buck. Crouch-walking blindly through the tall grass, guessing the direction of the buck and the large boulders at the base of the valley, he poked his head up several times re-calibrating his direction. The big elk buck stopped grazing and lifted its head. Its back was to Bill about sixty yards away.

At about ten yards from the rocks his wrist began to pulse. Someone needed him. He cursed life. Not only was his concentration broken, but he checked his health: gone—too much crouch-walking. He would never make it to camp *and* land the elk. He voiced the word "save" into his wrist.

Instantly, he was transported back to his virtual sphere. He released the Velcro cuffs on his waist, arms and legs and stepped down into his living room.

"Datanet data entry. This is Bill Z."

"Hello Bill Z_1, this is Jasonic L_3. I'm calling from Quality. We read you as having worked only twenty-six hours this week. It's nearly Thursday. Are you planning to put in time during the weekend? I realize you've just started with us, but as your welcome package states, 'a well-balanced work week equals a well-balanced you!' Let's try and get in those eight-point-nine hours per day ahead of schedule, okay?"

"Yeah, sure. Sorry."

"Oh and I know you understand our names convention. You're Bill Z_1, not Bill Z."

"I think I'm the only Bill at your company. Surely I can just be Bill Z, not Bill Z_1."

"We could hire another Bill Z sometime in the future. That would cause confusion as to your identity. It's hard enough to keep track of the hundreds of people who work for us in this sector, let alone our outside contacts, without messing around with our names. No. One person, one name. That's how it has to be. I'm sorry Bill Z_1. Listen, we can't have one group thinking they live with the morays of the 21st Century, while the rest of us are in the 22nd. No. One person, one name, shared burden. Understand Bill Z_1?"

"I guess."

"I knew you would, we only hire the finest employees, here at Datanet Subsidiaries. Thanks for your understanding. Have a great day Bill Z_1."

"You bet, Jase."

"Bill Z_1, it's Jasonic L_3."

Bill ended the call after Jasonic quipped some pleasantries about having to work hard to "keep the team strong."

Bill thought about whether he could get a shot off at the large elk buck from beside the big rocks. According to the game, he had failed: no supplies, not enough energy to get to the next campsite. Bill climbed back into the sphere and tightened the belts. He performed the hand movement that activated the game. A wave of euphoria went through his brain as he thought about his vertical leap earlier in the game. *And to think I'll be turning 50... Apex!*

* * *

Bill woke up and rolled in bed for two hours before starting the day. He finally pushed off the covers, dreading his required log time for work. In practice, a good eight hours with more work after dinner; in reality, as much time working as he could stand. He checked his inbox for jobs. Ten were waiting for him. A second group of ten were a quick e-message away. He never had to wonder about work; there were so many code monkeys writing scripts for everything from vacuums to elevators, all you had to do was read the script convention, whatever it described, then match the code groups to the order provided in the e-message. Then you just checked to see if the order matched the convention. Once it matched the order, it went on to the next higher level. Bill often wondered why they didn't have programs that could do what he did, but apparently they still got glitches occasionally. So, the whole populace—those who wanted to—could make a few credits checking for errant orders of scripts, never knowing how to write a single line of code, and making just over minimum wage: about 17 credits per hour.

After a few hours and his second group of ten from the inbox, Bill again weighed whether to give that buck another try. He couldn't figure how to proceed without energy or food in the game. His viewer just kept flashing "failed attempt" after a few minutes.

He fought off the temptation just long enough to decide to brave the out-doors in his backyard, air conditioned tent. Okay, technically his patio wasn't really a backyard, but it had a view. You could see a lot from the 62nd floor... well, mostly just a lot of other buildings. The plexiglass additions came with built-in condenser and coils and made for a nice, almost cool sit-ting area. He would often imagine the ground squirrels in a nearby meadow —once in a great while, he could see them—searching for food. There was a lot of talk of monkeys from South America making their way up to the Vir-ginias, but regardless of how many trees he looked at through his high-pow-ered binoculars, he hadn't seen any. It had been ground squirrels and starlings for years—or were they called crackles? It was always ground squirrels and starlings.

The city had pigeons (people called them doves) and near the coast, gulls had a new-found interest to birders who now called them by their species name: "Black-backs" and "Grey Beards" and "Samuel's Gulls," but never "seagulls," that was considered vulgar. You could attend seminars to learn the names and habits of the various gull species in your area. No one ever spoke about the old species they used to hear about from their grandparents: Purple Mittens, Bald Nuthatches or some such things, only saying, "they must've gone up north."

He drank his coffee substitute and sliced a bit of Meat TM to go on an all-grain cracker. Sensing time go by, he turned the temperature in the tent back up to 100 degrees and went inside, back to the *digital chains* of his computer.

* * *

Bill rode down in the elevator with a young couple he'd never seen before... but with a hundred floors, they could've been in the building for years.

"Have you see any monkeys?" they asked Bill when they noticed he still
had binoculars around his neck. "They're supposed to be here in Virginia
now."

"Not yet," Bill answered. "I'll keep looking though."

"Oh do let us know if you see one!"

The doors opened on the 50th floor and Bill began the trek to the store.
He had stopped using the moving platform for about a year now, determined
to build up his wind, if not get in shape. He never understood why anyone
would run around in circles at a track, accomplishing nothing, just for exercise. He likened it to living life in stasis. He often thought, *After all, the
world is so void of everything, new experiences are all we've got!*

"I can always count on you!" he barked at his inbox as he downloaded
another ten code projects on his wrist. He looked at the official timer, "Only
four hours of work done today. Shit, I will have to work over the weekend."

Neighbors floated by on the platform. Bill stopped and leaned against the
windows in the lobby, concentrating on his wrist.

He changed channels on the screen and typed "recurve bow" in the
search window. The Grid search brought up his favorite survivalist store:
Lost Civilians. He looked longingly at the wooden curved bow with a leather
handle. It was stained a dark cherry wood color and gleamed in the 3D window as it rotated.

"Someday, my friend," he spoke to the glistening bow. He looked up
quivers and found a dark red leather quiver that would match. *Oh that is so
perfect! All I need now are arrows.* He found them: long arrows, short arrows, four feathers, three feathers, standard heads, hunting heads. And so
many colors and designs: lightning bolts, flames, tiger stripes, zebra stripes.
He even found a Design-Your-Own-Arrow program. "Let's go with a black
arrow with dark orange flames and bright yellow flame lettering: Z. A. N. D.
E R. for identification," he mumbled. He put a vicious looking multi-bladed
tip on the thing. A picture came up with the finished image in 3D and a but-

ton that said, "Purchase?"

He followed the yellow flames that spelled out his name against an ebony background and of course the downright evil tip. He imagined it sitting on his shelf. A symbol of his true self. *How much was it? 20 credits. On sale!* He would pay 20 credits to touch his soul. Who wouldn't?

He clicked the purchase button.

* * *

It was only Thursday, of the next week, when the sensor in his kitchen showed that a parcel had arrived. Bill climbed in the elevator to go down to the 50th floor, the "convenience lobby" for those living in the top half of the building. You could get a few things in the store, get your hair cut, and eat dinner, ordering from several popular restaurant menus. You could also get your mail.

Inside the "Post" there were a few large packages leaning against the wall. Mailbox Q2 accepted his thumbprint. Bill reached inside the narrow box to retrieve a small blinking blue cylinder that read: "Oversized mail." As Bill pawed through the many parcels in the parcels bin, he hoped his arrow would've found a nice corner to rest in. Maybe it was upright, maybe lying down between a few other flat parcels.

Bill wasn't really surprised with the turn-around time. It was well-known the *old* Post had opened up the largest solar-run business in the US. They pushed the Green Revolution forward, first with Etrucks, then with Edrones. Unfortunately they were just in time to be packaged and have their assets sold off. But the amazing service they provided was demanded by customers nationwide and every moving unmanned vehicle: air, water, or road, not owned by a consumer, now also carried parcels that moved automatically from vehicle to vehicle.

Bill had reached the bottom of the pile, carefully moving parcels aside to scan them with the small cylinder. No green light, just a rhythmic blue pulse. Bill scanned the mailboxes one by one to see if maybe his package ended up in a neighbor's box by mistake.

Nothing.

Bill resigned to look through the parcels again, or maybe he would have to give the Parcel Company a buzz. Then he spied the larger packages leaning against the wall.

"That would be a hell of a lot of filling!" he said. *But it would guarantee a nice, unbroken arrow.*

Bill chose packages that were long and thin and waved the small cylinder.

No green light.

He chose another, and another: no green light.

"Talk about a pain in the ass!" *It's probably sitting across town, or a block from here... It'll be half an arrow by the time it gets to me!*

He wanted answers. He shouted at his wrist, "Grid. Open. Now!"

When he saw the screen illuminate, he yelled again. Search: Postal Company - cylinder code. A pretty middle-aged digital bot from the Postal Company appeared on the screen asking if she could assist with the process.

Bill, frustrated and losing steam, just said, "Search."

"Cylinder number please."

Bill pointed the small device at his wrist. The letters blinked once then appeared in the search field.

"Package delivered to 777 East Sycamore St. Pinnacle Tower #62Q2 Roanoke, VA. Oversize. Please use the scanning cylinder to verify your package."

"Wait, that's right. That's exactly right! Grid Off!"

He put his hands on his hips when he realized he'd *checked* all the packages. All the reasonable ones at least. He needed a new plan: a quick check of the remaining packages, then go to the ground foyer.

Bill looked at the packages lining the wall. "I don't care. I'll go left to right. Okay, looks like someone ordered a new headboard for their bed!" Blue pulse. "What's this, a flag pole?" Blue pulse. "Some kind of musical instrument?" Blue pulse. "Big old picture frame?" Green light.

* * *

Bill waited for the elevator with his surprisingly light box that was easily as wide and almost as tall as he was.

"Maybe someone sent me a full-length mirror? That's probably it. Cindy was trying to be helpful and sisterly and sent me a mirror." He wondered if it would be damaged. "Why would she send something like that through the mail? I'll call to thank her, but if it's damaged, I'll just recycle it. I really don't *need* a mirror."

The elevator chimed and he held the box carefully next to his body as he greeted several of his neighbors.

I can buy my own mirror, Cindy. I don't care if you are a big-time code monkey and can *afford it!*

* * *

Bill leaned the package against the virtual sphere and grabbed an old Leatherman tool that had been his great uncle's. The steel blade was dull, but it could cut through fastening tape well enough. He stopped to check the return address. It was missing. But his name and address were stamped on the front.

> William Zander
> 777 East Sycamore St.
> Pinnacle Tower
> #62Q2
> Roanoke, VA

Like any well-packaged parcel, tape gave way to the tip of the steel blade, but Bill had to be careful his enthusiasm didn't damage the contents. The final pop of breaking tape required muscles in more parts of his body than he'd counted on, muscles that hadn't activated in some time. As the box opened, he immediately saw his Z.A.N.D.E.R. arrow, but not just one. Ten flaming arrows were arranged neatly in a plastic tray, along with a dark cherry leather quiver. Ten matching tips in ten little boxes had their own tray.

What to feel? Happy? Shock? Both? Here was something he wanted—at least he thought he wanted. He just never imagined actually having them.

Was there some kind of sale? Did he misunderstand the build-your-own-arrow deal? *Was it some kind of promotion?* He checked the packing slip and bill of sale. 1 build your own arrow. 1 hunting tip. Cost: 20 credits. *It must be a mistake. Someone or something confused my wish list with the purchase! But if that was the case... Oh God.* Bill started to examine the structure of the box. There was a long straight square tube running the inside length. He lifted the tube upward. It unfolded and inside something gleamed a deep cherry wood color.

What now? He had it all: a bow, quiver and ten gorgeous monogrammed arrows. It wasn't supposed to happen this way. All he really wanted was an arrow. One beautiful arrow to remind him of the fun he had playing as a child.

It was just one dumb summer day, he thought. *Dad was showing me how to shoot and Mom was covering her eyes. Every time I pulled back the string, Mom would try to peek at me and dance around like she had to go to the bathroom. Which made Dad and I laugh so hard I couldn't aim. Dad told Mom to move behind us so I could shoot. It was just a really nice day. Mom cheered when I hit the hay bale. Dad showed me how to aim into the wind and sank the arrow in the bullseye. I couldn't believe he did that on his first shot. Well, he was probably a lot closer to the target than I remember. It was before the divorce.*

Bill realized he was sitting on the sofa holding the new bow, and that he was in a deeper mess than ever.

* * *

When would they find the mistake? Tomorrow? Next week? A year from now? He thought he should call to have it sent back. He wished he could afford the 1,000 credits it would cost to buy it. But he couldn't. Not now anyway. It was his dream come true and he'd have to send it back. *Maybe it was a sign. Maybe the universe was calling.* The universe might be calling but one part of him watched as the other part began typing in the Build Your Own Arrow program. He felt his dream slipping away as he rechecked the order in the Grid, and looked for the contact link. He found it much too quickly.

Hey, if someone sends you something you didn't order, isn't it yours? He thought he heard that somewhere. *Maybe those were the old rules when there was actually a U.S. Post Office, or maybe it's just an urban legend. It's not like it came out of the blue. You ordered something from them. It's not what you ordered. You would expect* them *to fix the mistake if it was the other way around.*

"Don't I deserve it?" He heard his mind echo his words. He looked around at his budget apartment, his sparse furniture, his familyless, significant-otherless, budget life and only one word came to mind: *yes!*

He needed a plan. A new way to be. A new place to be. A place where you can see more than ground squirrels and crackles and gulls. Since he was never one for the heat, there was only one answer: *up north.* He had a plan. He'd always had a plan, he just didn't know it. What would you do to grab a piece of your soul? *Almost anything.*

* * *

The next day he called the bank, packed a bag with his belongings, including his new bow and everything he ever bought from Lost Civilians, and made arrangements with a neighbor to sort his mail. He also cleaned out his fridge.

His first stop was the mall, his second the Vtrain. The only question now was which one to take? He could go straight north into New York State and make his way to Maine and then Canada; or he could go west to California, then turn north into Canada and Alaska. New York State would be cheaper and he could check out the East Coast for a trial run—get his feet wet. He could always take a tube west from there. He swiped his card to pay for the ride and entered a capsule for New York City.

Bill had never actually been in a vacuum train before so when the young, male attendant started giving instructions that Bill thought would be more appropriate for an astronaut, he couldn't help but open his mouth.

"This thing stays on the Earth, right?"

"Is this your first time using V-travel?"

"Yes, I'm heading north. I'm hoping to do some hunting."

"Hunting? This train is headed to New York."

"I hear there are some wild areas in northern New York. Then I can make my way to Maine. Surely the hunting is good there."

"Listen, I'm not sure what you were told but I ride these trains clear to the Canadian border and I've never seen more than a few acres of green here and there. I mean, they don't call it The East Seaboard City for nothing! I can't imagine they would let you hunt there. One second, let me get Old Jim. He likes to hunt. I'll be right back."

Bill thought about his new adventure. *How hard would it be to find a good place to hunt?* A tray of drinks was making its way down the aisle. Bill put up his hand and another male attendant asked Bill what he'd like.

"Just water, thanks."

The attendant held out something that looked like a shot glass.

"Water, I said water. I don't want to get snookered quite yet," Bill said, laughing.

"This *is* water, sir."

Bill took the diminutive glass and put it to his lips. *One swallow? Definitely recycled. They could have made it a little colder, but not bad.* "While you're here may I have another?"

"You may have another, sir, but we don't recommend it. The speed of the Vtrain requires passengers to refrain from unnecessary eating and drinking."

"I'll take my chances," Bill said, frowning at the attendant. Bill downed his second swallow of water.

* * *

The youngish train attendant came back with a tall man a few years older than Bill. The man had a salt-and-pepper beard just short enough not to look out of place in his uniform. The man bent down until his rough-hewn face was about two feet from Bill's. Bill noticed he had piercing green eyes.

"Heya. Hunter eh? Whacha after?"

Bill hadn't really thought about it. "I don't know, maybe a buck."

"A buck? Hell, you've got to go clear to Canada to get a buck!" The man folded his arms and pulled back his head. "It'll cost ya too! License, fees and whatnot. Why don't you stick with squirrels? You get three fat squirrels on the 'cue, that's a meal!"

"You hunt squirrels?"

"Hey, there's plenty of em, and it don't cost me. I'll hunt a rat too... if he's been livin' above ground for a while."

How would you know? "What do you use to get them?"

"BB's, snares, whatever does the job. I ain't picky. Listen, I hope you don't have nothin' bigger than a shotgun, cause anything with a rifled bullet is illegal pretty much everywhere 'cept up North. You can use any kind a hand gun though."

"I got a bow."

"Bow huh? Well, that's all right."

"Hey, I was wondering, maybe I should head to Alaska after I get to Canada for real big game."

"Alaska? Nah." Old Jim looked from side to side. "Place is shit. They ought to call it Alaska*land*. Feel free to bring your toddler. There ain't no big game up there. Just condos and malls, just like everywhere else. Developers and Oil companies chased everything outta there."

"Please secure your seats," said a voice from a speaker. "Movement in 100, 99, 98..."

"My advice, stay East, less popular. Hey don't forget the squirrels!" Old Jim turned and hurried back to the staff area.

"Thanks!" Bill called after him.

The lower the countdown got, the fewer people were moving around. Now he saw only two attendants, one on each side of the car, checking that passengers were belted in correctly. Bill downloaded not one but two emails worth of code to work on during the trip. He wasn't sure if he would have enough money for a license and such. He decided to get busy with work.

The Vtrain began to fidget at count zero. Then the Meat TM sub he had eaten in the mall made its way back into his mouth, accompanied, unfortunately, with the sour taste of stomach acid. Bill found the strength in his jaws to keep it from spraying onto the chair in front of him. After about five seconds the pressure on his restraints relaxed and he could once again swallow —eating his sub for the second time.

Bill had finished a little more than half of his first email group when the Vtrain slowed, threatening his stomach yet again. "That only took an hour." Bill pulled his travel bag and hunting pack out from under the seat. It was a good thing he had spoken to Old Jim. Maybe he should skip Maine all to-gether and go to Canada. It would save credits if he took one train instead of two. Bill synced his wrist to the station. There was a Vtrain to Newfound-land. *Surely, that would be far enough to find a place to hunt.*

Bill bought a ticket for Newfoundland and stood in a line behind about ten people whose possessions were being searched thoroughly.

"Wow, these Canadians are serious about terrorism." Bill knew terrorism still existed, but most people just stayed home. So, casualties were minimal. Once in a great while a security guard would pay the ultimate price. But now that they had anti-terror companies, they would rebuild or fix whatever was broken or blown-up in a few days. Bill would hum the jingles to himself in the shower sometimes—*they were such earworms!*

A man that looked like a commando in a straight-brimmed red hat tapped Bill on the shoulder. He had noticed Bill's long bag and asked about the con-tents.

"It's a bow and arrows for hunting." The man had a stern look and Bill was immediately asked to step out of line. Several officers in straight brimmed hats surrounded him. "Is there a problem officers?"

"Are you unaware that the Province of Newfoundland is a zoo?"

"I think I heard it had a very nice zoo."

"You've been misinformed, sir; the entire province is a zoo. Residents are not allowed to hunt. In fact, no weapons of any kind are allowed in the Province."

"I'm sorry, I didn't know!"

"We have the right to arrest you here and now. But since you were up-front with us, it's plausible you were not aware of our policy. We deal with poachers *very* seriously in Canada."

"Is there a place I *can* hunt?"

"The Hudson Bay area has a few hunting parks. If you show me your passport, I'll be happy to get you to the right Vtrain."

"Not that I'm interested in hunting anything *whatsoever*, mind you. But what type of animals do you have in the zoo?"

The Canadian officer looked at Bill suspiciously for a moment, then decided he was just curious. "We have various species of gull, doves, and squirrels. Residents have seen skunks and a fox on occasion. We are very proud of our population of rabbits. Our pride and joy is a small herd of caribou on permanent loan to us from the Inuit. You can visit us sometime, when you'd like to take pics, not pelts!" It was written in large red letters on a brochure the officer handed Bill.

He thanked the officer when he was directed to a Vtrain tunnel with plastic icicles hanging from the top and pictures of snowscapes, glaciers and a grizzly bear holding a sign saying "Up North."

"That's weird," Bill mumbled to himself. "They say it too?"

The Vtrain *Up North* was white as a ghost and covered in pictures of ferocious polar bears and mountain goats teetering on cliffs—even the seats were white with fake fur as if taken from a polar bear. It was filled with a lot of guys and gals carrying every conceivable weapon devised by man to hunt beast. One loud guy was from Louisiana, claiming he was "Gunna bag him a Woolly Mammoth!" Which caused snickers from some, and looks of jealousy from others. Bill looked at the gun the man brandished and decided: *If there were Woolly Mammoths up there, he could bring one down with the cannon he was holding above his head.*

The attendants were dressed in arctic-style camouflage and instructed all passengers to stow their cargo. This time when the water cart came by Bill passed it up altogether, not wanting a repeat of his earlier experience. When the countdown began, he felt excited at the prospect of hunting something, like the people who pioneered the world before cars and planes and markets and Vtrains.

* * *

After a much longer trip where Bill had had an easier time with his stomach, but was very much in need of a glass of water, the Vtrain jerked to a stop. Bill pulled his cargo out from under his seat and decided to follow the crowd wherever they went. The man with the elephant gun had been friendly enough before the trip started, but Bill was a little afraid of him and looked for someone else to talk to. As it turned out everyone was headed in the same direction so it was easy to blend in. He spied a compound bow hanging over someone's shoulder and walked more quickly to catch up.

Bill thought she was cute if it weren't for all the grease painted on her face. He thought a fellow bowman would be closer to his type of tempera-ment. But the way she held her mouth open on one side, as if holding a place for a future plug of tobacco, made him rethink his initial assessment. She started in with something about how many trophies she had and then moved on to the technical aspects of her bow, what it was made of, how she had it re-calibrated every season. "They can do it right here," she said.

They passed a statue of quite a realistic elephant. When Bill looked closer he saw it was covered in fur and had long twisting tusks.

"That's a Woolly Mammoth!" he said, quite taken back.

The grease-painted woman interrupted her explanation of her bow. "Watch how many point their weapon at it... Wait for it." Sure enough, at least ten people looked into their sites. Red dots gathered on the mammoth's heart, head and genitals.

In a voice that would carry clear across Canada, the grease-painted woman shouted, "We got noobs!" Her laugh was just as loud and made Bill's ear buzz. Variations on the noob theme popped up throughout the crowd, which made all the red dots disappear.

Now he could see the approaching structure. More statues of wild beasts surrounded the grounds and the large "Up North" sign, though covered in snowscapes and icicles, actually was striped in several settings: winter, desert, jungle, and grassland. Six lines of entrance were forming at the head of the group. As far as his eyes could see, barbed wire fences stretched out into the distance. Strategically placed signs said "Entrance 50 Credits + li-cense fees for what you hit." There was a long list of license fees from mar-tins and raccoon at 5 credits to mountain lions and polar bears at 300 credits. At the bottom in italics were things like tigers, elephants and Woolly Mam-moths, species Bill knew to be extinct, for joke prices, he imagined, of 4,000 and 5,000 credits respectively. Bill noticed a White-tailed Buck would cost him 175 credits, which made him swallow hard. At a minimum of 225 credits, it was doable, he would just have to watch his account for a while.

He paid the man, who looked a lot like the grease-painted woman he was walking with. Bill received his ticket, a program, and had his hand stamped.

All the six lines filtered into a giant cave with pictures of prey animals fleeing from springing predators. He felt cool air blowing from an opening ahead where everyone was headed.

As he neared the opening he began to brace, a bit, against the wind. His ears popped as he passed through and he no longer felt any wind. Nearly everything was covered in camouflage and hides of animals. Behind every counter, a wall was covered in a giant beast-skin: tigers, Kodiak bears and polar bears. *They must be worth a fortune,* he thought. In fact, it made him a little angry. *They should be in a museum!*

In the center of the vaulted room stood a full-size tree, growing right out of the tiled floor. It was larger around than a man's outstretched arms. *They must have built this place around it. They did a good job. It didn't look damaged or even trimmed.*

Bill felt pangs of thirst again and noticed bubbling piles of stones in every corner of the room. A man was helping himself to a drink, so Bill assumed it must be okay. Bill headed for another corner and let his dry mouth eagerly drink in the ice cold water. But after about three swallows, the familiar taste of recycling couldn't be hidden by the cold. Bill was very disappointed.

On the opposite side of the room a crowd was forming. Bill went to see what this was about.

There was a long desk where hunters were signing something on screens. In this corner Bill saw signs that said: "Danger Live Ammo" and "Look Before You Shoot!"

Bill watched as groups of hunters passed through yet another cave with their weapons pointed straight up at the ceiling. An attendant was counting heads and pulled down a gate after twenty people went by.

Another group of hunters went into an area under a natural-looking awning constructed of twisted branches, mosses and leaves. The whole area was held together with stripped hewn logs, notched and fitted together. There were seats oriented at different wall-sized screens. Here were the various hunting grounds that striped the outside area sign: winter, jungle, desert, and grassland. Cameras flicked from one area to another showing animals feeding, running, and being felled by hunters. This last event would cause a cheer to go up in the seats and speculation as to whether it was a heart, head or body wound. The camera would then jump to a new location with another scene.

Bill was starting to get excited; here were animals like he had never seen before: birds he'd never seen, wolves, bears, even beavers he had read about on the Grid. And there were bucks too with great pointing antlers. *No wonder people got excited coming here! Maybe I should get some greasepaint too—if it helps.*

He walked over to the long desk with screens where you can sign your name. It was a protection clause for the premises. There was a lot of lawyer-speak but in bold letters the screen read:

> *This establishment allows hunting using live ammunition. I understand that I am at risk of injury, including death, from falls, gunshots, arrow piercings and ricochets of my own and other hunters' ammunition, weapons, and any object that is part of the Up North Hunting Establishment. I hold Up North and its employees and associates completely harmless, and am hereby waiving my right to pursue legal action, as I am taking part in this activity completely at my own risk.*

> Signed_____ Date_____

Bill assumed this was all pretty standard. After all, they were guns, not toys out there. He signed the screen and stood in line with his cherry wood bow and arrow set strapped to his back, more anxious than ever for a chance at a buck. Bill heard the gate come down behind him and he made his way into the cave with nineteen other hunters.

* * *

Bill knew exactly where he wanted to go when the group divided into four lines. A grassland hunting ground was where he would find a buck. It was an opening furthest to the right.

He could see the yellow grass moving in the breeze through the opening as he approached. He thought of his virtual game at home. Here was a real-life version of it. His heart soared at the thought and he felt his soul singing. He knew it had all been worth it.

An attendant held a brightly colored vest in his hand with a number in large size letters. "You gotta put this on, okay sport?"

"Sure," said Bill.

"So what are you after today?"

"Maybe a buck, I hope."

"Awright, go gettem!"

Bill's foot stepped out on the pie-shaped grounds. A wall separated his grassland hunting area from the others, radiating out like a giant wedge. Another attendant pointed a path for Bill to take, separate from the other hunters. Bill unzipped his holder and pulled out the shining new bow. He grabbed a string from his kit and bent the bow to set it in its groove. He took a multi-bladed head from the box and placed it atop one of his signature Z.A.N.D.E.R. arrows. He felt a little silly and embarrassed at such a display, wondering if it was all caught on the giant screens in the room under the awning.

He headed on the vector pointed out by the attendant. But something was odd. He smelled grass and dirt but it was not like what he thought it would smell like. The grass brushing against his leg was stiff and didn't break in his hands. He crouched and examined the ground, but there wasn't any. There may have been ground underneath, but it was some kind of surface. Bill continued on for about a hundred yards through the odd grass. Then he saw the buck.

It was facing him about fifteen yards away with its head bent down as if grazing. Bill couldn't imagine what it was grazing on, certainly not the grass. When it lifted its impressive head he could see pocked marks on its chest. As it turned to show its flank, there were more pock marks. He thought the deer might be injured. Confused, he nocked an arrow and let it fly. A miss. But the buck just stood there. He nocked another arrow, hitting the buck full in the side. It fell. He'd done it. He'd got his buck.

Two attendants came out to carry the buck away.

"Hey, isn't that mine?" Bill asked.

"Yeah, sure bud."

One of the attendants handed Bill a plastic circle with a bullseye on one side and the word "Buck" on the other.

"Okay, good hit! Give this to the desk. You'll get your head... Hey listen, why don't you follow us—we've got a few too many hunters on the grass-lands. You can get right back in line, if you want."

Bill followed the men carrying his buck to one of the side walls of the enclosure. As they approached, three spots on the wall started to glow. At about five feet away, three panels of the wall opened, revealing a walkway that ran between hunting grounds. The men put the buck on a conveyor belt and activated the walkway, whisking the three of them back to the Up North Building.

"When do I get my buck?"

"Just give them—"

"I mean, do you guys have a service to ship the meat and such?"

"No meat, just the head on a plaque."

"What if I wanted to try the meat? I mean I did pay for the privilege, right?"

"Listen bud." He stopped the walkway then he stopped the conveyor belt. He took a utility knife out of his pocket and walked up to Bill's buck.

"Here's your meat!"

He sliced open the buck's flank before Bill could say a word. Underneath the furred exterior was smooth metal casing.

"We just pull a furry skin over the thing like a sock. We change it when it gets too many holes or gets too beat up."

Bill didn't know what to say; he'd gotten his buck, but not like he thought. He took his piece of plastic back to the building. One of the men let him back into the public area where he saw lines of hunters streaming into the building.

His wrist began to pulse. It was Cindy. "Where are you? My GPS must be on the fritz; it's showing you up near the arctic circle! Are you okay? Hey, I bought you a birthday present! Did it come yet? I hope you don't mind. I hacked into the wish list of Lost Civilians, that store you like, and found what you wanted. You're gonna be fifty, we have to celebrate!"

"Hi Cin, I'm good, I'm good. Thanks for calling..."

Bill handed in his piece of plastic and paid the man for his trophy head. He said it would arrive in about a week by drone. Bill walked back from the Up North facility in a daze. He got back on the Vtrain wondering if he should plan a trip south when he got home.

"Surely the monkeys are real... right?" He sat pondering. The Vtrain fidgeted then whooshed back toward home.

THE HOWLING OF THE STORM
BY SHELLI-JO PELLETIER

Outside the wind wailed but could not get in, blocked by shutters over the barred windows. Emma Nieve paused in the hall to listen to the force of the storm. If it blew its fury out overnight, they would leave in the morning. The thought was both exciting and nerve-wracking. Emma moved away from the chill draft and continued on her way.

The doorway at the end of the hall glowed warm and inviting. Sounds of laughter and clinking pottery spilled into the dark corridor along with the golden light from the room beyond. Emma stopped before she reached the open doorway. She could see the backs of several women within, orange firelight turning their forms to silhouettes. Boisterous stories and jokes drifted into the hall.

"I swear, this came straight from the mouth of a sailor in Red Harbor, I swear—!" That was DD, her loud laugh unmistakable. "Over there, that desert there, they've got giant worms there that spit fire, he says! From both ends!"

"The storm will end by daybreak, Garnet. Trust me on this. We'll leave on time—"

"Kath, move over. And gimme that. You're drunk as a fish—"

"Oi! Am not—"

Emma knew she could have stepped into the room and they would have moved over, made room for her at the fireside. She was the newest member of the team, and the youngest besides. Even so, they had all treated her warmly.

They were a close team, the Reds. A family that had been brought together through necessity and now stood with unshakable bonds. Observing them for the past three weeks had cemented that fact.

Though she had trained with them, preparing for the assignment tomorrow, Emma didn't feel confident that she could blend with these other women. She still felt like the outsider looking in.

Not able to bring herself to join the nightly gathering, Emma turned and retreated down the hall. At the end she slipped inside a room with two long rows of cots pushed against the walls. She didn't bother to light a lamp or a candle, feeling her way into the dark room and taking refuge under the quilt on the closest bed. Even with no windows in the room, she heard the roaring of the wind outside as it shook the snow down from the sky.

* * *

The day dawned clear. Emma could tell from the silence that greeted her when she opened her eyes. Several of the cots around her still had deeply breathing mounds upon them, but most were empty. She slipped from her bed and pulled on her other set of clothes. The water from the basin atop the room's single dresser woke her thoroughly, ice cold as she splashed it on her face.

Emma traveled the same corridor as she had the night before, passing the same reinforced window. Now the shutters were thrown open. Through the steel bars mounted into the concrete sill she could see the clouds hanging low, a ceiling of flat off-white but not the gray, heavy color that promised more rain or snow.

At the end of the hall the girl crossed through the doorway without hesitation. The room stole no confidence from her now that the team wasn't gathered there. Indeed, the kitchen was mostly empty. The fireplace in the center was banked low, an old aluminum coffeepot hanging near the center to keep it warm. One of the Reds, Rosie, was preparing her gear at a table against the far wall. The steady scrape of a rocking chair in the corner marked the presence of Sophie. Sophie wasn't a Red, just an old Grandmother without any family and so lived in the communal home in the center of town. Emma had been told to get used to this way of life. The Reds often stayed in the communal buildings of each town they came to, traveling with their assignments. Emma didn't mind it. It was far and away from the tiny cabin where she had spent most of her childhood with her father, and that was good.

Crossing to the larder built into the concrete wall of the room, Emma nodded to Sophie. "A good day for a convoy," she murmured as a morning greeting.

"Ha! Child, *you* don't remember what a good day is. None of y'do," creaked the voice in the corner, accompanied by the steady rocking of the chair.

Emma didn't refute the statement, though she prickled with the rebuke to a simple greeting. She reminded herself that the Grandmothers deserved respect, even though everyone was tired of hearing yet another variation on "memories of the old days." Emma had never seen sunlight catch on stems of tall green grass on a warm summer's day, but she could recite the memory perfectly (or a dozen others like it) thanks to a lifetime of listening to Grandmother Sophie and others like her who jumped at any chance to talk about the life they remembered before the world had changed.

"'Good day' indeed. No one should say 'good day' with a straight face nowadays," muttered the old woman, trailing off into other details. She mumbled mostly to herself, since Emma hadn't taken the bait and engaged her in conversation.

Across the room, Rosie chuckled but softly, below Grandmother Sophie's poor hearing, and didn't look up from her focused task. A series of short blades, one for each sheath slung around her hips and thighs, lay spread out on the table before her. Rosie the Ravisher gave them each her undivided attention as she sharpened the knives until they shone silver.

Emma glanced at Rosie, judging how soon they had to leave by how close Rosie was to finishing her task. She judged she should pick up her pace, so she reached into the larder and grabbed two handfuls of dried apricots to tuck into her pocket and a hard-boiled egg from the bowl on the middle shelf. It was still warm, and she gingerly picked the shell fragments off as she mumbled goodbye to Sophie and made her way out of the kitchen.

Emma returned to the cot where she had spent the night, grabbing her pack at the foot of her bed and shoving yesterday's clothes within. Packing was easy. The only other objects she owned were already outside, with her bike.

Emma slung on her pack and left the room, where the last Reds were finally stirring out of their beds. She made her way through the halls to the building's only exit, passing several empty rooms as she went, nodding goodbye to any people she passed. The Reds wouldn't be returning soon, if at all. At the front door she almost paused to give the building one more look, but instead steeled her spine and grasped the doorknob, turning the heavy door and shouldering her way out into the open air.

St. Jamestown bustled under the early morning light. Townspeople walked briskly from their homes, coats turned up against the chill air, eager to get their daily tasks done while there was light enough to leave. Snow piled up in random drifts, driven by last night's wind, between squat buildings. A mother kept her hand firmly on the shoulder of her young son, hurrying the steps of the boy to keep up with her pace as she crossed to the market square. Emma watched a baker laying out small loaves in the stall in front of his bakery, and a metalsmith carrying a bucket of steel shrapnel to the smithy. The morning air was quiet, save for a few low greetings heard when the breeze carried them to her ears.

Nightfall didn't belong to these people. Not like those in the city, MI

Cntr, where Emma had met and joined the Reds three weeks ago. In the city, people could brave the darkness with their power grid, farmers on the outskirts of the city with their own generators. But when the sun vanished from the sky here in St. Jamestown, everyone was safely behind reinforced doors for the night. Emma had grown used to it.

A figure appeared from between two of the stalls in the square, heading her way; Emma stood straighter even before she consciously recognized the figure to be her captain.

The short, compact woman wore only short sleeves against the chill, despite a bare head with just a hint of pale fuzz sprouting. The shiny skin of a jagged half-moon scar circled the left side of her scalp.

"Ready?" The captain didn't use three words when one would do.

Emma nodded, lifted her chin a fraction. She and the older woman stood eye to eye.

"Good. Wheels out in five. How's Rosie?" Pale green eyes flicked to the building behind Emma.

"Almost done, I think." Rosie was never late.

Captain Garnet nodded and strode away. Butterflies chose now as the time to cascade through Emma's midriff, though she knew she was prepared. Knew everything was ready. Knew she had been mentally preparing for this all morning. Still, it was her first assignment.

She turned from the square and strode as calmly as she could to the town entrance.

* * *

A ring of scrap wood and other building materials cannibalized from outlying town structures served as the town's wall. By the sole entrance, off to the side of the old asphalt road that passed through the barricade doors, Emma saw that the bikes had been wheeled out from under cover. Her bike stood at the end of the line, and she laid her hands on the worn handlebars.

It was a good bike. She was happy to have it. An old Yamaha R16, now painted matte black but originally blue (judging by a few places where the paint had chipped). She had been driving it for three weeks in preparation.

She had learned most of its little quirks, like how it pulled just a hair to the left if you hit the brakes in a hurry. It wasn't technically hers; it belonged to the Reds. She got to ride it now because they had been taking new recruits in MI Cntr. They had lost two of their point runners on their last assignment, and Emma had been adrift in the world with nothing in her life left to lose.

She hefted her pack and put her supplies in her saddlebags, seeing that her weapons sat well within. She made sure the handles were in easy reach before letting the leather covers fall down.

Emma took a moment to gaze at St. Jamestown's makeshift wall, at the old cracked road. Remembering why she wanted to do this. The pay was low but the respect they gained was equal to the danger they faced. Really though, that was only second and third to her initial motivation, which was the sight of the Reds as they rode together through MI Cntr. She could tell at first glance that they had been riding together for a while. She wanted that, someone to fight for and fight with.

Despite her lingering doubts, the team had been quick to pull her into the fold, complete with all the inappropriate jokes and teasing they gave each other. Don't be a firth, that was their favorite. DD, the remaining point runner, said it first, but the rest of them quickly picked it up. Firth was short for "first ride, last breath." Don't get killed on the first mission, they meant.

They also called her Little Red, which was supposed to be a term of endearment, she was sure. Emma still wasn't quite used to the close quarters, the lack of privacy, the back slapping and snickers just before you were out of earshot. But she was starting to like it.

Still, she appreciated the quiet moment now to center her thoughts and calm her stomach before the rest of the gang arrived. Emma didn't need to turn to see them. Rosie's footsteps fell hard and precise, like everything she did. Sandra clinked when she walked; she was the team mechanic and her jacket had about a thousand small tools in the pockets. Kylie's laugh was coarse, and DD talked too loud.

Silence fell, even DD trailing off, which meant Captain Garnet was walking up. Emma lifted her red leather jacket from where it hung on the handlebars and slung it on over her thick wool shirt. She imagined that she stood more steadily when the stiff jacket settled against her shoulders. She didn't need to look at the decapitated wolf head dyed onto the back to feel the connection the Reds shared.

She turned and looked when she heard the footsteps of the others falling into line. Seven women stood in a row beside her at attention. Their expressions were set and stern, but Emma could see the trace of amusement in their eyes. Her confusion faded. The team wasn't usually this structured, but with a sinking sensation Emma realized they were doing this for her benefit. She was the newbie. They were showing her the ropes.

Trying to control the heat rising to her face, Emma took the two steps necessary to join Kylie at the end of the line, folding her hands behind her back.

Captain Garnet looked them over. She had pulled on her own jacket, and the others had at some point as well. They weren't all exactly the same, but they were all red leather tops (some more patched than others). They were the closest thing to a uniform St. Jamestown had seen in a long time, Emma would have guessed.

"Right, listen," Garnet ordered shortly. "For Ms. Nieve, let's go over this once before we go." The roar of a diesel engine sputtering to life just outside the gate almost drowned her out, promising that this was going to be a short speech.

"You all know the drill," Garnet spoke, giving the line of women a look over. "We're running a standard convoy. Two tankers are waiting outside, both carrying gasoline. We'll be in the usual formation. DD's running point. Rosie, Kath, Kylie, stay in front of the tankers at all times. Emma, Sandra, stay near the rear of the second tanker, but don't fall behind me and Virgo. We bring up the rear.

"The destination is New Charleston, five hundred miles southwest. I don't need to tell you how necessary this gasoline is to their day-to-day life, and that we only get paid if it arrives safely. The plan is to get there in two days, no more no less. No unscheduled pit stops, and that includes for Wolves. Got it?"

Rosie grunted in a tone that implied, "Yessir" without actually forming a full word. Most of the others responded only with nods and Emma joined in, trying not to look embarrassed that the Captain singled her out to stay with the mechanic in the "safe zone."

There was no official ending to the talk; Garnet just turned and strode for her bike, a heavy black Silverwing. The other women each straddled their bikes and brought them to life, the movements smooth with familiarity. Kylie rode in a sidecar beside Kath. She couldn't steer and use her weapon of choice, a heavy crossbow, at the same time. DD's voice could be heard cajoling her bike, affectionately named Chariot, into starting without sputtering, but her exact words were drowned out by the general noise. Emma could tell their departure was attracting the attention of curious onlookers from the town, but they were all staying well back in the market area, away from the entrance.

Emma climbed on board her bike and started it up. Unlike some of the others, she hadn't bothered to give it any affectionate name. It was enough that it handled well and didn't give her any trouble. (Unlike Chariot, who was constantly demanding new parts from DD. But then again, she rode it a lot harder than the others did theirs.)

Now that Garnet had mentioned them, the Wolves were proving to be hard to keep off Emma's mind. Just the sight of a convoy was enough to keep away most of what passed for troublemakers in this area, the other Reds told her, the Wolves were another story.

They weren't really wolves, of course. At least, not according to the Grandmothers describing how wolves were supposed to be, from the before time. Emma had yet to see more than a few distant shapes moving against the white landscape, herself. But Grandmother Sophie painted a picture with her stories late at night that fused in Emma's mind. Eight foot tall when standing upright, with elongated forelimbs that they sometimes walked on, the Wolves looked more like ancient gorillas in body. But their heads were canine, predatory snout and teeth, sharp eyes and ears. Covered all over with thick white fur. They could blend in with the landscape so well that, come nightfall, the city walls were the only thing that kept Wolves from getting close enough to take someone unawares. There were a few other dangers in the area, but nothing a smart person couldn't handle if they got back inside the town before dark.

The Wolves were always hunting. The sight of a convoy wouldn't stop them from trying to attack two tankers, but steel and bullets could.

Through the open gates Emma could already see the two trucks pulling away, out into the road. The storm last night had been a mixed blessing, apparently. The wind had pushed much of the snow off the flat roads to pile up against the surrounding hills. DD opened up her throttle and peeled away from the group, overtaking the trucks before they got very far and passing them in a blur. Kath and Rosie followed, and the rest of the gang strung out in a line of sleek black shapes dotted with red.

Emma clenched her throttle and guided the bike as it surged forward, falling into line with the others as they set up a perimeter around the tankers. The landscape surrounding the town was mostly snow-crusted hills and frozen scrub brush. For Emma it seemed far too open and unguarded. The tension in her shoulders ratcheted higher.

No one wasted any time; they had only eight hours of daylight, at best. St. Jamestown and its wall disappeared behind them faster than Emma would have thought possible. She turned her blue eyes to the perimeter, forcing her mind to stay on her job. A flash of white motion on white snow would be the only warning they would get that Wolves were stalking them. Better to know ahead of time than fall into an ambush.

At first they made good time, the road around St. Jamestown still holding together fairly well. Later on, as they approached rougher, forested country, frost heaves and underground tree roots had so damaged the old asphalt that the tankers had to slow to a crawl or be forced to break an axle in a pothole. Their point runner produced a can of orange spray paint from her saddlebag. Soon the snow and road were marked with bright streaks of warning where the travel got particularly bad. This was the part of the journey that would take most of the day, and could end someone's life.

The darkening sky ahead had already set Emma's teeth on edge, and knowing it was just the trees closing in on either side of the road did no good. The forest was dangerous. They would ride out of it before nightfall and camp on the other side, but only if they didn't run into trouble.

Trouble found them long before dark.

* * *

Emma was guiding her front wheel around a bulging tree root and almost lost control of the bike when she heard the pop of gunfire up ahead. She whipped toward the sound, but the view was obstructed by the two tanker trucks in her way. A long roar from too close drowned out the sounds of the engines momentarily. Beside her, Sandra swore loudly.

Emma reached behind her back as she gunned her motor, steering around the first of the trucks and fighting to keep straight. She groped twice, a moment that felt like forever, before finally finding her saddlebag and then her palm slid around a comforting wooden handle within. She yanked the ax free as she rounded the second truck and came upon the scene.

Emma didn't have the luxury of freezing in terror, as her bike was carrying her directly toward the melee. Straight ahead of her a white mountain of fur was rising up, up, splaying front paws so wide they could have engulfed Rosie's head between them easily. Rosie the Ravisher yanked her handlebars hard to the right and swung a steel hammer with her left hand at the same time, clipping against the reaching claws before they could grab her.

There were other white shapes on the road—three, four, too many to count in a glance when Emma couldn't even look away from the one in front of her. Frustrated with Rosie's escape, the Wolf saw her coming and turned its upper body toward her eagerly.

Emma turned her wheel sharply to steer around the beast but in her panic she lost control. The bike slid and went down on its side, Emma leaping from it thanks to training, using her momentum to tuck into a tumble that unfortunately carried her not far from the feet of the Wolf. Its eyes tracked from the bike to her, deciding which was its prey in the short time she needed to roll to her feet. She raised her ax and swung. The creature checked its lunge at her, briefly cautious of the new weapon it hadn't seen before, which gave her the two seconds she needed to reach her downed bike and grab her second ax from the saddlebag. The two hatchets were a comfortable weight in her hands, compact but familiar. That and a childhood with her father, the wood harvester, gave her the strength to use them effectively.

Emma choked up her grip on her axes as she faced the creature, watching the signs she had been taught to see. The flex of the thick leg muscles that meant the Wolf was about to move. She dodged to the side and swung her ax, leaving a scored mark down the beast's reaching arm that started to bleed a few moments later.

"Get back on your—!" Captain Garnet shouted as she shot past on her Silverwing, carried beyond Emma's hearing before she could finish the command. Her glare was unmistakable in its meaning. It was easier fighting on the ground, though, and Emma trusted her axes.

"What're y'doing, Little Red!?" Chariot's sputtering roar almost drowned out DD's words as she whipped around in a tight circle next to the spot in the road where Emma stood. Emma had to dodge another swing of the Wolf and couldn't answer, but DD helped her out by tossing a wrench from her saddlebag at the beast's head. It bounced off the scalp between the ears, the Wolf unharmed but distracted long enough for Emma to lunge forward. Her axes bit deeply this time, sinking into the Wolf's chest in a fount of dark red. It let out a wet howl, claws spasming even as they continued to reach for her. But DD swung her bike close again, had another wrench or pipe or something in her hand that came down hard on the beast's muzzle as it was leaning backward from the force of Emma's blow. It fell down to the ground.

DD didn't stop to check if the few scratches on Emma's exposed skin where the Wolf had caught her were superficial. "On your bike!" she shouted as she shot across the road toward another Wolf that was bigger than the one Emma had faced and was driving Kylie and Kath back against a gnarled tree.

Emma obeyed this time, righting her bike and sliding onto the worn leather seat. Her axes went into her saddlebag. She aimed the handlebars to follow DD in helping Kylie and Kath but immediately had to swerve away as another Wolf she hadn't noticed jumped from the woods, almost landing on her front wheel.

Emma gunned the motor and shot away, fighting to control the bike and keep it from toppling. A game howl sounded right behind her—too close. It was giving chase.

She traded speed for agility, losing her momentum to swerve the bike left and right, forcing the Wolf to turn one way then the other in order to catch its prey. A raised root made her front wheel wobble; she planted one foot on the ground and shoved to clear the debris, but not in enough time. The bike lurched as heavy claws slammed into the rear tire.

Desperate to act before the Wolf got a grip on its prize, Emma twisted the throttle. The motor screamed and the bike shot forward, out of control. It jumped the edge of the road. Emma was screaming, or someone else was. The bike drove between two hedges of dead brush before the black trunk of a tree loomed suddenly up in front of her like a rearing Wolf.

Firth, Emma thought, and the word was a curse. Then there was blackness.

* * *

Emma woke with pain in her scalp and leaves in her face. She tried to spit, tasted copper. She opened her eyes. The world spun around her, but she could tell she was moving. The branches in the air above her passed from view, disappearing beyond her vision.

Wet cold was sliding up her back, under her jacket, the burning cold of snow against her skin. Her body was being dragged over the forest floor.

Other feelings in her body announced themselves to her wakening senses. A tight, hot feeling, spiking pain in her ankles. Wet crystals of ice against her fingers and the backs of her hands, which were up over her head. She struggled to lift her head and squint down to her feet, trying to make sense of this.

A mountain of white rose up as she lifted her head, passing between small, bent trees. Ice plunged through Emma, terror this time rather than the snow that crusted the ground. Thankfully the fear froze her throat as well, because the Wolf hadn't noticed she was now awake. Its giant paws were curled around both her ankles, pulling her deeper and deeper into the woods.

Emma realized the scene was silent, save for the sound of her and the Wolf's passage through the dead trees. She couldn't hear the sound of engines, or shouts of battle. How long had she been out? What had happened to the others?

None of this made any sense. Wolves were animals, they hunted in packs and gorged on whatever they killed. They did not take prisoners. They did not drag unconscious victims through the woods. Emma had grown up knowing that many of those that left a town or city without being able to return to safe walls before nightfall simply never returned at all. But there were no stories of being captured and carried off to parts unknown.

Questions and unknowing overwhelmed her for a time. It was so much easier to stay limp, to try to keep her breathing steady and even, to categorize the aches and pains in her body in preparation for when she would eventually act. The tight feeling in her ankles made her fear that she had a sprain or worse, not sure if they would support her weight if she got a chance to run. She didn't dare flex her legs to test the extent of the damage. Not until it was time for her to make her move.

Focusing on not panicking and staying still took enough concentration that the sudden stop took her by surprise, and her flinch might have been noticed if the Wolf hadn't immediately drop her legs and let them fall to the ground. Emma opened her eyes.

The shreds of the dead winter forest still surrounded them on all sides, the ground covered with leaf litter and a mantle of snow and ice. But in front of the Wolf was a perplexing structure, a huge square box of a building made of old plastered walls and a rectangular shadow for a doorway in front of them. She glanced at the beast, which raised its muzzle and sniffed the door frame with a long, ridged snout. Whatever it scented seemed to satisfy it, and it turned back to Emma. It growled and parted its jaws.

This was the time to move. Emma could tell that if she went inside that place she would not emerge again. She shoved against the ground, propelled herself to her feet. Her ankles ached but held her weight and she tried to run.

Moving with a speed that belittled its size, the Wolf had her in its arms in a fraction of a moment. Emma smelled musk and rot, gagged, and then it tossed her through the open doorway as if she weighed no more than a pack.

She hit the ground hard, the breath shooting out of her, but immediately she tried to scramble upright again. Her elbow complained where it had struck the ground, tingles traveling all the way to her fingertips, and her knees ached from her earlier spill from her bike. The cracked concrete floor was strewn with a few leaves and puddles of water from melting snow, but otherwise the room was empty. It was dim, the only light coming from the open doorway and small rectangular windows high up near the ceiling. Another dark doorway on the far side of the room led deeper into the building.

The darkness deepened when the Wolf swung a large metal door closed, sealing them both inside. Emma froze in the gloom, forcing her eyes wide, waiting for them to adjust to the small light coming in from the windows. She held her breath to listen for sounds of movement, and then could make out the shape of the white mountain near the door. It moved toward her.

Emma turned and ran.

The next dim room had the same small windows near the top of the walls, and the next did as well. Emma fled down a narrow hallway, pale day-light leaking in from open doors on either side, but she didn't stop to investigate. There was no sound of pursuit behind her, but that didn't mean she could take the chance of slowing down. She didn't understand anything about what was happening. Was it playing some kind of sick game with her?

The hall ended in another room, larger and lit better than the ones she had passed through before. Rows of larger windows lined the high walls, but still too far overhead for her to jump. No escape there. They were covered in years of dirt and sludge, leaves plastered to the dull streaked glass. Dust motes floated in the air from the light that managed to get through the grime.

The room was not empty, but it took her a moment to make sense of what she saw. It wasn't like anything she had seen before, but she could identify the rows and rows of metal boxes lining the walls, taller than she was, all standing together like good soldiers. Black glass rectangles made up the front surface space of many of them, dark and dusty and opaque, surrounded by rows of buttons and switches. Machines.

Emma didn't understand. Were they generators? Were they for making electricity? Out here in the middle of the forest?

Movement at the opposite end of the room and she froze. Two small white shapes moved through the beams of weak sunlight. Emma backed up, her hip hitting one of the machines. Furry figures, three feet tall with stubby muzzles and forelimbs, reaching out for her. Young Wolves.

A guttural howl echoed from somewhere in the building. Much too close. The two young stopped, their pointed ears swiveling to catch the sound, but their albino red eyes watched Emma.

She backed up another step and something crunched under her foot, and something else rolled away from her heel. Emma didn't dare look away from them to see what mess littered the floor under her feet. As the Wolf pups stalked toward her again her hands scrambled to grab something, anything in reach to use as a weapon. Clear plastic containers lined the front shelf of the machine she had backed up against. Whatever had been inside them had long ago turned to dust, but she didn't care about that. Without consideration her hands picked them up and flung them at the young Wolves. Brittle with age, some pieces broke apart. Others bounced against furry foreheads and rolled away across the concrete floor.

The diminutive monsters flinched back at first, but all too quickly they realized the random bits and pieces striking them did no harm and they started forward again. The sound they made as they circled toward her wasn't the deep growls or shuddering howls of the adults, but a broken almost hissing sound, like air escaping a tea kettle a bit at a time.

Throwing things was proving useless, and Emma paused when another howl from somewhere in the building reached their ears. This time it seemed to egg the young onward. They crouched down, muscles in their hind limbs bulging, about to spring at her. Emma didn't even bother to drop what was in her hand. She turned again and ran.

The Wolf pups gave yips of pleasure as they chased her, claws digging into a floor scoured with years of passage of such beasts. She fled from them across the room, into another darkened doorway. A shadow within a shadow told her there would be a door there.

Dust covered everything in this building, showing the passage of time, but the door swung open and then closed without more than a screech of complaint as she swung in a circle, flinging it closed behind her just as she passed through. She then leaped forward, pushing all her weight against the door just as the force of the two pups hit it from the other side.

Only as Emma raised her hands to push against the metal door did she realize she was still holding the last item she had grabbed from the machine in the other room: a strange orange loop of plastic as thick as her wrist but snapped in half. A tag hung from one end. Small, perfectly shaped letters were pressed into the plastic: EX-1-1-27. It meant nothing to her, other than it looked like something a dog might wear.

Emma dropped the broken loop as the young Wolves hit the door again. She looked down and saw a metal peg dangled from a short chain on the bar that crossed the center of the door. She had not seen the like before, but instantly it made sense to her. She grabbed the peg and jammed it into the tiny hole next to the dangling chain. The next time the Wolves hit the door, it didn't budge.

Emma stepped back and looked around quickly, but her rising hopes were dashed. There were no other exits to this room. Against two of the walls stood row upon row of black metal boxes, almost as tall as she was. Not machines, these instead looked like storage units. Handles on the front of each said that they probably had drawers that pulled opened. Metal cabinets. The last wall had the same high windows as before, crusted with filth, letting in a paltry amount of light.

She debated opening the nearest cabinet to look for weapons when suddenly a howl broke the air, so close it shook the door behind her, and a huge force slammed into it. Startled, Emma shrieked and leaped away from the door. She whirled to see it already had a dent in the center. Soon it would start to buckle.

With no more time for debate, the young woman grabbed the nearest cabinet and yanked, dragging it forcibly from the spot it had sat for many years. It screeched like a dying animal as she dragged it against the floor, straining to move the heavy object even a few scant feet to get it away from the wall and the other cabinets. Then she dodged around to the other side and pushed forward hard, shoving it up against the door.

The movement and growling on the other side had gone silent, perhaps unable to fathom the suddenly strange noises coming from within the room. Emma didn't pause to see if they would go away or overcome their reservations. She grabbed the next closest cabinet and started to pull.

Finally a long row of metal boxes stood in front of the locked door, barring the way should the Wolves muster the force necessary to break it down. Panting for breath, sweat pouring from her scalp and down her breasts, Emma collapsed against the far wall and sank to the floor in exhaustion. A thousand aches and pains that had been pushed from her mind as she worked tirelessly now made themselves loud. The muscles of her legs rippled like water. She couldn't move.

* * *

Emma wasn't sure how long she sat there in the small room, but she had intended to only rest long enough to get her wind back before planning her escape. She was delayed further when she grabbed the handle of the nearest cabinet to drag herself back up to her feet. The front of the metal box slid open when she yanked, revealing the start of a row of papers that were all filed neatly into slim folders of various thickness. The pages were packed in tight against one another, and they smelled of old paper, not mildew and dust. She pulled the handle of another cabinet close by and it slid open to reveal the same.

The idea of stacks and stacks of paper hiding in all these cabinets was surprising and intriguing; it was not at all what she had been expecting to find. Emma grasped a handful of papers and pulled out the first folder closest to her curious fingers, began pawing through page after page of densely packed writing, wondering what could have possibly been housed in a place such as this.

As she poured over the pages, her curiosity only grew. Though the words were in her language, they made no sense to her. She tripped her way through paragraphs of nonsense, picking out the occasional concept. Here were some words about weather patterns, cloud density and atmospheric pressure and wind speed. And here further on was something about plants and growing time and "variables."

In another cabinet altogether were words that seemed to her to be about animal husbandry, reproduction and traits. She found pictures that showed canines that grew bigger and heavier with each generation, diagrams of forced changes to their skeletons, the twisting of limbs to create something new and strong and deadly.

Slowly, though Emma grasped the theme of only one page for every dozen she skimmed through, the picture in her mind began to clarify. These

were words written by someone—by many someones perhaps?—who intended to learn to control the weather, the earth, even the very seasons. To
guide and change the world.

The dates on the papers she found were very old. From the before time.
Looking at the sheer number of cabinets in the room, it was surely many,
many years of work. A lifetime of work.

Something vital was recorded here.

Emma was only able to rouse herself after it had all sunk in, after the
thoughts had chased themselves around her mind and fallen out like glass
marbles. She had never thought about this before. She was no philosopher or
cleric, to spend her days trying to reach a higher understanding on why the
world was the way it was, what god had decided it would now be harsh and
forever cold when before it had been green and warm and life had been easy.
Nor was she like the Grandmothers, who spent their days bemoaning their
fate and yearning for what had been before, always looking back and never
forward.

For Emma it was pointless. She always faced forward, walked forward in
life, not looking back. Her father had taught her that, carrying nothing more
than a pair of hatchets through his days, going out to cut wood and bring it
back to the city. Captain Garnet had taught her that, taking her in and giving
Emma a chance even though she was young and untrained, after her father
had gone out one simple day and never returned.

So why did this come to her now, when she didn't need it? Didn't need a
sudden revelation. She needed to get out of this dungeon without alerting her
jailers, needed to get through the forest before it got dark or she would be a
dead woman before she found civilization again. She needed her bike and her
axes, and to tell Garnet that she was still alive. That was what she needed,
not all this.

Emma stood and looked around the tiny room, several sheets of paper
clutched in her hand. She wasn't even sure what was written on these in par-
ticular; all the words and concepts had blended together after scanning so
many pages. But she curled them up and shoved them into the back pocket of
her pants as she surveyed just how high the windows to the room really were,
and gauged how many stacked cabinets it would take her to reach them.

Then she got to work. She had many miles to go before it got dark, and the papers would be important to someone.

* * *

The sound as she dragged more cabinets across the concrete floor to the space under the windows was horrendous. Before long the howling on the other side of the barricaded door returned. She tried to ignore them as she worked, tried to assure herself that the row of cabinets would hold and that the Wolves weren't clever enough to figure out what she was doing. Finally she wiped grime and sweat from her brow and stepped back, surveying the cabinets she had maneuvered on top of one another. It was a precarious mountain of metal, but it would have to do.

Emma picked up a thick metal pole, one of the cabinet's interior parts. She brought one hand up to shield her face, hefted the pole like a javelin, and threw it at the closest window with as much force as she could.

Quickly the girl turned away from the windows as the crash of breaking glass—terrifying and loud in the small room—smashed across her senses. Shards rained on the back of her jacket, but she didn't allow herself time to flinch. Emma shook her head, causing a tinkling of glass to fall from her short hair. Every second that passed now was borrowed. A sound like that could attract anything from outside. Thick riding gloves and pants protected her body from more broken glass as she grabbed for a handhold and pulled herself up to the second cabinet.

She picked up the metal pole, which had fallen on top of the cabinets after striking the window. She used it to knock out what glass pieces remained around the edge, then grabbed the frame and pulled herself up.

Anxiously she scanned the forest area below as she balanced precariously on the window frame. Years of drifting snow and tree litter had built up on the ground around the building. She thought perhaps she had a ten foot drop, which she could survive without injury as long as she was careful to absorb the fall with her body and not her legs.

No living thing met her searching gaze, but the Wolves behind her had fallen silent. There was no way to tell where they were now. She had no time. Emma launched herself forward, the Reds' imprinted training kept her body tucked. The impact was jarring, but no more or less than the shock of cold snow pressing against her body as she landed.

Emma shook it off and stumbled to her feet. Her hatchets were gone, lost back at the battle site, along with her bike. She was defenseless, but she had a mission. To survive, to report to her captain, and to share what she had found.

Gaining her sense of direction from the patch of clouds that seemed the brightest, hiding the position of the low sun behind them, she ran for the trees and left the Wolves' den behind.

* * *

Emma didn't bother hiding her footprints in the snow, speed being more important than disguising her trail. Wolves tracked with scent more than with sight.

As daylight expired, every cracking twig or moving shadow became Emma's enemy. She didn't know in which directions St. Jamestown or New Charleston lay. She could only run vaguely southward (or jog when running became too much), basing her path on the fact that the Wolf had been dragging her north when she awoke in its claws.

Puzzles and mysteries helped keep the terror at bay. She turned over what had transpired as she traveled. Though comprehension of the grand picture was a bit beyond her, she could feel the weight of importance in her discovery. Her hand reached to her pocket countless times, touching the papers there, making sure they hadn't fallen. Could it be someone who remembered the before times, a Grandmother or Grandfather in some town or city, would be able to read and understand the papers Emma was bringing out of the forest? Could a big enough team, equipped and prepared, make their way back to the den and reclaim the rest of the knowledge the cabinets contained?

The wind picked up with the dying of the light. Emma felt another unexpected storm brewing in the wet air that struck her face. Her knees felt like jelly and the breath was raw in her lungs but she pressed herself faster. It was possible a storm might keep the Wolves from hunting this night, but if so it would kill her as surely as anything that ran on the ground.

The next thing she heard was not howling of the wind, but the baying of a creature on the hunt.

There were trees all around her, dead gnarled fingers reaching for the sky, shaking with the force of the wind. She didn't try to climb or to hide. It had been pressed upon her during training, in Garnet's succinct voice and DD's boisterous tales. The only way to survive the Wolves was behind safe community walls, or to kill them before they killed you.

Emma thought she could hear them moving in the trees. She ran.

A black, snow-edged ribbon appeared in the woods before her. She tripped and fell upon the road, climbed back up to her feet, turned and faced back the way she came. She searched for white moving shapes in the evening gloom. This could be a place to make a final stand. If someone found her body on the road, maybe they would find the pages in her pocket and under-stand their importance. Maybe she would get a burial.

The roaring of the wind changed direction, pressing against her ears and bringing with it the stench of animal and rot. Snowdrifts moved next to the road—what she had taken for snowdrifts. Too close.

Piercing light struck her like a beacon. Emma cried out, fell back and covered her face with her arms. The roaring sound of the approaching storm was now something familiar and impossible. Revving engines surrounded her. Unbelieving, Emma tried to tell herself she wasn't hearing the captain's heavy Silverwing or Chariot's sputtering throttle. She opened her eyes and saw the beasts rearing up on the side of the road, reaching for them in the gathering gloom, but then Emma was tipping backward as Kylie pulled her into the little sidecar and they tore away.

The storm unleashed a torrent of rain as the team of bikes took off down the road. They moved as a single unit, Emma clinging to the warm body squashed into the car next to her. She raised her voice to be heard over the sounds of weather and machines. "You're alive!" She still didn't quite be-lieve it, wondered if this was the afterlife and her real body was now nothing more than meat on the side of the road.

"I could say the same for you, Little Red!" Kylie returned, wearing a cheeky grin below her thick glass goggles. She had a thick scratch at her temple, crusted over with dried blood, to testify to the battle in the woods. Emma realized she must look frightful herself. "Been searching for hours! Didn't think we had a chance!"

"But—but—"

Kath shouted as she steered the bike and sidecar through the downpour. "Well you didn't think Garnet was going to leave you behind, did you? After she saw them drag you off into the woods? Here, this is yours!" She reached into her saddlebag and pulled out another impossibility. A worn, comforting ax, which Emma took wordlessly and clutched to her chest.

She *had* thought the Reds would continue their assignment without her. She had assumed she was on her own, that she would have to make her own way to New Charleston and hope to meet up with them before they left for another job. She had thought the assignment was everything.

But the tankers were nowhere in sight now, and Emma realized the Reds must have either turned them back to St. Jamestown or sent them on ahead alone. So the Reds could stay behind and search the forest for Emma, whom any sensible soul would have known was nothing more than a dog's dinner at that point.

The young woman looked around as they continued to put distance between themselves and the hunting pack, left far behind. Garnet and Rosie rode nearby, shouting back and forth about the likeliest place to camp for the night and get out of the storm. Kylie in the car next to her cheerfully chatted about finding her another bike in New Charleston, since her own had met its end against a tree trunk. The other three women rode close behind, all a tight group of warriors with headlights cutting through the oncoming night.

THE JOKE

BY RICHARD VEYSEY

R alph surveyed his humble living room. He gave a small nod of approval to the neat TV stand. The cloth in his hand was brown from the dust he had removed from the 32" LCD TV, cable box, and stand itself. The clutter of DVDs that once littered the stand were now put away in their drawer.

Jack would arrive any minute. It was rare for Ralph to have guests, so the apartment had needed quite a bit of work before he would feel comfortable having company. Some of his friends teased him about his etiquette. It was something his mother drilled into him as a child: no friends until the house was clean.

Ralph walked across the room to the window in the corner. Most of the windows in the apartment were secured to only partially open. The building was built years before many safety regulations were put into effect. When it had changed hands decades earlier, the new owners had taken minimal steps to ensure they would be safe from fines if an inspection took place.

He pushed the living room window up until it locked into place. He then reached a hand outside, gently pulling at the sash, jiggling it from side to side until the piece that secured it to the window frame came loose. Ralph pulled the lower section of the window into the apartment carefully. He imagined that a combination of the elements, as well as years of neglect and rot, had warped the old wooden window frame.

Ralph turned to look at the coffee table by the couch. He had removed the empty soda cans and the dirty dishes, leaving a small pile of mail and the remote for the TV. He sorted through the clutter, pulling out the advertisements and throwing them into the half-full garbage bag by his feet. As he picked up the remaining envelopes, all of them bills, a few overdue, he noticed that the mail had been covering a small book.

"Ah, that's where it's been!" Ralph picked up the book and flipped through the thin pages. His mother had sent him this bible as a Christmas present months ago. It had belonged to her parents, and she felt it was time to pass it on.

"If you don't find Jesus now," she had written in the card that had accompanied the present, "I'm afraid you might never find His light."

Ralph appreciated his mother's faith and the gesture the present represented, but it wasn't enough to convert him. He had barely thought about God since he moved to the city and began going to college. Nearly a decade without religion had made him secure in his agnosticism.

Ralph picked up the bible with the letters and placed them on his bedside table next to the lamp. He made sure the overdue bills were on top of the pile. This way, he wouldn't forget to take care of the most important things first.

He heard a knock on the door. Ordinarily the doorman would have called Ralph to verify any guests coming in to the building, but he had told her that Jack was coming and asked her to send him right up.

Ralph took a quick look in his bedroom mirror. With a few comb strokes he covered his small bald spot. The thick, black hair around it was still enough to conceal this first sign of his approaching middle age. He adjusted his collar slightly, making sure the blue button-up shirt was perfectly straight. As he crossed the living room, he noticed the trash bag still sitting by the coffee table. Uttering a brief curse, he picked it up and ran to deposit it in the kitchen before returning to the door to unlock the two locks that functioned as his security system.

"Come in, Jack!" Ralph greeted his friend with a smile. "It's good to see you. It's been, what, since last January, right? How have you been? Come in, sit down! Can I get you something to eat?"

Jack nodded at Ralph, smiling as he came into the small apartment. He sat in the plush leather chair by the door. "Yes, it was January. I'm glad you were free today. I needed to talk with someone. Have I ever mentioned how good of a friend you've been to me all these years?"

Ralph stood by the kitchen door, fidgeting. "Thanks, Jack. I know we lost contact after college, but it's been good to be in touch with you again and see you. Man, those were some wild times, eh? Can I get you something to eat?"

"What do you have? I've been so busy I haven't had a chance to get a bite to eat. My stomach has been grumbling up a storm."

Ralph chuckled. "I can cook up some hamburgers and fries if you'd like."

"That sounds good. Can I get a cup of coffee, too? I was up late last night."

"Of course, of course." Ralph zipped across the small kitchen, preparing the coffee maker and the food. "You shouldn't stay up so late; it's bad for your health."

"It doesn't happen often. Usually I get plenty of sleep. I just had a lot to do last night."

"Doesn't this remind you of our college days? We drank coffee by the gallon and ate pizza, hamburgers, and ramen all the time. Do you ever miss those days?"

"Yeah. Things were so simple. We partied and drank all the time, didn't have to worry about work, got laid all the time."

"Oh, I remember one time you wanted this chick, and her boyfriend got up in your face and you clocked him." Ralph punched the air. "Knocked him out cold. Did you ever get anywhere with that girl?"

"Nah. She left after that, remember?"

"Oh, yeah, I remember now. We were worried she was going to call the cops on us and get us busted." Ralph walked into the living room with two cups of coffee. He set them both on the table.

"Thanks." Jack took a sip of the coffee. "Oh, this is a good roast. What is this?"

"I get it down at that organic food shop." Ralph walked briskly back to the kitchen, returning with a small bag. "It's expensive, but I don't mind pay-ing a lot for a good cup of coffee." Ralph handed the bag to Jack and re-turned to the kitchen. "These burgers are almost done. You want anything on them?"

"Cheese, ketchup, and mayo."

"Wasn't that what you always had back in college, too? Not much changes in five years."

"Things are always changing. It's one of the few constants in life. Change can take years or happen overnight, but it happens."

"I don't remember you as one to wax philosophical. I guess things really can change. I mean, look at us. When we lost touch, I got a good job and you found a wife. Speaking of which, how is she doing? More importantly, how is that whole situation going? You told me it was pretty rough last time I saw you." Ralph walked into the living room slowly, balancing two plates of food. He set them on the table and sat across from Jack.

"I took care of it last night, just like you said I should." Jack took a sip of his coffee and examined the food in front of him. "Guess it took me a while, but you were right."

"What do you mean? I don't remember much about the conversation. I mean, I remember you said you thought she was cheating on you, and she was always asking for money and being rude, but I don't remember—"

"You said I should kill her," Jack said.

Ralph was aware of the humming of the fluorescent bulb overhead. It sounded deafening in the sound vacuum of the room. Then he laughed vigor-ously. "Oh, man, that was a good one. I remember now. You told me how bad it was and I said, 'Well, you could just kill her.' Oh, wow. So, how are you and her, really?"

"I just told you. She's dead. I did it last night. I killed her, took the corpse out to the woods a few miles away and buried her." He took a bite of the hamburger. "This is really good, Ralph. Man, it's been a while since I had a good, home-cooked burger. Seems like lately I've been eating fast food every day of the week."

Ralph felt like the chair wasn't holding him up, as if he was sinking into it. He watched Jack slowly, casually savor the hamburger. "You can't—I mean, that's not something—what are you—"

Jack set the remainder of the burger down, "Could I have a napkin? This burger is amazing, but I'm making a mess over here." He gestured to the ketchup that dripped from his fingers onto his white khaki pants.

"A napkin?" Ralph felt his legs shake as they pulled his body upright and across the floor to the kitchen. He returned with a handful of napkins and sat back in his chair. "You're being serious? You really killed her?"

"Yeah. Turns out she really was cheating on me with some asshole she met online. I looked through her e-mails and found out everything. She was going to leave me in a few weeks. Last night after she went to bed I just grabbed her by the neck and squeezed." He held his hands up, miming the action as he described it. Then he lowered his hands and smiled. "I mean, I suppose stabbing her or shooting her would have been easier, but then there would have been such a mess and the noise." Jack chuckled and shook his head. "No, I knew I wanted to do it clean, quiet, and easy. She really put up a fight, though." Jack pulled up the sleeves of his shirt, revealing fresh, raised scratch marks. "They bled something awful. The sheets are probably ruined."

"Why are you telling me this? What am I supposed to do?" Ralph stood and walked toward the kitchen. He stopped and turned, walking back to the couch with his eyes on his feet. He looked up at Jack. "That's just awful. That's a really, really horrible thing you did, Jack." Ralph could feel a drop of sweat slowly sliding across his temple.

"Was it? I mean, she was cheating on me, that makes her a bad person.

That asshole she was sleeping with, she probably would have cheated on him, too. I did him a favor. No, I think I did a good thing."

"How can you rationalize it like that?" Ralph's voice shook, its timbre rising and falling. "You killed someone, Jack. She's dead. Doesn't that bother you at all?"

"Should it? It's over and done with. I don't really feel anything. Just glad she's gone." Jack popped one of the fries into his mouth.

"I don't know what I'm supposed to do." Ralph sat close to the arm of the couch clutching his hands tightly in his lap. "I mean, shouldn't I call someone? Shouldn't I be telling this to the police?"

Jack stopped eating mid-bite. He finished chewing and swallowed. "I came here because I thought you'd understand. You were the one who suggested I do it."

"It was a fucking joke, man! I didn't think you'd actually do it. A normal person—"

"What do you mean, 'a normal person?'" Jack's voice was as calm as Ralph's was frantic. "Are you saying I'm not normal? That's not a nice thing to say to a friend. It hurts my feelings."

A normal person couldn't commit murder and feel nothing, Ralph thought. "I'm sorry; you're right. That was rude of me."

"It's fine." Jack finished the last bite of the hamburger. "People say things sometimes; they just slip out. I know you didn't mean it. You're just over-reacting a bit. There's no need to get so emotional about it. It doesn't affect you, does it?"

Ralph closed his eyes and took a deep breath, "I really appreciate that you trusted me enough to come here and tell me what you did. I think we should both walk calmly down to the police station and tell them exactly what happened—"

Jack sat up, "So they can throw me in jail? They won't care that I was justified! They'll just see me as another murderer and put me behind bars." Jack slowly relaxed into the chair. "I don't want that. If you're really my friend, you wouldn't want that, either."

Ralph shook his head, "Of course, I didn't think of that. I'm sure they'd lock you away for life." He sat with his feet close together, leaning forward, hands on his thighs. "What do you think we should do, then? Why did you need to tell me all this?"

"This was a huge, life-changing event; I had to tell *someone*." Jack popped another fry into his mouth. "Of course, you can't tell anyone. You won't tell anyone, will you, Ralph?"

Ralph shook his head. "Of course not. You can trust me. Uh—did you want to go out and do something? Maybe head down to the bar, grab a few drinks?"

Jack chuckled. "I outgrew that phase a long time ago. Is there a game to-day? I wouldn't mind sticking around to watch a game with you. That brings back memories, doesn't it?"

Ralph forced a smile. "Yeah, like that tailgate party we had at Ronnie's. Wasn't that the night your girlfriend got totally wasted?"

Jack chuckled. "That was one fantastic night." He made a lewd gesture that made it clear exactly what kind of night it was.

"Hey, I think Pat lives not too far away," Ralph said, standing. "Should I call him up and see if he remembers you and wants to come by? I can ask him to bring some beer and we can make a night of it."

Jack nodded. "Sounds good. Give him a call. I didn't know you still talked to any of them. I lost touch with almost everyone after I graduated."

Ralph shrugged. "I talk to them from time to time." He pulled his phone from his pocket, forcing his hands to be steady as he searched for Pat's number.

"Hello?"

"Pat? It's me, Ralph Hamm, from school. We met a few times at Ronnie's parties, remember?" As he spoke, he wandered toward the kitchen doorway.

"Oh, yeah. The guy with the crazy friend. What's going on?"

Ralph leaned against the empty door frame and paused. "Yeah, you remember Jack, too? He's over at my place and we were wondering if you wanted to come over and watch a game with us. If you bring over some beer, we can pay you back."

"Are you kidding?" Ralph could hear an edge in Pat's voice. "I always thought there was something off about Jack. Ronnie thought so, too. I'm not too keen on seeing him again."

Ralph forced a laugh, "Yeah, he's here right now; I was really hoping you'd want to stop by. It would be nice if it were more than just the two of us."

The phone was silent. Ralph was afraid Pat had hung up.

"You're acting kind of strange, is everything okay?"

"No, no," Ralph said, "In fact, if you want to bring anyone else along, that would be fine, too, right Jack?" He looked over at Jack, who smiled and nodded his assent.

"Do you want me to call the police?"

Ralph tried to hide the relief in his face. He turned his back to Jack and exhaled. "Yes, please. And I'll pay you back for it when you get here. Oh, you probably need my address. Do you have something handy to write it down?"

"Yeah. Give me the address and I'll send the cops down. I don't know what's going on, but tell me later, okay?"

"Sure thing. I live at 1000 12th St., Apt 1410. It's on the 14th floor of the building. I'll see you soon." Ralph returned the phone to his pocket and walked back over to the couch. When he sat, it was less of a conscious movement than his knees simply giving out beneath him.

"He's on his way, then?" Jack finished the last of his fries.

"Yeah, he should be over soon. Let me just find a game that'll be starting up. Maybe there's something good on pay-per-view." Ralph grabbed the remote from the table and began slowly looking through channels.

* * *

Ralph glanced out the open window. The sun hadn't fully set, but little of it was visible through the tall buildings, and the long shadows made it appear as though night had already fallen.

"Everything okay? You keep looking outside." Jack's eyes narrowed.

"Yeah, just keeping an eye out for Pat." Ralph turned his gaze back to the street below.

A police car pulled in on the side of the street, its lights dancing across

the surrounding buildings. Ralph heard the brief siren blip of a second com‐
ing from a few blocks away.

"What's going on, Ralph?"

Ralph turned. The lights from the police car reflected off the windows
across the street, dancing across the walls of the apartment. Jack stood by the
door. Red and blue light alternated across his face.

Ralph chuckled weakly. "They must be here for someone else in the
building. I swear there's a cop here almost every day. I hardly notice them
any more."

"I don't believe you," Jack said. "You called them, didn't you? You
weren't really on the phone with Pat, you were calling the police."

"No, Jack. I was on the phone with Pat. I'm not lying."

"Then he must have done something!" Jack's calm demeanor was a dam
through which anger could burst at any second. "I'm not stupid!"

"Calm down, Jack, they aren't—" Ralph felt his heart pounding.

"They're going to throw me in jail!" His voice was frantic and fright‐
ened. "Why do you think I should be calm?" Jack's eyes opened wide. There
was no more fear now, only rage. "I'm going to go to jail because of you!"

Ralph's eyes swept the room, his mind's eye penetrating the walls and
seeing the layout of the entire apartment. The window in his bedroom over‐
looked a rusty fire escape, but the window was closed and locked. He could
try to open it, but Jack would reach him before he could get out. The only
other exit was through Jack.

"Do you have anything to say for yourself?" Jack took a step forward.
His voice was as calm as the sea before the breaking of a tsunami. "You've
been a good friend, but perhaps it's time we terminated our friendship." He
took another step forward.

Ralph tried to back away but he only managed to collapse back onto the
couch. He thought he could see a second set of red and blue lights flashing
across the walls. He could feel his clammy palms sticking to the leather
couch.

There was a knock on the door.

"See, they're here to take me away, now." Jack's voice was a low whis‐
per. He took another step forward, moving around the table. "They're going

to throw me in a cell for the rest of my life and it will be all your fault."

If Ralph were standing, he might have had time to run around the other side of the table, to reach the door before Jack could get to him. Sitting, though, he would barely have time to rise before Jack's hands were around his throat.

There was another knock. "Ralph Hamm? This is the police."

"I'm not going to let them take me." Jack closed the distance between them and grabbed Ralph by the shirt, lifting him to his feet.

"What are you doing, Jack!" Ralph shouted as he rose. His legs were unsteady. Were it not for the hand holding him up, he would have collapsed back onto the couch.

"We're breaking down the door!" A solid thud reverberated through the room.

Jack slid around behind Ralph, wrapping his arm around Ralph's neck tightly, squeezing. With his free hand he grabbed Ralph's wrist and held it firmly against his upper back.

Ralph winced in pain, trying to breathe normally against the pressure on his windpipe. Any movement was met with increased pain and reduced air.

There was a second thud.

Ralph could see the hinges of the door push out. He tried to shout but all that came out was a hoarse squeak.

The door slammed into the apartment. Two police officers, guns drawn, stepped through the doorway. They aimed at Jack.

"You're not going to put me in a cell to rot. You're going to lower your weapons slowly and back out of the room."

The officers didn't move. "Release your hostage and put your hands above your head."

Ralph felt the grip on his throat tighten. He gasped for air, but nothing reached his lungs.

The officer who had spoken lowered his weapon and stepped back. The other watched out of the corner of his eye, then followed suit.

Ralph felt the grip on his throat loosen. He gulped for air, relishing the feel of it in his lungs as he never had before.

"He killed his wife!" Ralph shouted, "You've got to—" He gagged as the pressure on his throat returned.

One of the officers pulled a small canister from his pocket. He stepped forward, holding it in front of him.

Ralph heard a hiss. He closed his eyes as the cloud of spray spread toward his face. He coughed and gagged as it seeped into his nostrils and filled his lungs. He could hear Jack behind him similarly afflicted. The pressure on his neck and arm lessened.

Ralph stumbled backward. He felt something, probably the palm of someone's hand, strike his arm and grab hold. His legs failed to keep him upright. There was a momentary pressure against his back as he fell. His head struck something solid.

* * *

Ralph slowly opened his eyes. It took him a few moments to recognize the layout of the unfamiliar room in which he found himself. An IV line ran into his arm, feeding his veins with a clear fluid. The bed beneath him was hard as a rock, but the sheets and pillows were soft enough to make it comfortable.

"Are you back with us, Ralphie?"

Turning his head, he saw that he was not alone in the room. His mother sat in a chair beside him, leaning forward, her eyes wide with concern. Her hair was in disarray, as though she'd just woken up. The only jewelry adorning her body was a necklace with a silver cross.

Behind her, he could see the first hints of sunrise playing above the rooftops and through gaps in the taller skyscrapers.

"Yeah, I'm awake." Ralph tried to sit up. A dull pain throbbed across his temples at the effort, so he lowered himself back down. "What happened? How did I get here?"

"The officers sprayed you with pepper spray. You fell back and hit your head against the window sill. It was a hard blow, knocked you unconscious pretty quick. Looks like you got a decent concussion. They've been pumping you with pain killers and keeping an eye on you through the night."

Ralph remembered the blow. He thought back, remembering the events of the previous evening. "What about Jack? He went crazy. He killed his wife and—" He stopped at the look on his mother's face.

"Ralphie, hun. Jack's dead." She placed her hand on Ralph's arm. Her eyes were full of love and sympathy. "He was behind you when you fell backward. The window was wide open. They say he was in the room and suddenly he was gone, fourteen stories down. He died when he hit the ground. I'm sure he didn't suffer. He's in a better place now."

Ralph felt a surge of relief at the news, then revulsion at his reaction. "I killed him!?"

His mother patted his arm, "No, no, no. It was an accident. It wasn't your fault. It was just his time, I guess. The police told me about what you said he did. They've confirmed that his wife has been missing. They're searching for her body now. They were going to ask you some questions when you woke up."

"But he's dead and it's my fault." Ralph remembered the happy times they had together in college. In hindsight, he could recognize the signs of Jack's budding sociopathy, but he hadn't really been a bad guy. He needed help, he didn't deserve to die.

"God called him home, Ralphie. You couldn't control that."

"He killed his wife in cold blood and had no remorse. He could have killed me, too. Do you really believe there's a place in your heaven for him?"

"He was sick. It wasn't really his fault."

"Whose fault was it? Did God make him that way? Are you saying that this God that you worship would intentionally make a man so twisted that he thought it okay to take a woman's life just because she cheated on him?"

Ralph's mother looked down at him, her eyes filled with love and pity. It was the look she always gave when he spoke something that clashed with her beliefs. "God works in mysterious ways, sometimes. We don't understand His plan, but we have to trust that He has one."

"Why? It doesn't make sense. Why does this have to be part of some grand plan?"

"What if it wasn't? What kind of world would we live in if there were no grand plan?" Ralph's mother reached her hand out to him. "Without God, what meaning would our lives have?"

Ralph closed his eyes. To accept that some God made Jack a sociopath would be to acknowledge that this same God creates evil. It went against everything he had been raised to believe, against everything his mother believed. What was the alternative, then? Does one believe that God is capable of evil or believe that there isn't a God at all, or at least not one that is going to directly intervene in human lives.

"Are you okay? You're sweating." Ralph's mother put a hand on his forehead.

If there's an impartial God judging people, sending them to heaven or hell for their deeds on Earth, would Jack be damned for the murder he did, even though he was created to do it? And what of Ralph? Jack's death may not have been intentional, but Ralph caused it, felt relief in it. He wasn't even sure if the remorse he felt was honest or out of guilt.

Ralph wiped the palms of his hands against the sheets. They left small wet streaks on the fabric.

But what was the more frightening thought, that there was a God judging his actions, or that everything was random? The idea that in a world of seven billion people, each one was part of some huge plan seemed hard to imagine. With so many people, how could one life, one action, have any meaning, at least on a grand scale, at all? How could mental disorder and murder fit into any kind of benevolent plan?

The alarm on the heart monitor by Ralph's bed chimed.

"Ralphie, I think there's something wrong. I'm going to run and fetch the doctor."

Ralph closed his eyes. He could hear his mother's rapid footsteps out the door. He took a deep breath and held it, then exhaled. After a few more, the alarm returned to the steady beep of his regular heart rhythm.

The Fear left him. It was gone for now.

Dappil Goes To Hell

by Jamie Alan Belanger

The Caretaker

Dappil slammed his little fist on the counter, the sound barely making any noise in the expansive room. He had to stand on his toes to do it, because he was the exact height of the counter in this human-run library. Gnomes were admitted here, as were all citizens of Haven, but most avoided the library because they could only reach the first two shelves of books and often required a stool for even that second shelf. The management didn't take kindly to gnomes climbing up the bookcases to reach the upper shelves.

Dappil's eyes barely rose above the edge of the counter, but still he attempted to glare at his new adversary. "Seven?" he screeched, slamming his fist on the counter again. "What do you mean, *seven*?"

The aged caretaker stared at Dappil over the rims of his glasses. He furrowed his bushy white eyebrows and huffed. One of the Caretaker's many jobs was helping people find and read books. Occasionally, he had to go above and beyond the call of duty. This appeared to be one of those days. "I mean there are... seven."

"Seven hells?" Dappil said.

"Yes, seven," the Caretaker said with a sigh. "Which one are you interested in learning about?"

"I—I don't know..." Dappil said, returning to the flats of his feet and pondering the question. He scratched his little chin and shook his head, his ponytail brushing his neck as it swished side to side. "Which do you think is nicest this time of year?"

The Caretaker raised an eyebrow. "Er..." he said. "My guess would be... none of them."

"Lot of help you are!"

"Sir," the Caretaker's assistant said, "please, you are holding up the line."

"Yeah," said the burly man behind him. "Hurry up, you little runt."

"Don't call me names!" Dappil said, shaking his fist at the burly man. "I'm just trying to get some information. You'll see how unhelpful this guy is when it's your turn. For now, just stay quiet and let me think."

The burly man stared down at Dappil and shook his head. "Go to Hell," he said.

Dappil lowered his hands and stared at the man, open-mouthed. "That's what I'm *trying* to do!" he screeched. "Everyone keeps recommending I go there, but nobody will tell me *how*!"

The Caretaker rose from his seat and gestured to his assistant. "Please come with me, little sir," he said. "My assistant can handle the inquiries of the other patrons."

Dappil huffed, thrust a hand into his backpack to ensure all of his things were still there, and followed the Caretaker through stacks of books. The Caretaker walked slowly with an intermittent limp which actually helped Dappil keep pace with the man. As a gnome, the man would have been young, perhaps in his prime. For a human, he was ancient. Dappil guessed the man was pushing triple digits in age, but he had learned long ago not to ask. Or was that one of those rules of society that only pertained to women? Or only to elves? Or only to women elves? All he knew was that Fdiariel hadn't taken too kindly to his inquiry, and since then he decided it was best not to ask.

"Here," the Caretaker said, indicating a small room adjacent to the entrance. "This room contains all the knowledge in the world on the planar realms. Follow me."

The Caretaker led Dappil into the room. Dappil stood in the center and looked around. The room was small, but by gnome standards, it could have been a palace. The ceiling stretched a full six gnomes above him. Thirty gnomes could sleep on the floor; more if they didn't mind being stacked. The room was circular, in a jagged sort of way, with walls that seemed composed of bookshelves. Dappil counted twelve shelves on each of the eight bookcases. Above them was a ceiling built from stained glass, various colors reflecting the light from the midday suns, casting shadows that danced on the walls.

"This room is pretty," Dappil said.

"Thank you," the Caretaker replied. "I designed it myself. It seemed... fitting, in a way. This room has all the books known to exist on the gods, the Void, the Seven Heavens, the Seven Planes, and the Seven Hells."

"I had no idea there was so much to the afterlife," Dappil said.

"Most people don't think about it. They're pretty busy with their current lives."

"Like that guy in line behind me," Dappil said. "What an impatient jerk."

"Indeed," the Caretaker said. "I suggest you start with this book." He reached up and pulled down a massive volume, grunting with the effort. He slammed the giant book on a nearby table and pulled the chair out.

Dappil hopped up, standing on the chair, and leaned forward to look at the book. The cover binding was elaborate. The predominant color was the black, tanned skin that bound the book together. But on top of that was an intertwining maelstrom of melted colored wax. "It's beautiful!" Dappil said. "It looks like someone ate an entire box of candles and vomited them up."

The Caretaker shook his head. "I can't imagine—"

"Is the whole inside done like this too?"

Dappil opened the book and frowned. "Oh no," he said. "Oh dear, oh dear."

"What is it?"

"Words!"

"That is what one normally finds inside of books."

"I can't read *these* ones. What language is this? Do you have any books with pictures?"

The Caretaker sighed. "A Traveler's Guide to the Realms of the Gods," he read, then turned the page. "Part One: The Void."

"What's that?"

"Intrepid travelers who wish to journey into the forbidden realms will first venture into a vast nothingness, a contradiction of existence—"

"I don't need to know about this," Dappil said. "Skip to the Seven Hells, that's where I'm trying to go."

The Caretaker turned pages. "Seven Heavens... Seven Planes..." He continued turning pages until he was almost at the book's end. "Ah, here we go, 'The Seven Hells,'" he read. "'Simply put, those wishing to see these places should *not*. Mortal eyes cannot comprehend the extent of these realms. The Seven Hells are barren landscapes ripe with hatred and suffering.'"

"That doesn't sound very nice," Dappil said. "Why would people keep telling me to go there?"

"'The Seven Hells,'" the Caretaker read, raising his voice, "'are where the wicked go to be punished. For all eternity, their souls suffer and lament the state of their existence. Traveling to the Seven Hells is not advised. However, should people wish to ignore these words—'"

"Yes, yes," Dappil said, stomping his feet on the chair. "Ignore his words. What are the Seven Hells like? Maybe there's a good one that people are thinking about when they keep telling me to go."

"'The Plane of Disease,'" the Caretaker read.

"Oh no," Dappil said. "Not that one. Doesn't sound like fun at all. I had this infection once—"

"'Plane of Fear—'" the Caretaker read, raising his voice to drown out Dappil as much as possible.

"No thank you!"

"'Plane of Lust—'"

"No. Eh," Dappil looked at the picture under the words. "Ye—no, no, I really shouldn't."

The Caretaker turned the page. "'Plane of—'"

Before he could even get the word out, Dappil looked at the picture and his eyes grew wide. "No way, notachance, next one! Next! Turn the page, please!"

The Caretaker shrugged and turned the page. "'Plane—'"

"Nooooo!" Dappil screamed, hiding from the picture by sticking his head under the table. He sobbed, wishing the image could be removed from his mind. "Nonononono!"

The Caretaker turned the page. "I'm sorry," he said. "I should have warned you about *that* one. There are some things that mortal eyes just cannot unsee. Ah, here's one that doesn't sound so bad. 'The Plane of War.'"

"Plane of War?" Dappil said, removing his head from under the table. He looked at the picture and shrugged. "Why would anyone want to live in a perpetual war?"

"Well, it certainly seems nice after the last two hells," the Caretaker said.

Dappil pondered this. "Yes, I suppose you are right. That is the best one so far. Why don't we bookmark that one and come back later."

"There's only one left," the Caretaker said.

"I said bookmark it," Dappil said, pressing his fists into his hips.

"Fine," the Caretaker said. He reached into the folds of his robes and retrieved a small slip of paper. He placed that in the binding and turned a few pages. "Ah, the final hell. 'The Wicked Streets.'"

"Interesting..." Dappil said. He looked at the picture. "Those streets don't *look* that wicked. Look here," he said, pointing at a man in the foreground of the charcoal drawing, "that man is handing the other one a bag of money."

"No, I believe he just *stole* it from him," the Caretaker said.

"Huh. I suppose you're right. The other man *is* facing the other way. Sort of hard to see the detail in this drawing. Still, it looks like just about any street in Haven. What do the words say?"

The Caretaker cleared his throat and read. "'The Wicked Streets are a perverted version of the City of Judgment, where followers of Emirokol—the god of retribution and trickery—spend all eternity robbing and murdering each other and anyone foolish enough to—'"

"That sounds *just* like Haven!" Dappil said. He slapped his little hand on the page. "That's the one everyone must want me to go see. *That's* the hell I'm going to!"

The Caretaker sighed. "Very well."

"So how do I get there?"

"The book does not say *how* to travel to these places, just what is there."

"But how—"

"Please," the Caretaker said, raising a hand in front of Dappil's face. "I am just a librarian. Your best chance to travel there is to talk to a wizard."

Dappil wrapped his arms as far around the Caretaker as he could reach. "Thanks a lot, mister. I know a wizard who can help me, I'm sure of it."

Dappil jumped off the chair and walked out of the room with a bounce in his step. He whistled and skipped as he left the library. On the way, he bumped into the burly man after turning a corner too quickly.

"Hey," the burly man said.

"Hi!" Dappil replied. "I'm Dappil! You remember when you told me to go to Hell?"

The burly man furrowed his brows. "Er... yes..."

"Well, I'm *finally* on my way. Wish me luck!" Dappil resumed whistling and walked—more slowly this time—out of the Great Library.

The Wizard

On the streets of Haven, Dappil glanced at street signs, trying to gain his bearings. Most of them had only words. He had to cross a few of the cobble-stone streets before he found one with pictures, but using that picture and a nearby tavern sign (for one of those places that refused to serve little folk), he was able to orient himself. Moving north through the streets, he whistled a happy tune. He was finally going to Hell. Dappil was eager to see what all the fuss was about. Humans on the street scowled at him.

"Ain't you in the wrong section of town?" one man said.

Dappil stopped and looked toward his destination. "No," he said, "I don't think so. The magic school is right over there, isn't it?"

The man frowned. "Well... yes, it is," he was forced to admit.

"Good, then I'm definitely in the right section of town. But thanks so much for helping me make sure!"

The man scratched his head and mumbled something Dappil couldn't hear. Dappil shrugged and continued walking and whistling. A horse thundered by, shaking the stones on the street, and Dappil was forced to move more carefully.

When he reached the end of the street, he could see the magic school ahead of him. It was a small building, one built just to house the neophytes who were in Haven preparing for one of their many tests. The building was supposedly filled with beds and books and desks that the students used while studying magic. Dappil had met a student wizard here a while back, and was hoping that she could tell him how to get to Hell. The steps were too tall and he was forced to use all four limbs to climb up. He reached the top and knocked on the door. He waited, but there was no response. He leaned back and could see a door knocker positioned a full half-gnome above his reach.

"Well that's just great!" he said after a few jumps that fell short. He pounded his fists on the massive door and yelled. "Hello!" he shouted. "Hell-llooooooo!"

Finally, as one sun was setting and the other started to rise, the door opened. Dappil had long since given up and was sitting on the top step, staring at the people in the streets. He heard the door open and jumped to his feet. "Finally!" he said. "Do you have any idea how long I've been sitting here? It's been all day, well all Solday anyway. Now it's Elday and I'm starting to get hungry. Do you have anything to eat?"

The young human man standing in the doorway blinked a few times and shook his head. "I'm sorry, who are you?"

"Oh dear, oh dear, where are my manners?" Dappil composed himself, thrust his hand out before him, and ran at the young man. "Hi!" he screamed enthusiastically. "I'm Dappil!"

The young man stumbled back a step, then slowly reached out and grasped Dappil's hand. "I... I'm Tomas," he said.

Dappil vigorously shook Tomas' hand up and down. "So pleased to meet you!"

"Is—is there something I can help you with? You don't look like a student."

"I'm here to see Nariah," Dappil said.

"She's studying. Come in," Tomas said, backing up.

Dappil walked into the lobby. He looked around but the inside of the building wasn't nearly as impressive as the outside, and the outside wasn't that impressive to begin with. The interior looked like any of a number of inns he had seen. Small lobby, sparse with furniture and no decorations. The only thing remarkable about the interior of the building was that it was very well-lit. "I like the... lighting," Dappil said, feeling suddenly awkward.

"Thanks?" Tomas said. "Please wait here, I'll see if I can fetch Nariah."

Tomas walked through a doorway and into another section. Dappil watched him walk down a hallway and turn into a side room. From what he could see, the hallway was just as drab as the lobby. He whistled a little, but noticed that no sound echoed in this lobby, which was very disappointing. The acoustics should have been better, but he supposed wizards didn't whistle very much. They always seemed so nervous.

From down the hallway, he heard a familiar yet muffled voice say, "Oh, no!" There was a growing sound of rustling robes and then Nariah walked into the hallway. She was wearing a purple robe today, one that Dappil had never seen before. Her orange-golden hair was tied up in a bun. For an elf, she was beautiful. By gnomish standards, she would never be married. But Dappil found he liked her just the same.

"Hello, Nariah!" Dappil called, waving to her.

"Hello, Dappil," she replied. "I'm trying to study... what do you need this time?"

"I'm trying to go to Hell," he said.

She stopped, still standing in the hallway. She stared at him, then leaned against the wall with one hand. "Excuse me?"

"Hell," Dappil said, trying his best to speak slowly. "I want to go to Hell."

Nariah dug in her ears with her fingers. "I'm sorry, I believe I misheard you."

"Hell," Dappil repeated. "Everyone keeps telling me to go to Hell, and I really do want to see what all the fuss is about. So I'd like to go."

"Why are you telling me this?"

"You're a wizard, aren't you?" Dappil said.

"Well, yes, sort of..."

"I'd ask your sister, Fdiariel, but she's so far away. Besides, she's not a wizard like you, and the Caretaker said I needed a wizard. Can you send me to Hell?"

"No, I can't, and you probably don't want to go either."

"I'm sure I want to go," Dappil said. "I'm tired of people suggesting it. I think it's time I did some traveling. Please send me to Hell."

"I don't have that kind of power, Dappil! I'm just a student."

"Is there someone here who can? Please, I really want to go."

Nariah rolled her eyes and slapped her forehead. "Oh fine, whatever will make you go away and let me return to my studying."

Tomas was standing behind her. Dappil saw his eyes grow wide. "You can't be serious!"

Nariah turned on him and whispered something. Tomas looked at Dappil and shrugged. She said something else and he said, "Fine," and walked past Dappil and left the building.

"Come, Dappil," Nariah said. She took his little hand and led him down the hallway. At the end, they walked up a set of stairs. Dappil was pleased to see that the interior stairs were more gnome-friendly than the ones outside. He wondered if they ever had gnome students, and if so, how did they get into the building? Was that the first test of their magical abilities? He thought of asking Nariah, but something seemed to be agitating her. She got like this, at times, and he found when she was in one of these moods, it was usually better for him to leave her alone. She pulled him along a new hallway that was just as nondescript as the one downstairs. One more flight of stairs and they were on the top floor, which had a short hallway that ended in a single door. Nariah knocked on the door three times.

"Come," said a male voice from inside.

"Say nothing until I've introduced you," Nariah said. "*Nothing.*"

Dappil nodded. It was not wise to upset a wizard, and if he was about to meet Nariah's master and teacher, then he was going to be a very powerful wizard indeed. Nariah opened the door and led Dappil inside. He let himself be led as he searched through his entire wealth of knowledge for anything that would mark him as a civilized, respectful citizen. Today, he would be on his absolute best behavior.

The room was huge, and not very well decorated. One entire wall was devoted to benches and beakers and vials that bubbled with colorful liquids. Another wall was filled with enormous tomes, all with the same blue velvet binding and a silver icon and lettering on each. There was a desk against the far wall, and a man seated before it wearing a velvet blue robe.

"Master," Nariah said, bowing deep. "This is Dappil. He wishes to travel."

"Oh?" came the response. The man dipped a quill into an inkwell and scribbled some words on a paper. "I believe I will have time later today, once I finish this scroll work. Where does the little gnome wish to go?"

"How did you—" Dappil said, then clapped a hand over his mouth.

The man chuckled. "I am Kalor of the Spire. I see much that is hidden, gnome. Where is it you wish to go?"

"Hell," Dappil responded in his usual cheery voice.

Kalor's hand stopped, poised above the inkwell. He turned his head to the wall and Dappil could see one of his eyes. It was opened wide, staring, and was a dark gray color he hadn't seen before. "Excuse me?"

"Dappil wishes to go to Hell, Master," Nariah said.

Kalor dropped the quill into the inkwell, turned all the way around in his chair, placed both hands on his knees, and leaned forward. "You may return to your studies," he said, his eyes focused on Dappil.

Nariah released Dappil's hand, bowed to her master, and exited, closing the door softly behind her. Kalor continued staring at Dappil. The moment the door closed, he leaned back in his chair. "Which one?" he asked, casually.

"The Wicked Streets!" Dappil said. "That one sounded the most interesting. Some of the others just sounded awful."

"They are *all* awful," Kalor said. "Why would you want to go to *any* of them?"

"Everyone keeps suggesting I go to Hell, so I did some research and the only one that sounded like it would be the right Hell to go to was The Wicked Streets. I do *so* want to go," Dappil said.

Kalor raised an eyebrow and chuckled. "I do not think that is what they meant," he said.

Dappil wagged a finger at the master wizard. "Don't you start talking like that. I've spent a lot of time researching this and I'm absolutely sure I want to go. Can you send me or not?"

Kalor shrugged. "I cannot send you to Hell. I can *take* you there, but we will be linked. You will have a short time to explore. Spend any longer and I will be forced to abandon you there, forever."

"How long?" Dappil asked.

"Minutes," Kalor said. "But, believe me, it will feel like *days*."

"Sounds like fun," Dappil said. He patted his small pouches and smiled. "I'm packed and ready. When can we go?"

Kalor stood slowly. Dappil wasn't sure if the creaking and cracking was from his bones or his chair. "Why so eager?"

"People have been telling me to go to Hell for years, and now I'm finally going to get there. I'm so excited!" Dappil considered rushing forward to hug Kalor, but decided against it. "Can you imagine how wonderful it is to finally get a chance to do something people have been suggesting for such a long time? It's such a wonderful opportunity. I thought it was great when I finally figured out *which* Hell they wanted me to see. I didn't even know there were *seven* of them. But now I guess it makes sense."

"Indeed," Kalor said. "One for each of the gods. I should finish this scroll first—"

"Can we go now? Really, it's wonderful that you're taking me, but I'm so excited I don't think I could wait another minute."

"There is one more thing I need to—"

"Please? Please, can we go?"

Kalor grumbled. "First, there is the matter of payment."

"Payment? Oh, yes, of course. I was expecting that. How much does a trip to Hell cost these days?"

"I require two strands of wire, one silver, one gold. And a flawless pearl the size of... well, the size of your fist."

Dappil clenched one fist and looked at it from every angle. "Oh my, that is quite a large pearl. Where could I possibly find something like that?"

"I... I do have one left, but it is a very valuable item. It would cost almost nine thousand gold coins to replace it."

Dappil's eyes grew wide. "Nine *thousand*?"

"Yes," said Kalor, "and there's also a fee for the power expenditure and my time, which comes to an additional one thousand gold."

Dappil opened his pouches one at a time and rummaged through them. "Oh dear," he said. "I could possibly come up with ten gold coins, but not ten *thousand*. What about this gem? Could you use this instead?" Dappil held up a small blue gem the size of a marble.

Kalor glanced at the gem and was about to wave his hand dismissively when he stopped. He stepped forward and seized the gem. Turning it over and over in his hands, he gasped.

"I know, it's very small, but it is quite pretty," Dappil said.

"Where did you get this?" Kalor demanded. "Where in the world did you come across a Cerian Wish Gem?"

"A what?" Dappil said, scratching his little head. "I found it when I was visiting my friend Fdiariel down at the Spire of Sorcery. Funny story, she's Nariah's sister. Although I really don't see the resemblance. Maybe you have to be an elf to see that—"

"You *stole* this from an enchantress at the Spire?!"

"Stole? What? No, me?" Dappil waved his hands in front of him. "She dropped it and I found it. I was going to return it, but then she was busy and I... well, I just sort of wandered off. Found myself in a weird dusty old room with no doors or windows—that was a strange trip—then when I made it back to her, and she was still busy. I've been meaning to get back there to re-turn it, but things have just been so hectic."

Kalor lowered the gem and looked at Dappil. "I—*I* will return it for you, if you like."

"You will?" Dappil said. "Oh, thank you so much, that really would be lovely. Now I just need to figure out how to pay for the—"

"Don't worry about the cost of the pearl," Kalor said, carefully placing the small blue gem into a velvet-lined box on his desk. He closed the lid and waved a hand over the top of the box, which glowed with an eerie red aura. "I will gladly take you to Hell, for free."

Dappil ran forward and wrapped his arms around Kalor's legs. "Oh, thank you thank youthankyou!" he said. "You really are a very nice wizard to do that for me. Oh boy, I can't wait. I'm finally going to get to see Hell!"

Kalor untangled his legs and pushed Dappil away. "All right, fine, just stop hugging me."

"Huh? Oh, sorry," Dappil said.

Kalor retrieved a staff that was leaning against the wall by his desk and moved to the room's center. He reached down and retrieved a pinch of sand from the floor. Waving his hand and the staff before him, he mumbled an incantation and released the sand. In the air, the pinch multiplied, raining a few pounds of fine sand on the stone floor. Kalor held his palm out over the pile of sand and it stretched out into a fine, thin layer. He grasped his staff in both hands and drew a circle in the sand.

"Stand in the circle with me," he said. "And do not leave the circle until I say so, no matter what happens. Stand still, and be quiet."

Dappil did as he was told, standing beside Kalor inside the circle. Kalor raised both hands and the staff stood before him on its own. He spoke strange words in a voice that grew in volume until the stones of the building shook. A large pearl extracted itself from a coffer on the bookcases and flew to his left hand. From the desks against the right wall, two small threads looped through the air to his waiting hand. Kalor continued chanting, and as Dappil watched, the pearl crumbled to dust. He gasped, but said nothing. Then, suddenly, the whole room was gone.

The Void

Dappil looked around, but there was nothing to see. He was standing on nothing, surrounded by nothing, with nothing above him and nothing to his sides. Kalor stood beside him. Between them, Kalor's staff hung in the void. Kalor opened his eyes and handed the silver strand to Dappil.

"Take this," he said, "and do not lose it. This is your way back home."

Dappil took the strand and looked at it. "How does this get me back home?"

Kalor pushed Dappil, sending the little gnome flying through the void. Dappil screamed, then giggled. It was a strange sensation, twisting and tumbling end over end. The only thing to give him a sense of distance or location was seeing Kalor grow smaller with each revolution. He had no fear, no way to stop, and he wasn't accelerating or decelerating. It felt like the times he'd leapt out of trees or off buildings, but without a ground rushing toward him and no fear of impact or pain.

"Pull the string!" Kalor shouted.

Dappil pulled on the string with both hands, stretching it as far as he could. "I don't see—" he said, then realized he was once more standing beside Kalor. "Oh!" he said. "That is interesting."

"Watch the strand," Kalor said. "It will get shorter with time. If it disappears, you will be stuck here, forever. If you lose it, you will be unable to ever leave. When it has shortened so far that you can barely grip it with both hands, then pull, and you will return to me. Then we leave this place using this golden strand." He opened his hand to show the golden strand. "This is our way home."

Dappil nodded and looked around. "These don't look like streets," he said. "There's nothing wicked about this place at all."

"This is The Void," Kalor said. "It is a nexus, of sorts, a place where all the realms of the gods link together."

"This isn't at all where I wanted to go," Dappil said. "What are you trying to pull here?"

"Be silent, and listen," Kalor said. "You can reach any of the planes from this place. The Void is nothing, and everything, at the same time. It is the ultimate expression of paradox, an endless expanse of nothing that—at the same time—contains everything else. No god lives here, yet *all* gods live here." He waved his staff in the air and spoke strange words again. "Here is your portal. Remember the silver strand. Check it often."

Dappil turned and saw a glowing portal floating in the nothingness before him. It bounced in a slow rhythm, up and down and side to side, growing and shrinking with a steady pace. He peered inside, seeing streets. They still didn't look very wicked, but they were definitely streets. "All right," he said, not quite convinced. The streets looked deserted. There was no sound and no scent that he could detect. "I'll be back," he said.

Dappil stepped into the portal with one leg. Feeling solid ground on the other side, he leaned into the portal and brought his other leg in. Everything seemed to swirl around him, pulling him in several directions at once. He gripped the silver strand tighter, not wanting to let go of it. But at some point, he felt it fall from his grasp. He was falling, twisting and turning, tumbling end over end, for a very long time. Then he slammed into the cobblestone streets and felt pain surging through his body like he'd never felt before.

The Wicked Streets

When he realized that the pain had stopped, he rolled over and looked at the sky, which was a shade of red he hadn't seen before. Somewhere between red and pink, the sky pulsed with occasional sparks of heat lightning. Dappil sat and looked around the street, which looked like any major city he had visited. It most resembled Haven, given the way the cobblestones fit and the look of the buildings. There were signs here, too, but he still couldn't read them, and they had no pictures like they did in Haven. Stores along the sides of the street all appeared to be closed. Dappil pushed himself to his feet and started walking. He found he had a slight limp and a shooting pain in his right hip whenever he stepped. So he made a hopping game out of walking down the street, which set him to giggling. A scream echoed down the streets, silencing him. He paused and listened to see if there would be more, but the only sound he detected was his own breathing.

Dappil set off once more, hopping and giggling, and once more a tortured scream filled the air around him. This time, Dappil stopped and looked around, peering into store windows and down alleys. "Hello!" he called out. "Is someone there?"

Something hissed behind him. Dappil turned around and smiled. Before him stood a creature, which he felt was an appropriate word, for it was no ordinary thing that he saw. This creature stood taller than a human, and was as plump as a well-fed barmaid he once insulted unintentionally. The creature dripped with ooze from orifices in both heads, and had three large arms that ended in claws. It had orange and green patches of skin that appeared to be covered in translucent scales. When it talked with one head, it hissed with the other, alternating every few words.

"What is that infernal racket?" it hissed.

Since the creature had two heads, Dappil was having trouble figuring out if it was talking to him. He looked around twice but the streets appeared to be empty. "Who, me?" he said. "Hi! I'm Dappil!" He thrust his hand out to the creature.

The creature recoiled from the proffered hand and hissed. "We care not what its name is, just that it remains silent!"

Dappil retracted his hand with a sniff. "Well, now, that's rather rude. I'm just trying to be friendly."

"Bah!" one of the creature's heads shouted. "There is nothing friendly on these streets," said the other head.

"Oh, right," Dappil said. "The Wicked Streets, was it?" He looked around and shrugged. "Doesn't look that wicked to me. I was once stuck in Kerendas for six days, now *those* were some wicked streets. All sorts of mean people, and I'm not talking about the thieves and murderers. They were actually kind of nice, when I think about it. It's the shop-keepers who were wicked! Everywhere I went it was always 'We don't serve gnomes,' and 'Get out of here, you runt,' and 'Go to Hell.' Well now, here I am, finally in Hell. Quite frankly I don't see what all the fuss was about—"

The creature screamed, which shook the ground and rattled the windows. Dappil clapped his hands over his ears and waited until the sound subsided.

"Quiet!" both heads hissed. "Silence," one head said. "Or be silenced," added the other.

Dappil removed his hands and wagged a finger at the creature. "Now, you listen to me. I lost my little stringy thingy, or I would just leave here right now. This place is absolutely dreadful! And I don't mean it's like torture or maiming or anything. This place is positively *boring*. I thought Hell was supposed to be interesting. Why else would so many people tell me to come here? So far all I've seen is you, and—let's face it—you are really not that nice."

The creature howled and picked up Dappil with two of its arms. It used the third arm to cover his mouth. Dappil squirmed but all he could do was slide away from the third arm over and over again. "Silence," the creature said, "or you will summon the—"

The creature stopped and all four of its eyes grew wide. It dropped Dappil onto the stone street and ran into an alley. "They come! They come!" it howled.

"How rude!" Dappil said. He stood and tried to brush the ooze off his shirt, but it just spread around. "Oh, that's just great. I had this cleaned a week ago."

A new sound emerged from the alleyways, a scraping that grew louder from every direction. Dappil whirled, over and over again, eager to see what was coming. He stood in the center of the street, and had a good angle, regardless of which direction the owner of this new sound would arrive from. The sound grew louder and soon was accompanied by a stench that made Dappil's eyes water. He pinched his nose. "Oh, dear gods," he said, coughing. "Now *that* is certainly more like it. Finally, something wicked about these streets."

The owner of the scraping sound emerged from the alley in front of him, but the scraping continued, and another emerged to his right. Dappil turned and saw more creatures filtering out of the alleys into the streets. Each of the new creatures was identical, standing about as tall as an elf, but twice as wide, and with huge fangs that protruded from their shoulders. These strange creatures all held weapons of various types—swords, axes, morning stars, and flails. When they stopped pouring out of the alleys, Dappil counted three dozen creatures in all, half on each side of the street.

"Mordrekan," one of the new creatures said.

"Taelian. The time has come to finish this," Mordrekan said from the other side of the street. "My might will prevail!"

Dappil continued to clench his nose with one hand and held out the other to the newcomers. "Hi!" he yelled as best he could. He wanted to be heard, but found it hard to speak around his hand. "I'm Dappil! Have any of you seen my—"

"Your army is weak, Mordrekan. Let us end this," Taelian said.

On both sides of the street, the creatures raised their weapons and charged. Dappil, still standing in the middle of the street, ducked and curled into a little ball. One of the creatures tripped over him and screeched as it was impaled on an enemy's sword. Dappil watched the battle through his fingers, still clenching his nose since the stench had grown so powerful that he could smell it even with his nostrils closed. He gagged and watched as the creatures fought. Heads, arms, and legs flew in various directions. Skulls were bashed in. The street flowed with their stinky blue blood, filling the cracks between the cobblestones. Dappil attempted to crawl away, but bumped into one of the creatures, which was knocked off balance. The creature named Taelian fell forward with arms flailing, swinging its weapon as it fell to the pavement. On the way down, its sword cut one of the other creatures. Dappil whimpered and waited until the battle was over, and then rose. He looked around and counted the bodies. All were dead, except for Taelian, who was rising and surveying the remnants of the battle.

"Victory!" Taelian shouted. "At long last, the streets are mine!" Taelian stomped over the corpses and walked the way Dappil had come, laughing and raising his weapon in the air, shouting about his might and his victory over Mordrekan.

Dappil removed his hand from his nose, gagged, and replaced it. The stench was even worse now that the creatures were dead. He moved down the street, putting as much distance between himself and the battlefield as possible. Further up the street, the city looked the same as the area where he had first arrived. Closed stores, empty alleyways. One store he came to had a smashed front window, and it appeared as if the place had been looted. Dappil looked around the store but there was nothing left. It was once a blacksmith's storefront, judging by the layout. He had been hoping to at least find a Hell weapon to keep as a souvenir, but it appeared those hopes were dashed. There were plenty of weapons just laying around on the street behind him, but he had no desire to return to the presence of that stench.

"Hold it right there," said a female voice from behind him as he stepped out of the store.

Dappil turned and smiled. "Hi!" he yelled at the dwarf woman. "I'm Dappil! Say, that's a mighty nice beard you have there. Really brings out the color in your eyes."

She frowned and huffed. "Be quiet, you," she said, then reached up and scratched her beard. "Does it?"

"Oh yes," Dappil said, nodding vigorously. "Say, have you seen any wicked streets around here? I've been trying to find them, and I really don't think I have."

"Wicked... streets?" she asked. She lowered a dagger that Dappil hadn't even seen and scratched her beard again. "I kina thought we were *in* tha place."

"No," Dappil said. "Oh, no, we can't be. The only thing wicked about *this* place is the smell back there."

She looked at him and sniffed the air. "Ugh," she said. "Smells like Mordrekan and 'is ilk."

"Yes, I believe that is what he said his name was."

"Oh?" she said. "Introduced 'imself, did 'e?"

"Not quite," Dappil said. "Technically, he ignored me, and threatened someone on the other side of the street. Then they fought and most of them died, except that Taelian guy. He wandered off."

"What?"

"They fought—"

"—and Taelian lived?"

"Yes. It's a big, stinking mess back there. Someone really should clean it up. I thought Taelian would, but he seemed intent on walking away from it all. Say, have you seen a small silver string about this big?" he asked, holding his hands apart.

She huffed. "Well now... Taelian lived... ain't that curious."

"What do you mean?" Dappil asked.

"Normally, none o' them lives. They fight, all die, then are reborn to fight again. But Taelian lived, you say?"

Dappil nodded. "Yup."

"Curious," she said. She glanced around and resumed scratching her beard. "So's this."

"Oh?" Dappil said. "Why is this curious?"

"On a normal day, I rob someone. Sometimes I kill 'em, sometimes they kill me. Never stood around *talkin'* before."

"Would you prefer taking a walk?" Dappil asked. "I was looking for a wicked street, maybe we can find one together. And if you see my silver string, please point it out. It must be around here somewhere."

She pondered this, shrugged, and sheathed her dagger. "A'right," she said.

Dappil took her hand and together they walked down the street. Dappil told his new friend stories about his time in various cities around Palamar, and she listened, and chuckled at all the funny parts, and sniffled at all the sad parts. Whenever Dappil asked about her life, she ignored him and stared at the sky or the stone. So Dappil continued talking, until a thought occurred to him and he stopped. "Wait," he said. "I never did catch your name."

"Name?"

"Yes, your name," Dappil said. "I'm Dappil. What's your name?"

She released his hand and placed one of her hands on her forehead and the other inside her beard. She cried a little, then pouted, and finally released her head and shrugged. "I—I don' know. I canna remember. Did I have a name?"

"Everyone has a name," Dappil said.

"I canna remember mine," she said, looking very sad.

Dappil stared at her and frowned. "Hmmm... I can give you one, if you'd like."

She shrugged.

"You remind me a little of an old friend. Friend of a friend, really. Okay, I barely knew her, but she had pretty eyes like you. So until you can remember your *real* name, I'll call you Dora."

Dora smiled and nodded. "A'right," she said.

Dappil took her hand and together they continued down the street. He had to teach her how to skip several times before she got the hang of it. She started laughing and hugged him several times. Together, they skipped over enough distance for three gnomish towns, when suddenly Dappil stopped.

"Hold up," he said, looking very serious.

"What is it?" Dora asked.

Dappil knelt and touched the cobblestones. He sniffed the air and looked around. "There," he said, pointing at the stones a few feet in front of them.

"What?" Dora asked.

"It's a trap," Dappil said. "That loose stone is a pressure plate. Step on it, and the rope looped around it will grab your foot and swing you—" he stood and pointed down the alley to their right "—down there."

"Ack!" screamed a very frustrated creature in the alley. It stormed out and roared at Dappil. It wasn't much taller than him, but it looked a lot less friendly. Rows of teeth glistened in its gaping maw as it panted and drooled on the street. "You ruin Gerson's trap!" it screamed.

"Oh, calm down," Dappil said.

"He saved me," Dora said. "I would have stepped on that for sure."

Gerson stomped and howled. "You ruin! You ruin!"

"I'm... Dappil..." Dappil said, tentatively, holding out his little hand.

Gerson ignored him and stomped the ground again. "You ruin!" it said again.

"Yes, yes, I know and I'm sorry," Dappil said.

Gerson stopped and stared at him. "Sorry? Sorry..." it said, scratching its chin. It looked around and peered at him. "What is 'sorry?'"

"It was an... accident," Dappil said.

Gerson looked at Dora, who shrugged. "Me catch dinner here, ever day. Me set trap, me catch dinner, me eat. Now you ruin. Now me no eat!"

"That's another thing awfully strange about today," Dora said.

"Gerson," Dappil said. "Is it this time that you normally catch dinner and eat?"

Gerson thought and patted its midsection. "Me hungry. Time me to eat."

"Oh dear," Dappil said. "You aren't... I mean, you don't... not us?"

Gerson waved its hand before him. "Me no eat you," it said. "You no dead. Me set trap. Something trigger. Something die. Then me eat. Now, me *no* eat."

"Have you ever not eaten for a day?" Dora asked.

"No," Gerson said. "Me eat ever day."

"Strange," Dappil said.

"Very strange," Dora agreed.

"What me do now?" Gerson asked, and looked as if it were about to cry.

"Come with us," Dappil said. "One of these stores has to be open. I'm sure we can find something for you to eat. Or at least maybe we can find out who's in charge around here. I'm still trying to find The Wicked Streets. Have you seen them? Oh, and I had this silvery string. Have you seen that?"

Gerson looked at Dappil and shook its hands. "Me no see," it said.

"Well, come along," he said. Dappil took Dora's hand in one of his, and tried to take one of Gerson's hands but Gerson didn't understand and swatted him away. Dappil and Dora took off down the street, skipping and singing a little tune. Gerson followed behind at what it considered to be a safe distance from the strange pair.

Emirokol

At the end of the street, a dense fog lingered, pouring out of the alleys on both sides. As they watched, discussing what to do, the fog lifted, revealing a massive obsidian fortress that stretched as far as they could see, into the red lightning sky. Dappil leaned back and tried to see the top, but it was too far. "Fascinating!" he said. "Let's go see if there's anyone inside."

Dora gripped his hand tight as he led her to the entrance. Behind them, Gerson continued following them. Dappil led the way to what appeared to be the entrance. Dozens of black steps stretched all the way up, and Dappil started the long climb. The steps were shiny like black glass, and very smooth, but he found that his shoes gripped them well enough. At least they were more gnome-friendly than the steps at the wizard school in Haven. Dora slipped at one point, but holding onto Dappil's hand helped her regain her balance. Onward and upward they continued until they were very tired and had to take a break. Dappil looked down at the city, then turned and looked up at the fortress.

"Oh dear," he said. "We aren't even half way there!"

"I am ready to continue," Dora said, rising from her seat on the step.

Dappil glanced down at Gerson, who lingered half a dozen steps behind them. "Come on, Gerson, try to keep up."

Gerson hissed, but was otherwise silent.

Dappil and Dora continued up the steps, huffing and puffing all the way to the top. They stopped there, standing at the base of a giant pair of doors. Dappil pounded on the door. "Hello!" he called out. "Hello?"

The doors opened, slowly, creaking with the effort. When they finished opening, lights flared inside, illuminating a massive hall that stretched into the building. Deep inside, they could see a giant humanoid sitting in a chair on a raised dais. Dappil held his hand out and ran down the hallway, his little footsteps barely making a sound in the massive chamber. "Hi!" he screamed at the top of his lungs. "I'm Dappil!" He found that running was altering his voice in a very humorous manner. He stopped at the edge of the dais and giggled. He watched the figure as it stared down at him. Each eye was bigger than his entire body, and shone like black ice, reflecting the hall. The giant was clad in a suit of obsidian plate mail that glowed orange-red, as if the body inside were on fire. Dappil lowered his hand when he realized there was no way the gigantic creature could possibly shake his hand. "You're huge!" Dappil said.

The giant sighed. "You have ruined everything you've found here," it said in a booming voice.

"What? Me?" Dappil said. He glanced around and saw Dora and Gerson behind him, cowering from the massive creature. Dora was on her knees and weeping. Gerson saw this and it, too, fell to its knees. "What ever are you two doing?"

The giant stood. It took a step forward, and when its foot was about to crush Dappil, it shrunk to a human-sized foot, planting onto the floor. Dappil looked up from the foot and saw that the giant's entire body had shrunk to the same scale. It was now the size of a typical human, and not nearly as intimidating. "They are paying fealty to a god, and you would be wise to do the same." His size had shrunk, but his voice had not; it echoed around the chamber the same way.

Dappil looked at the man and his eyes grew wide. He smiled and thrust his hand out. "I'm Dappil!" he shouted. He was excited, for now that this person was a man and not a giant, he could properly introduce himself.

The man scowled at him. "I am Emirokol, god of retribution and trickery. Deceiver of armies, scourge of goodness and light. You will bow, mortal."

Dappil retracted his hand, frowned, and bowed. "Okay, I'll bow, but I really don't underst—oh, wait, I get it! Wow, are you really a god? I've never met a god before. This is suddenly more exciting. And here I was beginning to think this entire place was terribly boring. By the way, have you seen The Wicked Streets? I've been looking for them."

"You are in The Wicked Streets. This is my domain."

Dora started sobbing, rocking back and forth and mumbling something Dappil couldn't understand.

"Really?" Dappil said. He placed his fists on his hips. "You can't be serious. It's really not that wicked."

"You have ruined everything you have touched here," Emirokol boomed.

"What do you mean?"

"The Stoorlach you first met is a fearsome creature that hides in the shadows, slinks in silence, and stalks its prey at all hours. You offended him with your incessant babbling. Now he is not stalking his prey; he is hiding in silence and weeping."

"Oh, come now. Incessant? Surely you must be joking," Dappil said. "There's nothing at all incessant about me. I'm not like other gnomes! Really, I'm not. By the way, have you seen—"

"Enough!" Emirokol said. "Next you foiled a perfect battle of vengeance in my streets."

"What? A battle? Do you mean those smelly guys? Seriously, that stench was the only thing wicked about these streets."

"Their battle is eternal. Always they fight, and always they die, never to know which army or which general is greater. Your intervention resulted in a victory for Taelian. Now they are all being tortured in the understreets. The covenant has been broken. It will take a thousand years to purge the memory of victory from their souls."

"It can't be all that bad," Dappil said.

"Next you met a cunning thief who is supposed to spend all eternity killing and being killed. Every day her destiny changes, but always she robs the same person, and one of them survives. Today, they both survived, and Jerudian the thief is broken. She has song in her heart, a dance in her step."

"Who, Dora?"

"Jerudian must be rebroken now. Another four thousand years in the torture chambers should be enough to harden her heart once more. You have brought this fate upon her."

Dora cried and begged for forgiveness. Emirokol scowled at her and demanded her silence.

"What?" Dappil said. "No, please don't. She's a very nice dwarf, whatever her name is. Why would you do that to her?"

"Finally, Gerson's pact is also broken. You found his cunningly hidden trap—"

"Oh, please, that rope and the loose stone?" Dappil huffed. "You must be joking. I've crafted better traps out of grass and cheese."

"Silence!" Emirokol shouted in a voice that made the columns and floor stones shake. "Gerson's pact is broken and he has not fed. His soul needs to be fed the blood of the innocent every day. That is the bargain he has made, the price for the vengeance I have granted him in life. Now, that covenant is also broken. He, too, must be cleansed again in the understreets."

"You aren't very nice," Dappil said.

"Foolish mortal," Emirokol replied. "I would keep you here and torture you for all eternity. However..."

"I wish I had my string," Dappil said. "I would just pull it and be back with Kalor. This place is terrible. I really don't know why everyone kept telling me to come to Hell. Dreadfully *boring* place."

Emirokol shook his head. "I cannot imagine putting up with *you* for all eternity. I would only be punishing myself. I foresee thousands of years undoing the damage you have already done to my domain. Every day you spend here will corrupt the evil I have wrought, forcing me to waste thousands more years undoing the damage. For that, I will spare your soul."

"Does that mean I can go home now?" Dappil asked, suddenly very ex‐cited.

Emirokol reached out with his hand, showing a shrinking silver thread. "Here—"

"You found my thread!" said Dappil.

"Fool!" boomed Emirokol. "I stole your thread when you entered my do‐main!"

"Now why would you do a mean thing like that?" asked Dappil.

"I will give you the thread and send you home," Emirokol said. "In re‐turn, I ask one favor from you."

"Of me?" Dappil said, smiling widely. "What could a god possibly want from *me*?"

Emirokol leaned forward and whispered to him, "Live a *good* life. I do not ever want to see you again."

Dappil snatched the shrinking silver thread and was about to pull it when a thought occurred to him. "Wait, why would a god of evil want someone to live a good life?"

Emirokol laughed. Dappil was surrounded by darkness and felt himself falling.

Home

Kalor was muttering, writing on his scroll, and looking very nervous. His papers rustled and he felt a chilling breeze. Turning, he watched as Dappil materialized in his office and fell two feet to the floor, sending a small cloud of sand into the air.

"Oomph!" Dappil said.

"You!" Kalor said. "You made it out... *how* did you make it out?"

"No thanks to you," Dappil said.

"You didn't return in time, and I was forced to leave. I waited as long as I could."

Dappil patted his pouches and sighed. "I'm sorry, I didn't mean it. I lost the string."

"The silver strand? Lost? Oh dear..." Kalor said. He looked as if he was about to say something, then waved it away. "No matter, it shouldn't be a problem. But how did you get out of there?"

"I met some giant who said he was a god," Dappil said. "He said he took my string, and—"

"Emirokol!" Kalor screeched. "How did you survive?"

"He said I ruined everything, but to be honest, the streets weren't all that wicked to begin with. Except the smell of that one group. That was simply *awful*."

"But how—"

"I should get going. Thanks for bringing me there. It wasn't quite what I was expecting, but I really do appreciate you taking the time out of your day. I'm suddenly very thirsty."

Before Kalor could gather his thoughts, Dappil opened the door to Kalor's private study and bounded down the hall. He walked down the stairs, singing a little song. On the second floor, he peeked into several rooms but in each room someone shooed him away. Back in the lobby, he thought of talking to Nariah, but he figured she was very busy, with all the studying she had to do. Dappil couldn't figure out why she wanted to be a wizard. It seemed like a lot of time spent reading. Conjuring fire and ice would be fun, but there was far too much preparatory work involved. So Dappil bounced out into the street, jumping down the too-big steps of the wizard school. When he reached the bottom, he bumped into a man, who pushed him to the ground and scowled.

"You little runt," the man said. Then he kicked Dappil. "Go to Hell."

Dappil sat on the ground and looked up at the man and sighed. "I've *been* there," he said, much to the apparent surprise of the man. "It's really not all that special."

ABOUT THE AUTHORS

Jamie Alan Belanger earned a bachelor's degree from the University

of South Florida in Computer Science and worked for a small software company in Tampa for eight years before moving to Maine to pursue his own projects. He currently works for a company he started with his brother Paul, Lost Luggage Studios. His interests include computers, writing, photography, and designing worlds he'd rather live in.

Shelli-Jo Pelletier has been determined to write stories for book-eager

children ever since third grade, when a teacher assigned her additional coursework because she "read too much." Born and raised in southern Maine, she received her bachelor's in creative writing from the University of Maine at Farmington. Her previous publications include a chapter in "Telling Their Stories: Women Business Owners in Western Maine," a project by the Western Mountains Alliance to honor women entrepreneurs.

ABOUT THE AUTHORS

D.L. Harvey has a degree in Anthropology-Geography with a side focus in economics that helps with creating her universes. Her pursuit of a Master's of Psychology aids in both the development of her fictional characters and in managing her real life family of five. She has an eclectic range of interests from genetics to psychics, from singing to quantum theory, from linguistics to motorcycles. She hopes her writing shows that the universe is an amazing, beautiful, and scary place, worthy to be explored and shared.

Steven Inman finds his many jobs to be an interesting diversion from his writing obsession. He lives in Portland where his B.A. in Classical Literature comes in handy in his daytime maintenance work, where he reads Candide to air handling units. He has worked in cemeteries, hotels, churches, shelters, and M60A1 tanks. In his spare time he reads, writes, runs, eats meals, plays with old movie projectors and office equipment, and eventually goes to work.

ABOUT THE AUTHORS

Timothy Lynch is a Reference Librarian at The University of Southern

Maine. He graduated with a BA in English Literature from St. Bonaventure University and an MLS in Library and Information Science from Simmons College. He enjoys reading, writing and walking around Back Cove in Portland. At least once a month he can also be found swimming mythical rivers and hiking the endless trails of dreams.

Richard Veysey is the youngest member of the Greater Portland

Scribists and our current leader. He has been telling stories since he could put words together to form a sentence, and writing since he learned how to read. In his free time, he likes to write, program and play video games, make all-natural moisturizers, face washes, etc., and hang out with his friends. He also hates writing about himself in the third person.

Greater Portland Scribists (GPS) is a group of speculative fiction writers who live near Portland, Maine. We formed in 2011 with the intention of publishing an anthology, which we have done every year since. We meet throughout the year to discuss writing, publishing, and to submit our stories to intense group workshopping sessions. Creating worlds and crafting stories is a fun way to live, and we do our best to help each other become the best writers we can be. Plus our discussions tend to go off-topic on some pretty epic and entertaining tangents.

To learn more about GPS, visit our blog at
http://scribists.blogspot.com

Be our fan on Facebook at
http://www.facebook.com/GreaterPortlandScribists

Purgatory Beckons (by Paul J Belanger)

In a world descending into moral depravity, it seems Evil has won. After a botched arrest attempt, Detective Debbie Mason's life begins spiraling out of control, forcing her to question whether fighting crime is worth the effort. But nothing could prepare Debbie for the arrival of Garrett Carmichael, a stone-cold killer sent on a mission of mass homicide by his mysterious employer.

Pariah (by Jamie Alan Belanger)

Neil Roberts, a programmer for the largest software provider on the planet, stops in a bar and witnesses a murder. His once boring life changes drastically when, through a twist of fate and a realization that his life has no purpose beyond his job, he leaves the scene of the crime and becomes a suspect. Neil's life shifts from protecting people to becoming that which he most despised... a hacker.

Fireteam Zulu (by Jamie Alan Belanger)

The year is 2254. Humanity has expanded into our solar system. But we've spread too far, too fast, and the military cannot police the solar system. Hopeful colonists are preyed upon by pirates who take what they can with little opposition. Fireteam Zulu is a group of ex-marines who help those people, hunting pirates wherever they find them. Then one day they discover that *they* are being hunted.

The Sol-Bect War, Part 1 (by Paul J Belanger)

Humanity is near the tail end of an intergalactic war that we are losing. After a rough skirmish, a strange object is picked up by the United Earth carrier Ticonderoga. Within, the ship's scientists find something even stranger: a man, cryogenically frozen and shot into space more than 300 years ago. The fact that he's still technically alive raises questions of Fate's hand in life and war.

The Sol-Bect War, Part 2 (by Paul J Belanger)

The war against the Bect rages on. Humanity is now on the offensive. The Bect send larger forces against us. Our weapons and tactics may have improved, but our forces are beginning to dwindle. And the strange newcomer who showed us a path to victory, Peter McCabe, is Missing-In-Action and presumed dead. Can the human war machine complete what he started?

The Sol-Bect War, Part 3 (by Paul J Belanger)

Six years after the Sol-Bect War's end, peace is still elusive. While the Bectolothian home world is torn apart by civil war, their military ignites another conflict with the Terrans. A Bect spy betrays Peter McCabe, and Terran and Bect forces converge on Vale-4. With war on every front, spies on every side, and the lines of friendship so blurry, how can Peter know who to trust?

Scribings, Vol 1

The first volume of short stories compiled by the Greater Portland Scribists, a group of speculative fiction writers in the Portland, Maine area. This compilation contains eleven pieces of fiction written by members Lee Patterson; Cynthia Ravinski, MA; Jamie Alan Belanger; and Richard Veysey.

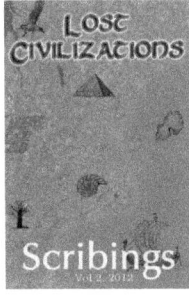

Scribings, Vol 2: Lost Civilizations

Join the Greater Portland Scribists on a journey into lands long lost. Scribings, Vol 2: Lost Civilizations contains eight stories about Ancient Egypt, the Vikings, Atlantis, and even a few completely fictional civilizations. Written by members Richard Veysey; Cynthia Ravinski, MA; Jamie Alan Belanger; Christopher L. Weston, and Timothy Lynch.

Scribings, Vol 3: Metamorphosis

Change is inevitable. Everything that happens in your life alters you, forever, for better or worse. Whether the change occurs to one person or to a whole society, it eventually affects us all. Scribings, Vol 3: Metamorphosis contains six stories from the Greater Portland Scribists that explore changes, from the self-inflicted alterations of a glory seeker to a victim forced to learn how to live his life all over again.

Scribings, Vol 4: Miscreations

Miscreations are things that should not exist, but do.
Scribings, Vol 4: Miscreations contains twelve stories from
the Greater Portland Scribists that explore these oddities.
Errors in evolution. Discoveries in supposedly clean rooms.
Extreme memory loss. Appliances that are a little too smart.
Mythical beasts reborn. And one joke that went way too far.

Terran Shift Anthology, Vol 1

The Terran Shift Anthology, Volume 1, the first collection of
stories set exclusively in the Terran Shift universe, contains
seven science fiction stories from five authors set in all four
eras — from Bio-Tech dystopia to The Sol-Bect War era.
This anthology includes The Sol-Bect Setup, the thrilling lost
chapter in which Peter McCabe visits the past to lay the
groundwork for his future.

Terran Shift Anthology 2: The Bio-Tech Era

Terran Shift Anthology, Volume 2: The Bio-Tech Era is the
second collection of stories set exclusively in the Terran
Shift universe. The collection contains seven science fiction
stories from five authors, focusing entirely on stories set in
the Bio-Tech Era, a plausible near-future where humanity
becomes even more dependent on technology.

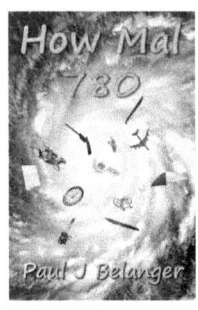

www.ingramcontent.com/pod-product-compliance
Lightning Source LLC
Chambersburg PA
CBHW061132200626
46817CB00016B/1051